Sheridan's Fate

What Reviewers Say About BOLD STROKES Authors

KIM BALDWIN
"*Force of Nature* is filled with nonstop, fast paced action. Tornadoes, raging fire blazes, heroic and daring rescues…Baldwin does a fine job of describing the fast-paced scenes and inspiring the reader to keep on turning the pages." – L-word.com Literature

ROSE BEECHAM
"…her characters seem fully capable of walking away from the particulars of whodunit and engaging the reader in other aspects of their lives." – *Lambda Book Report*

GEORGIA BEERS
"Beers weaves a tale of yearning, love, lust, and conflict resolution. She has constructed a believable plot, with strong characters in a charming setting." – *JustAboutWrite*

RONICA BLACK
"*Wild Abandon* tells how these two women come to realize that 'life was too precious to be ruled by…fears, by…demons.' While these two women struggle with their issues, there is some very, very hot sex. If you enjoy complex characters and passionate sex scenes, you'll love *Wild Abandon*." – *MegaScene*

GUN BROOKE
"*Course of Action* is a romance…populated with a host of captivating and amiable characters. The glimpses into the lifestyles of the rich and beautiful people are rather like guilty pleasures…a most satisfying and entertaining reading experience." – *Midwest Book Review*

CATE CULPEPPER
"…an exceptional storyteller who has taken on a very difficult subject …and turned it into a spellbinding novel. As an author, she understands well that fiction can teach us our own history." – *JustAboutWrite*

JANE FLETCHER
"*The Exile and the Sorcerer* is a mesmerizing read, a tour-de-force packed with adventure, ordeals, complex twists and turns, and the internal introspection of appealing characters." – *Midwest Book Review*

JD Glass

"*Punk Like Me*...is different. It is engaging. It is life-affirming. Frankly, it is genius. This is a rare book in that it has a soul; one that is laid bare for all to see." – *JustAboutWrite*

Grace Lennox

"*Chance* is refreshing...Every nuance is powerful and succinct. *Chance* is not a novel about the music industry; it is about a woman discovering herself as she muddles through all the trappings of fame." – *Midwest Book Review*

Lee Lynch

"Lynch, with a dozen novels to her credit dating back to the early days of Naiad Press, has earned her stripes as a writerly elder. She was contributing stories to the lesbian magazine *The Ladder* four decades ago. But this latest is sublimely in tune with the times." – *Q-Syndicate*

JLee Meyer

"*Forever Found*...neatly combines hot sex scenes, humor, engaging characters, and an exciting story." – *MegaScene*

Radclyffe

"...well-plotted...lovely romance...I couldn't turn the pages fast enough!" – Ann Bannon, author of *The Beebo Brinker Chronicles*

Susan Smith

"This disparate duo's lush rush of a romance - which incorporates reincarnation, a grounded transman and his peppy daughter, and the dark moods of a troubled witch - pays wonderful homage to Leslie Feinberg's classic gender-bending novel, *Stone Butch Blues*." – *Q-Syndicate*

Ali Vali

"Rich in character portrayal, *The Devil Inside* by Ali Vali is an unusual, unpredictable, and thought-provoking love story that will have the reader questioning the definition of right and wrong long after she finishes the book." – *JustAboutWrite*

Visit us at www.boldstrokesbooks.com

Sheridan's Fate

by
Gun Brooke

2007

SHERIDAN'S FATE

© 2007 BY GUN BROOKE. ALL RIGHTS RESERVED.

ISBN10: 1-933110-88-0
ISBN13: 978-1-933110-88-2

THIS TRADE PAPERBACK IS PUBLISHED BY
BOLD STROKES BOOKS, INC.
NEW YORK, USA

FIRST EDITION, SEPTEMBER 2007

CREDITS
Editors: Shelley Thrasher and J.B. Greystone
Production Design: J. B. Greystone
Cover Graphic: Sheri (graphicartist2020@hotmail.com)

By the Author

Acknowledgments

Nothing and nobody can sustain life in a vacuum, and thus, I want to express my heartfelt thanks to the following people.

My beta reading team! Pol, Lisa, Sami, Georgi, Ruth, and Jan, your shoulders must be strong and broad, ladies, since I am able to stand on them so confidently. And the ones who read and cared, Jay and Carol, thank you so much for endless support.

My family, who remain ever proud of me, Elon, Malin, Henrik, and Mom; it is wonderful to have people rejoice in the fact that I am living my dream.

I am so happy, and so fortunate, to belong to Bold Strokes Books, who nurture, and inspire, their authors the way they do. Shelley, my editor, you are perfect for me, and you know my writing so well by now. Radclyffe, thank you for your continued faith in me. Julie, thanks for your eagle-eyes. Sheri, you are so cool to work with. And thank you to the crew that proofs, etc., to quote Stacia, "you are our gods!"

And lastly, my readers. I write for myself, for my own enjoyment, but ultimately, I write for you.

DEDICATION

This book is dedicated to everyone living with a disability. Especially close to my heart is a group of people that gathers online under the name Sverige_MS_Support.

PROLOGUE

Pain, beyond anything she'd ever felt, seared Sheridan's body. Her stiff neck burned, and her chest constricted as her whole system convulsed. She tried to cough, but the pain overwhelmed her. The heat on her skin seeped further into her body. *This is it. I'm dying. No one can live through this.*

Hands pulled at her, voices came and went, one moment startlingly close only to shift and grow distant the next. Sheridan tried to move her arms, to make the voices understand that she needed help, needed someone to stop the agony, but nobody listened. She tried to call out, but her mouth was dry, her tongue stuck hopelessly to the roof of her mouth, making it impossible for her to create the tiniest squeak.

Eventually, and Sheridan didn't know if it had been minutes or days, the pain subsided as she finally just shut off. As Sheridan relaxed, the voices around her seemed to grow more frantic, but she finally found some comfort. She couldn't understand why this break from the torment would upset anyone. Couldn't they see she was finally through the worst of it? All she needed was some sleep, a little rest, and then she'd speak to them, answer all their insistent questions.

Sheridan floated, content and without any discomfort, and a childhood memory of a shiny yellow balloon made her smile weakly. The balloon danced up, up, and bounced against the ceiling. Sheridan looked up at her mother, beautiful and laughing as she helped Sheridan manage the bobbing balloon. Falling through soft clouds, clutching at the string unafraid, Sheridan listened to her mother's voice. "Hold on. Don't let go now. Hold on."

❖

"Damn it, what the hell's going on here?" the physician growled and gazed at the monitors above the woman's still body. He didn't like what he saw. "Push more Ringers, we need more fluids in her." The medical staff swarmed around the bed in an organized chaos, administering medicine and carrying out orders.

"Temperature 106.5. BP 60 over 40. Respiration 85, shallow. Pulse 140, fluttering." The nurse to the physician's left rattled off the information, her dark eyes concerned above the mask.

"She's septic." He bent over the woman on the bed, his trained eyes taking in the signs of shock. "Her kidneys are failing, and other organs are shutting down as well. We need to regain control. Prepare her for dialysis and intubation."

Another nurse pressed an oxygen mask over the woman's face and began to compress a breathing bag. Leaning over the patient, she looked shocked at how fast the woman had deteriorated. "Hold on," the physician heard the nurse whisper. "Don't let go now. Hold on."

CHAPTER ONE

I told you after my last assignment, no more working in private homes. Ever." Lark Mitchell ran a hand through her short, light brown hair, as she glowered at the employment agency director. Having known Roy Vogel for seven years, Lark recognized the corpulent man's amicable, convincing look.

"Lark, please hear me out," Roy said, his face serious as he sat behind his desk. "Trust me, I know what you said, and I respect it—"

"I don't think you do, since you're asking me to do it—again!" Lark heard her own voice escalate and took a deep breath to calm down.

"This is different. I promise. No nosy relatives, no God's-gift-to-women dads, and more importantly, three times your last salary."

The money didn't tempt Lark anymore. She had made enough over the last seven years to render her financially independent for at least a decade. Right now she enjoyed being back in Texas. Her last assignment in Dubai had taken its toll on her, because she had been on call more or less around the clock. "What do you mean, no relatives? Who is this person and why do they need a physical therapist?"

Roy shrugged, his familiar grin showing he was pleased that he'd managed to stir Lark's curiosity. "I can't provide you with any details unless you choose to take the assignment. Patient confidentiality. All I can say is that this is a high-profile, extremely well-paid job, which would make it possible for you to take a long break from everything once you're done."

Lark rose, nervous energy making it impossible for her to remain in her seat. "And where is it?"

"Right here in San Antonio. Alamo Heights."

Ah. Old money. "And for how long, initially?"

"One year."

"I'd want it stipulated in my contract under what circumstances I could quit and still be paid throughout the ongoing month." *I can't believe I'm even thinking about it, even discussing terms!* The fact that it was in town, close to her family in Boerne, made a big difference. After a two-month extended leave, Lark had begun to climb the walls, and not even helping out in her mother and stepfather's gallery did any good.

"Of course. Anything you want to put in there. They really need someone with your experience and expertise."

"No working on weekends. I want to be able to go home to Boerne then and be with my family." Lark glanced over at Roy, to make sure he knew she meant it. "I can make a few exceptions, if there's an emergency, but I want a five-day working week."

"You'll still be putting in long hours," Roy said. "I can probably negotiate your conditions for weekends off, but the patient requires a lot of help and training."

"Is he, or she, elderly?"

"No." Roy checked his computer. "Thirty-eight."

"Any other people employed to help with ADL?"

"She has a live-in staff of three, but as for the Active Daily Living training, that's the physical therapist's responsibility, together with an occupational therapist, who's available when necessary. There's also always a nurse on call." Roy frowned at his document. "Apparently, the patient is reluctant and impatient when it comes to aides and training, traumatized by the repercussions of the illness."

Lark's interest grew with each word, since this sounded like one of those challenging cases she used to find fascinating, and so rewarding, when she was a new physical therapist. Lark had dreamed of helping people regain a good quality of life, making them more independent and facing a new future. This case was beginning to interest her, despite its conditions.

"Very well," Lark agreed, intrigued, but apprehensive because she hadn't stuck to her plan.

"Excellent!" Roy beamed. "I'll recommend you and call ahead. As far as I understand, they want you to start right away. Ms. Ward has been without a PT for more than two weeks, and you know that's not good."

"Ms. Ward?" Lark straightened in the chair. "As in *the* Wards?"

"Ward Industries, yes. As high a profile as you can have here in San Antonio, I imagine. You'll be working out of their Alamo Heights mansion, of course."

"Of course," Lark echoed as her mind reeled. The Wards had lived in San Antonio since Texas became a republic, and the term "old money" was never truer. "So, when do I begin?"

"Barring hang-ups, you'll start Monday."

Today was Friday, which didn't give Lark much time to prepare. "I need to read Ms. Ward's medical records."

Roy scratched the side of his neck. "Ah, hmm, that may be a problem. Ms. Ward's pretty careful with information regarding her condition. You'll receive a full report once you get there, and I have to warn you, you'll find extensive confidentiality clauses in your contract. Ms. Ward's assistant specifically told me about this issue. Guess she's big on privacy, and who can blame her?"

"I suppose, with her background." Lark nodded, wondering what had happened to Ms. Ward. Vaguely, she remembered how the media circus had focused their attention on the Wards a few months ago, but she couldn't recall exactly what they'd reported. It wasn't the first time the Wards had been in the media's focus. "I won't sign anything until I know how extensive the confidentiality clauses are." Lark glared at Roy. "You know my work ethics. I take them very seriously."

"Believe me, I know, Lark. The Wards have been pretty badly burned during the years. The tabloids never seem to give them a break, and the business magazines are after them for other reasons."

"All right. When would they expect me?"

Roy checked his watch with exaggerated movements before assuming a sheepish look. "Your interview, which is only a formality, is in ninety minutes."

Lark sat up. "You've got to be kidding me!" Her thoughts whirled. Was she prepared? Dressed well enough? Presentable? She looked down at her tailored slacks and short denim jacket. *Yeah, presentable enough. This is Texas, not Dubai or the Côte d'Azur.*

"Don't freak out. They're only twenty minutes from here by car. You have enough time if you want to spruce up, I'd think," Roy said. "You're pretty as you are."

Surprised at Roy's unexpectedly familiar remark, Lark slowly shook her head and smiled. "Why, thank you, sir. Not true, but I guess I don't send herds of cattle stampeding, at least."

Roy looked as if he meant to say something more, opened his mouth only to close it again while shaking his head.

"I rest my case." Lark grinned and checked her watch. "Okay, eighty-five minutes now. Better run."

"Good luck. I know you're the best one for this job." Roy got up and shook her hand. "Call me later."

Lark agreed and left the agency in deep thought. Uneasy that she'd gone back on her vow never to accept another assignment to work in yet another wealthy private home, she pulled out her cell phone and dialed her parents' house. Her stepfather, Arthur, answered.

"Hi, Dad," Lark said and pressed the phone closer to her ear, "you're not going to believe this."

"You've got a new job," Arthur said, sounding matter-of-fact.

Lark smiled, despite a faint feeling of dread. "Yeah, I do. But at least it's in town."

"San Antonio?"

"Yeah. Alamo Heights."

A moment's delay. "A private home?"

"Yes. I know what I said—"

"Are you sure about this, Lark?" Arthur's worry was obvious. "It's only been a month."

"I know, I know." Lark reached her Lexus and climbed inside.

The Bluetooth system in her car radio kicked in, and Arthur's voice came through strong over the speakers. "Just as long as you know what you're doing."

"I know, Dad." Lark pulled out into the busy rush-hour traffic. "I guess Roy made me an offer I couldn't refuse." Feeling her grip on the steering wheel tighten, Lark forced herself to relax. "It really sounds like an interesting case. And good money."

"You know, that shouldn't influence your decision, sweetheart."

"And it didn't. I mean, that wasn't the main thing. Roy has no idea how much I've put away, so he tried to make that the selling point. But really, Dad, something about the fact that my new patient has no close family intrigues me. At least that's what the tabloids report about her family situation. I know very little for sure, but something told me that this person truly needs me." Lark knew that if anyone understood this point, Arthur would.

"All right, Lark. I trust that you know what you're doing. Wait a second...what?" Arthur spoke to someone in the room with him. "Your mother wants to know if you'll be back for dinner today. I'm cooking."

"I'll be there. I'm on my way to the interview now, but it shouldn't take all that long. I'll be home by five, six at the latest, depending on traffic."

"All right, sweetheart, see you then."

Soft country rock music replaced Arthur's deep voice automatically as the speakers shifted to her favorite radio channel. Patsy Cline's voice filled the car, soothing Lark as she drove toward Alamo Heights. Uncertain of who, and what, to expect, she sang along with the lyrics of "Crazy."

❖

"Fuck!"

Sheridan harnessed the overwhelming desire to toss the Pocket PC phone across her office, and instead she placed it carefully on the large desk in front of her. Leaning back in the wheelchair, she rubbed her aching neck while she tried to calm down. She was pretty sure that her staff had heard her profanity, which made her cringe. Known for her ice-cold perfectionist approach and the fact that she never let anything faze her where business was concerned, Sheridan was sure the people around her saw this lack of self-restraint as a sign of weakness.

Her staff acted increasingly cautious around her, which only confirmed Sheridan's suspicion that they thought she definitely had lost some of her usual composure. She noticed something in the way they acted around her—wary, and with a look of infinite pity in their eyes.

A knock on the door made Sheridan straighten up so quickly in her chair that her neck smarted again, sending flashes of pain up the back of her head and down her shoulders. Refusing to moan or twitch under the sharpness of the ache, Sheridan folded her hands in her lap. "Enter."

"Ms. Mitchell to see you about the position as physical therapist." Erica, her secretary, stood in the doorway.

"Ah. Well, send her in."

Erica stepped aside and a slender young woman with short, light brown hair entered. The sun streaming through the panoramic window ignited golden highlights as Ms. Mitchell pushed longish bangs out of her eyes. She strode across the room and extended an almost fragile-looking hand toward Sheridan.

"Ms. Ward, it's a pleasure to meet you. I'm Lark Mitchell. Roy Vogel of Vogel Health Professional Agency sent me."

"Of course. Please, sit down." Sheridan motioned toward the chair across the desk from her. Lark Mitchell sat while she unbuttoned her denim jacket. She wore a crisp cotton top underneath, its sheer material barely revealing a white bra. Embarrassed for the way she stared at the other woman, Sheridan found it impossible not to sound annoyed as she continued. "Mr. Vogel assured my assistant that you're the best among the best, Ms. Mitchell."

"Lark, please. And yes, I'm good at what I do."

"Very well. Lark. Mr. Vogel faxed us your résumé only a few minutes ago. I browsed through it. Impressive." The words came out staccato, and the pain in Sheridan's neck and shoulders threatened to turn into one of her awful headaches.

"Thank you. I know I will be able to make life a little easier for you, Ms. Ward." Lark leaned forward, examining Sheridan with kind brown eyes. "Forgive me, but you seem to be in quite a bit of pain. May I help you with that? I mean, right now?"

Stumped, and amazed at Lark's audacity at skipping any preliminaries, Sheridan didn't answer.

"Ms. Ward?" Lark seemed to take Sheridan's silence as a yes. She rose and rounded the desk. "Is it your neck?"

"How did you know?" Sheridan mumbled under her breath, bracing herself for the searing pain she feared would be unavoidable even at the lightest touch. She knew from experience how she paid the price for any manipulation by a physical therapist.

"Your posture. Let me know if this hurts too much." Lark skimmed warm fingers along the rigid, swollen muscles that led up from Sheridan's shoulders and attached to the base of her skull on either side of her spinal column. "Oh, yes, there's the problem, right there."

Sheridan held her breath, determined not to show any weakness, no matter how bad the pain became. Lark found the sore spots at the base of Sheridan's skull and began to massage them with mild insistence.

For a few seconds the pain peaked and Sheridan nearly pulled back with a growl, then suddenly it became duller and the whole area nearly numbed. Lark's thumbs pressed the sore spots harder against the base of Sheridan's skull, as if flattening the ligaments.

"God." Sheridan's self-restraint crumbled for a few seconds. She had not expected any relief, only more pain, and unless it was sheer coincidence, this demonstration might prove Lark's skill, compared to that of the other physical therapists she'd fired, one after another. "Thank you."

"I suppose you've tried heat to alleviate some of these stress symptoms?" Lark asked as she returned to her chair.

Sheridan glanced at the small hands that had manipulated her with such strength and proficiency. "I used a special heat lamp, a Japanese invention." She shrugged, again stunned at how loose her shoulders felt. "Didn't do much good."

"Well, I'm more for the low-tech solutions that I know work, rather than fancy equipment that regular people can't afford anyway."

"I'm not regular people." Sheridan nailed Lark, who didn't even flinch. Her self-confidence was quite impressive.

"Not so very regular, when it comes to your circumstances. Very regular, when it comes to your body. We can all become ill, Ms. Ward."

"Sheridan. If you're going to be my PT, you need to call me by my first name. I get enough of the title thing at work." Hardly anyone called her Sheridan anymore. Sheridan wasn't sure why she suggested that Lark use her first name. She hadn't even thought to bring the subject up with her predecessors.

"Sure, Sheridan. That will actually make our work easier."

"Oh? How so?" Sheridan knew her raised eyebrows could make any one of her employees nervous.

"I may have to pull rank and be really tough at times, and using your first name makes that a whole lot easier. It's my experience that no matter how good our intentions are, most patients reach a point when they just can't see the light at the end of the tunnel, to speak in clichés. It's up to me to see it for you and keep you on track."

Nobody had ever cared to explain that point to her, or, Sheridan mused, perhaps nobody had *dared* to explain it. "I don't intimidate easily, Lark," she said and clasped her fingers on the desk.

"It's not a question of intimidation, but more of persuasion."

Lark's voice, clear and unwavering, made something stir inside Sheridan. It didn't sit well with her, this feeling of embryonic trust, and she pushed her shoulders up, disregarding the renewed pain her action caused.

"All right. I take it that it's no problem for you to start right away? My assistant suggested you're…between jobs."

"Right away, as in Monday." If Lark caught onto the needle prick, she didn't let on. "I wish to discuss some of the conditions in my contract—"

"You can do that with Erica. She's familiar with my terms and can answer any administrative questions you might have. I wish you could start tomorrow." Sheridan was eager to test this new physical therapist and discover sooner rather than later if she was as incompetent as the previous ones. She fully expected to be let down.

"Tomorrow is Saturday, and I don't work weekends, unless you have an emergency." Lark spoke clearly, but not unkindly.

Oh, for heaven's sake. "I see. Very well. Until Monday, then." Sheridan wished she could rise to show that their meeting was over. Instead she waved her hand dismissively and pulled the Pocket PC phone to her, tapping it twice with a stylus.

"Thank you, Sheridan. Have a good weekend."

"You too," Sheridan replied, careful not to look up. For some reason she was furious and felt as if her nerve endings were exposed to the world. She couldn't risk showing even a hint of frailty, not to anyone. If she had to be perceived as a corporate witch, so be it.

When Lark didn't make a sound, Sheridan finally glanced up from her phone, only to find her new physical therapist gone.

❖

Lark found Erica pleasant and easy to deal with, unlike her boss. Sheridan seemed anything but easy, and Lark had to admit this might prove to be her most challenging case to date, even counting the Henderson twins. The thought of the identical twins, born with identical birth defects and subjected to multiple surgeries during their seven-year life span, made Lark smile. The twins had become as precious as her nieces and nephews.

"Ms. Ward employs three assistant nurses, who between them tend to her around the clock. She doesn't use them as much as she could," Erica said apologetically. "Ms. Ward is a private person, very independent. She prefers to manage on her own as much as she can."

Lark had noticed that. The tall, pale woman in the inner office had tried to act as if nothing was amiss in her life, and she probably had no idea how obvious this charade was to Lark. When she first met a new patient, she could read between the lines. She saw pain where others saw false bravery, and she spotted the cause, whereas others chose to take things at face value. *It's easier to assume that things are just as fine as the patient implies.*

"Let me call the housekeeper, who can show you around. That way, you can check out your room and make sure everything is as you like."

"I wasn't sure yet if Ms. Ward wanted me to live here or commute from Boerne." In fact, Lark was relieved that she was going to be a live-in PT, since she anticipated that she was going to need her energy for things other than sitting in the "parking lot" that I-10 turned into every rush hour.

"Ms. Ward was absolutely clear on that point," Erica said, her hand hovering over the receiver. "She always sets high standards for her employees and demands twice as much of herself. Her former PT didn't live at the mansion, and Mrs. Ward was constantly frustrated when she had to wait more than an hour for the PT to get here. It was hard for the rest of us to watch her suffer a lot of unnecessary pain." Erica looked darkly at Lark.

"I have no problem with staying here," Lark stated calmly. "In fact, at the beginning of a case, if I can be available when I'm needed the most, my job is easier and the patient benefits. Apart from the physiotherapy program I'll design for Ms. Ward, I know how crucial the working relationship is between a seriously wounded or ill patient and their PT." Lark knew she sounded serious and confident, but inside she wondered if Sheridan Ward really could be counted among the average cases. She seemed to be the one to call every single shot, including her own treatment.

The housekeeper, who introduced herself as Mrs. D, looked nothing like the stereotype for her line of work. Tall and slender, with iron grey hair, she could easily model mature women's wear. "Welcome," Mrs. D said and shook Lark's hand firmly. "Come with me, and I'll show you to your suite."

Suite? Lark had lived in several luxurious homes, and so far her quarters had been everything from a room above the garage to a bungalow on a wealthy Arab family's estate. This was, however, her first suite.

The mansion boasted a wide marble staircase as well as a spacious elevator.

"The elevator was installed for Mrs. Olivia Ward, Ms. Ward's mother. No one used it much before Ms. Ward became ill. Now…I guess it's good that we kept it in working order."

Mrs. D's voice became muted, and Lark saw what she interpreted as true worry in the housekeeper's eyes. She knew words were not enough and merely nodded as they walked up the stairs.

In the middle of the north wing, Mrs. D held open the door to a large living room. "Here we are then," she said and motioned for Lark to step inside. "I'm sure you'll be comfortable here."

"I'm sure I will." Lark studied the room that held both contemporary as well as vintage furniture, all in mint condition. Dark red walls, floral wallpaper on the ceiling, and accents in gold and black, together with an open fireplace, made for a cozy, warm ambience. A door at the far end led into a large bedroom, with a king-size four-poster bed as the focal point. The fireplace opposite the bed and the room's moss green, gold, and ivory color scheme made the room seem like something out of a Victorian novel.

"Your bathroom is over there," Mrs. D said and pointed toward a door in the far left corner.

Lark entered a white and gold bathroom consisting of a Jacuzzi tub, glassed-in shower stall, two pedestal sinks, and a toilet behind yet another door. White marble, faintly lined with light grey streaks, created a stunning effect.

"It's beautiful. I'll be beyond comfortable." Lark found her surroundings opulent, but knew better than to voice such thoughts. The rich and privileged took these things for granted and found it curious, almost suspicious, if a person revealed her more humble beginnings by being too impressed.

"Excellent, Ms. Mitchell—"

"Lark, please. We're going to be working under the same roof for a while."

Mrs. D frowned. "I don't mind being on a first-name basis, Lark. It's just that I'm Mrs. D to everyone."

"I have no problem with that." Lark smiled broadly. "I should get going. Lots to do before Monday."

"Monday?" Mrs. D. looked surprised. "I thought you were starting tomorrow."

"No, Monday. I won't be working weekends unless Ms. Ward's condition requires it. Here's my cell phone number, in case you need to reach me. Don't hesitate to call if something comes up."

Mrs. D. regarded the business card that Lark handed over. "Very well. I appreciate that you are so clear and up-front about this arrangement. It makes it so much easier to plan for Sheridan's care."

"Good. We have an understanding then." Lark smiled and placed a gentle hand on Mrs. D's arm. "Thank you for showing me around. The rooms are lovely."

"You're welcome. Let me walk you to the door."

"No, that's all right. I'm sure you have a lot of things to do. I'll find my own way out." Lark hoisted her bag onto her shoulder. "See you Monday."

Lark walked through the broad hallway and down the marble stairs. Passing the half-closed doors to Sheridan's study, she couldn't help but stop and glance inside. Sheridan sat in her state-of-the-art wheelchair by the window, apparently lost in thought. Her fists lay tightly curled on the armrests, and something about her profile startled Lark. As forceful as Sheridan had come across during their conversation, she now looked vulnerable and frail.

Instinctively, she knew that if Sheridan realized that Lark had seen her during an exposed moment, their future working relationship could be damaged. She stepped away from the door and headed toward the main entrance. Pushing the heavy oak door open, she walked down the limestone stairs to her Lexus.

Lark thought of Sheridan, sitting in solitude by her window, perhaps even watching her drive away. Suddenly eager to return to the Ward mansion the following Monday, Lark accelerated down the driveway toward the automatic gate.

CHAPTER TWO

I can't do that. Not yet." Sheridan looked up at the stubborn woman next to her. Lark had put a harness around her waist and now looked expectantly at her.

"Yes, you can. You proved your arm strength to me on the bench press before. You can easily carry your own weight on these bars." Lark placed her hands on the double bars in front of them. "The harness will be secured to the bars, and I'll be right in front of you and Cecilia behind you with the wheelchair."

"I shouldn't have to repeat myself," Sheridan said between clenched teeth. "I thought you read my medical charts. My legs are... dead. I can't stand up, let alone take a single step."

"I've read your file, Sheridan." Lark spoke kindly, but with an annoying assertiveness. "Come on. Cecilia's ready and so am I."

Sheridan wanted to send a scathing glare at the young nurse behind her, whom she knew she could easily intimidate, but something in Lark's challenge kept her from following her first impulse. "Fine." Small drops of perspiration dripped down the small of Sheridan's back as she grabbed the bars. Her hands slipped and she yanked them back. "Damn!"

"Here. Baby powder. You'll be fine." Lark puffed some powder onto Sheridan's palms. "Try again."

Sheridan grabbed the bars and pulled herself forward. Sure she was going to fall and become suspended in the harness, she gasped when Lark stepped in and held her upright.

"There you go. Find your bearings and secure a good grip of the bars. I'm here and I won't let go."

Sweating profusely, Sheridan found that Lark was right; she had no problem holding herself up. She had lost a lot of weight during the last few months, of course, but it still baffled her that she could keep herself erect like this. None of the other physical therapists had ever convinced her to go through with this particular exercise. Instead, Sheridan had trained her arms as if to compensate for not being able to do anything about her lifeless legs.

Sheridan stood practically surrounded by Lark's arms, certain that they'd both fall any second. "You better let go. I can't hold on much longer."

"Yes, you can. I'm backing up a step. Swing your legs forward and try to put weight on them."

"Why? They're dead!" Sheridan's heart was pumping fury-filled blood through her body.

"Because every time you put weight on them, and we'll do that more in a few days once the right equipment arrives, you'll build stronger bones. Stronger muscles and tendons." Lark still held Sheridan's harness with steady hands. "Good. Try it now."

Sheridan hated the calm, encouraging tone in Lark's voice. It was obvious that the other woman didn't understand the severity of her condition. Lark came strongly recommended by many of her previous patients, but at this point, Sheridan couldn't see what made them give her such enthusiastic reviews.

"All right," she muttered, her pride kicking in. She pressed her arms down and lifted her dangling feet off the floor. Trembling all over, she managed to swing them forward and carefully put a little of her weight on them. The braces around her knees kept them from folding, but only Lark's firm hold kept her from plummeting to the floor.

Standing close together, chest to chest, Sheridan noticed that Lark was at least four inches shorter than she. She inhaled deeply to dig into the reservoir of her strength and found that Lark smelled of something clean and fresh, reminding her of new linens, with a trace of lavender. The surprisingly intoxicating scent filled her senses, and Sheridan pulled herself up once more and managed yet another step, her lower body swinging forward before slumping into Lark's arms.

"Great! You're doing fine," Lark said as she held on to Sheridan. "Cecilia, the wheelchair, please. Thank you."

Sheridan felt the seat of the wheelchair at the back of her knees and sat down with a thud.

"We have to work on that too. You'll be able to get in and out of this chair with much more grace than that." Lark smiled reassuringly. "You're off to a very good start. If you do this well during all our sessions, you'll see a significant improvement in your muscle tone in just a few weeks."

"Really." Sheridan tried to catch her breath. Blaming the strenuous physical therapy, she refused to listen to the small voice that told her that the closeness to Lark and her enthralling scent had something to do with her being so affected.

"Really." Lark walked out from between the bars. "You've had enough for now though. I want you to rest. This afternoon, I'll bring my notebook and we'll go over your ADL status, Active Daily Living, and what you need to learn to make your days easier."

"Like comb my hair?" Sheridan huffed. "I can take care of myself. I don't require any such assistance."

"No, not easy tasks like that. I mean personal hygiene, dressing   "

"You have a way of not listening, don't you?" Sheridan's anger escalated. Lark stood there, so calm and professional in her blue-grey sweats, and seemed so damn superior. "I *don't* need help. I am perfectly capable of taking care of myself."

"I beg to differ." Lark obviously didn't budge. "I don't mean that you can't do anything on your own. In fact, I admire how independent you are, and how far you've come these six weeks you've been out of the hospital. You're without doubt a fighter, and that's what's going to make all the difference for you. Some people in your situation give up. The future seems so dark, and it's all so overwhelming that they think it's not even worth it to try." Lark quieted and a slight frown appeared between her dark brown eyebrows. "The only thing I notice about you is that you seem to have given up on the use of your legs."

"They're dead. I have the medical charts to prove it. The neural paths were destroyed by the meningitis." Sheridan's voice sank an octave. "Nothing to do about that."

Lark pulled up a stool and sat down, directly in front of Sheridan. "Listen to me. The dead nerve cells are gone. That's correct. But, and I'm sure your doctors told you this, other neural paths will step up to the plate and take over. Not entirely, that's true, but well worth training for. The more you train, the more your body recognizes what needs fixing. We all have a wonderful ability to heal." Lark leaned forward.

"I'll be honest with you. You'll probably never be able to run, or even walk without support, but you can improve so much more. Trust me, and I'll prove it to you."

Lark sounded so convincing, so sure, but her optimism went against every pragmatic cell in Sheridan's body. She thought about the bacterial meningitis that had wrecked her body six months ago. After six weeks in the ICU, when the bacteria seemed to defy every attempt to eradicate it, she'd spent another long two months in a private rehab clinic where she'd finally accepted that she was now confined to a wheelchair and would never walk again.

Now she looked around the large room that she'd had Mrs. D and her first physical therapist turn into a gym. It contained every piece of training equipment known to man and an in-ground pool with a newly installed lift, which she hadn't used yet. Not comfortable with water even before her illness, she certainly wouldn't go near it now. *I'd look like an idiot, trying to stay afloat just by using my arms.*

"You sound awfully confident," Sheridan said, nailing Lark with her best glare, which normally sent people running out of the room.

"Only because of my experience and training. You've been through a lot, and I'd really like to see you begin to go forward rather than dwell on the past. But recovery is a process in itself, and you can't skip a step. If you do you'll only have disappointing setbacks."

"What do you mean?"

"You'll make progress, and sometimes it'll be hard to see that, since it'll take some time—"

"You have three months," Sheridan interrupted Lark.

"What?" Lark blinked.

"I became ill five months after our previous stockholder meeting, and I need to be in the best shape possible for the next one." Sheridan injected a scornful tone in her voice in a desire to rattle the collected woman in front of her. "That won't be so hard for someone with your experience, will it?"

Lark recognized a challenge when she was thrown one. Three months wasn't long, but they could do it. "All right. But you misunderstand something. *I'm* not the one that has a lot of work to do during the next few months. You do, Sheridan. This all depends on you. I can guide you, show you, nag, and push you—but ultimately, you're the one responsible. Are *you* prepared to work that hard? To give yourself this chance, this opportunity?"

Sheridan sat up straight in her wheelchair, obviously struggling to keep her posture, to remain the epitome of the CEO, the boss, despite her trembling muscles. "If you knew me, Lark, you wouldn't ask that. If you had any inkling of who I am, and what I'm about, you'd know—"

"I don't know you. Yet. But give me a chance to." Spontaneously, Lark took Sheridan's right hand between hers. It was ice cold and she automatically tried to warm it by stroking it. "Let me in and let's work together. If you fight me, like you've done so far by questioning every single thing that I want you to do, it's going to take a lot longer than three months."

Sheridan stared at their joined hands, speechless all of a sudden. "I suppose you have a point," she conceded after a while. "It's just my normal MO, to not take anything at face value."

"Which probably is a great trait in the business world. I understand that. This is different. Without mutual trust, the result will be…less than optimal."

A flicker of something unreadable passed across Sheridan's face. It might have been remorse, or confusion, but it was gone before Lark could decipher it.

"All right. What's next?"

The curt tone of voice made Lark let go of Sheridan's hand. It dropped back onto her paralyzed legs and remained there as if it was also affected by the cruel disease.

"I want you to rest, as I said, then we'll meet again after lunch, when it's convenient for you, and I'll give you a massage."

Black, well-plucked eyebrows rose in disdain-filled surprise. "A massage?"

"Surely you got massages regularly at the rehab clinic?"

"Yes, of course, but—"

"Apart from the fact that it will stimulate and increase the blood flow to the dormant muscle groups in your legs, it'll provide me with information about the areas where you might be heading for trouble. Other muscles are already compensating for the ones that are not functional. If you use them wrongly, you'll create a whole new set of aches and pains which could be prevented."

Sheridan merely nodded, apparently not in the mood to volunteer any information regarding the neck pain she'd suffered last Friday during their meeting. "Very well. I have a teleconference at one p.m., so how about two thirty?"

"Good. I also need access to your schedule, so I can plan ahead. I suppose Erica can fill me in?"

"No. No, I'll do that myself. Erica knows of my business schedule, but I have some…personal engagements that I keep track of myself." Sheridan suddenly looked exhausted and leaned against the backrest for the first time during their conversation. "I'll e-mail you the hours I have free during the day. Early mornings and late afternoon mostly. I hope that'll be sufficient."

"That should work. The morning sessions will be the tougher ones, while you're still energetic and up for them. The late-afternoon ones will consist of more relaxation, pool sessions, and massage. Some ADL training perhaps." Lark watched Sheridan's eyes glaze over a bit while she talked and knew she was too tired to retain any more information. "If you have time for a power nap, that'd be good," she said. "You look bushed."

Closing her eyes briefly, Sheridan nodded, surprisingly candid. "You're right. This did me in for a bit. I'll see you at two thirty, then."

"Want me or Cecilia to wheel you back?"

This question obviously overstepped a boundary. Sheridan's shoulders went up and her back was once again ramrod straight. "Certainly not. I'm fine."

Of course you are. Lark watched as the proud woman wheeled toward the door. The near desperation in her arrogance tugged at Lark's heart. An unexpected part of her wanted to shield Sheridan and remove the pain and worry that was obvious in her eyes, despite her formidable persona.

Annoyed and startled at where her thoughts were going, Lark stood and faced Cecilia, who had put away the equipment and disinfected everything they'd used. "How's the lunch at this place?"

Cecilia, short and plump in a very pretty way, smiled, showing cute dimples. "Mrs. D makes sure the staff has lunch between noon and 2 p.m. We use the dining room in the southeast wing, on the first floor. Want me to show you the way? It's a bit of a maze here, until you know your way around," Cecilia said and winked.

As adorable as this young woman was, she wasn't Lark's type. Sometimes Lark wished that she'd find these seemingly more free-spirited and uncomplicated girls attractive, but so far she'd mostly fallen for the tall, dark, and brooding type.

Lark halted and closed her eyes. *Dark and brooding. Oh, no. No, no, no.* Sheridan Ward's beautiful, austere features seemed etched on the inside of Lark's eyelids.

"You okay, Lark?" Cecilia interrupted her thoughts.

"Sure. Yes. Just thought of something." Lark mentally shook her head and strode toward the door. "Let's go. I'm starving."

CHAPTER THREE

Sheridan closed the telecommunication software on her computer and let her head fall back with a deep sigh. This was not going to be easy. She had spent the better part of the last six weeks talking with every member of her board of directors, and today it seemed that she'd hardly made any progress at all. Men and women, most of them older than she, had obviously—infuriatingly—decided to treat her as a child, with all the patronizing that came with such an attitude. Only when she infused her voice with her infamous cold, controlled fury did some of them relent. She had three months to convince them that only her legs had suffered any damage. It was apparent that her disease had rattled the stock market as well as the boardroom.

Sheridan had rested for half an hour after a shower and a quick lunch, but trying to relax had only created more tension. Lark Mitchell's words, honest and blunt, swirled in her head. Was it really possible for her to regain some of what she'd lost? The doctors had been carefully optimistic the first week after she regained consciousness. Frightened and bewildered, Sheridan had hidden behind a proud façade, asking all the right questions and showing very little feeling in the presence of the health-care professionals. Only when Mrs. D had visited her, which she did every afternoon, had Sheridan been unable to hide the torment in her soul. With a shudder she remembered clinging to the hand of the woman who had been part of her household for more than thirty years. Sheridan wasn't ready to share how she felt, not even with Mrs. D.

Disease was something she'd been taught to ignore or, even more so, disdain. Her father had displayed only contempt for human physical frailty, which had turned Sheridan into a stranger after her mother died. Sheridan swung her chair around and faced the window. When she noticed that it was time to go to the gym, she surmised that Cecilia had shown Lark the room with the massage bench.

Sheridan's arms seemed heavier than usual as she wheeled toward the end of the corridor, took a left, then stopped just outside the door. A golden-brown head appeared instantly.

"I thought I heard you. Ready to begin?"

Resisting an instinctive "no," Sheridan merely hummed in vague consent and followed Lark into the room. At the far end, next to the pool, another door led into a spacious room that now held a massage table.

"I've lowered it to the same height as your bed. I want to see how you move over on your own." Lark motioned toward the table. "The bench is firmer than your mattress, but it should be okay."

You've been in my bedroom? When? "All right." Stiff, both emotionally and physically, Sheridan pulled up next to the bed. Using all of her arm strength, she pushed sideways over to the massage table, then tried not to seem as out of breath as she was.

"Not bad, but it can improve a lot," Lark stated. "First of all, hasn't anybody showed you how easy it is to remove the armrests on your wheelchair? Like this." She tugged at the armrest closest to the table and pressed a small knob at the same time. "There. Now try scooting back."

Sheridan obeyed and, to her surprise, had to exert only half the effort to slide sideways back into the chair. Two seconds later she had refastened the armrest and removed it again. "I'll be damned."

Lark laughed out loud, "If you could see the look on your face!" There was no malice in her laughter.

"Enjoy the moment." Sheridan gave a faint smile, but thinking about what Lark had confessed earlier, she slowly grew serious again. "Tell me, when were you in my private rooms? I'd appreciate it if you didn't snoop around without my consent."

Staring at Sheridan with a completely blank look on her face, Lark then shook her head. "What do you mean? I haven't been to your rooms."

"You know what my bed looks like." Somehow Lark's deceit hurt more than Sheridan had bargained for, and she realized she had harbored a faint hope that Lark would turn out to be different.

"Only because I asked Cecilia during lunch. I was thinking of different ways to begin the ADL training, and moving in and out of the chair to and from different kinds of furniture is pretty basic." Lark's brown eyes darkened to almost black.

Taken aback, Sheridan glanced down at her hands before she met Lark's eyes again. "I apologize," she said stiffly. "It…I got the impression that you—"

"Took the opportunity to snoop around a big house that belongs to one of the rich and beautiful." Lark pursed her lips. "Well, who can blame you?"

Beautiful? Did she realize what she just said? Sheridan could only stare for a few precious seconds, then saw a pink blush creep up Lark's neck and flood her skin up to her hairline.

"I'm sorry. I—" Lark coughed, obviously embarrassed. "I spoke before I thought."

In other words, not beautiful. Sheridan smiled wryly. "No need to apologize. I see my reflection every day, and I know I look like a barely warmed-up corpse these days."

"What?" Lark looked stunned at Sheridan's attempt to defuse the situation. "No, you don't. A bit pale, but you look fine."

"Fine?" Sheridan remembered only a short time ago when she'd been considered not only one of the richest and the most influential business tycoons in Texas, but also the most stunning. Men and women had always found her attractive, and if it hadn't been for the fact that she'd married her conglomerate of businesses a long time ago, she could have had a new date on her arm each Saturday. Those days were over now.

"Yes, fine. Let me help you up on your stomach. You really need that massage now."

"Thank you." Uncertain how exactly this massage was going to take place, Sheridan waited while Lark pushed the wheelchair out of the way.

"You need to remove everything but your panties. Do you need help? Is it warm enough for you in here?"

It was suddenly too warm. Irritated, Sheridan told herself that Lark was merely another health-care provider, yet another stranger who gained access to her body, whether she liked it or not. *And to think I used to be such a private person. Kind of hard when you need to let people do the most intimate things to you.* Sheridan sighed and began to tug at the zipper of her sweat jacket. Undressing wasn't as invasive as the examinations, probing, blood samples, and other tests done in one of those machines, each more futuristic-looking than the next.

"I'll give you some privacy. Shout if you need help." Lark stepped out of the room and left the door ajar a few inches.

Silly tears rose in Sheridan's eyes at the simple courtesy, and as she tugged at her clothes her hands shook a little. Only when she came to the sweatpants did she eventually have to give in. She pulled a terry-cloth towel around her upper body. "Lark?" Her voice was husky and she hoped her tone wasn't too obvious.

"Right here. Oh, you did very well, considering that I stuck you on a table with nothing to hold on to. Here. Lie down." Lark's gentle hands guided Sheridan onto her back. Within seconds she had efficiently rolled Sheridan back and forth and liberated her from her pants. "There we go. And the socks." Lark placed a warm towel over Sheridan's legs and one over her upper body. "Better, huh?"

"Thank you." All covered, Sheridan began to relax as Lark reached for her left arm and began to carefully manipulate it. "You have good muscle tone in your arms. Let's see. Does this hurt?" She pressed down on several points around the elbow, and Sheridan was glad to honestly say that it didn't.

Methodically, Lark went over every muscle in Sheridan's arms and legs, then ended her assessment of each extremity with a gentle, soothing massage. "I use grape-seed oil," she explained. "Best thing, in my humble opinion."

"Grape-seed oil? I've had a lot of massages at day spas and so on, but I've never heard of it."

"All I ever use."

"None of my other PTs ever suggested a massage." Sheridan felt she had to break the comfortable silence or she'd fall asleep. "Especially not Frau Kreutz. She was just as hard-boiled as the name suggests."

Lark snorted. "Oh, really?"

"I hope she's not a valued friend and colleague of yours." Sheridan grinned, happy that Lark caught on to her attempt at a joke.

"Never heard of the esteemed Frau Kreutz. What did she do to you? Push-ups?"

"Yes."

Lark's hands stopped what they were doing. "What? You're kidding?"

"That's not all she did. She wrapped me in wet, hot towels too. The day she actually scalded me was the day I called the Vogel Agency. I'd had it."

Lark still wasn't moving. "I thought you were kidding. Honestly."

"Nope. Frau Kreutz turned out not to be licensed in the US to practice her…trade. In fact, she didn't have a license to practice in *any* country."

"How did you end up with such a character?" Lark began to massage Sheridan's left leg again, which wasn't numb. Indeed, when the pain seared her legs during the night she wished they were.

"Believe it or not, a friend of my father recommended her. That should have been my first warning, but I was just home and had fired the first PT already."

"Wow." Lark's hands reached Sheridan's thigh, and the insistent massage ignited small sparkles across the skin that sent goose bumps from her thigh to her knee. "How many PTs have you sacked, by the way?"

"Five."

"One per week. Interesting."

"Why's that?"

"Because I intend to be the exception to the rule. Time to roll over. I need to do your back. Something tells me that's where your problems are."

"All right." Was she as breathless as she sounded? Sheridan struggled to turn her upper body, not even bothering to hold on to any of the towels. She was much too busy trying not to fall off the table. Since Lark was busy guiding Sheridan's legs, the top towel fell unattended to the floor.

"Oops. Here's another one." Lark placed a folded towel across Sheridan's lower back and began to work on her shoulders. "Oh, my. You're so tight here that I could use you as a cutting board. And your muscles are completely in knots. I bet this hurts."

"It's not…so…bad." Sheridan tried to speak evenly, but Lark's ministration across her trapezius muscles, all the way from the back of the neck and down to each shoulder, made her squeeze her eyes shut.

"Need me to ease up?" Lark's hands slowed down.

"No. Well, yes, perhaps a bit. Didn't know I was so sore."

Lark's movements remained slow, but she went deeper and deeper into the muscles with skilled hands. Finding every knot and aching ligament, she focused on the shoulders for at least fifteen minutes. "Can you feel yourself loosening up?"

"Yes." Sheridan's shoulders burned with hot sensations that traveled down her arms and up her neck.

"You'll probably feel quite sore tonight and tomorrow. If you do, and if you're too uncomfortable, let me know, and I'll give you some heat treatment." Lark palpated the muscles down Sheridan's back with gentle hands. "These aren't as bad, and I don't want to do too much on our first session. Let me help you up."

With a few swift operations, Lark assisted Sheridan into a sitting position. Feeling utterly vulnerable, perhaps due to the warm, relaxed awareness in her shoulders, Sheridan clutched the towel to her chest with one hand and steadied herself with the other. "Thank you." The towel slipped and Sheridan pressed it closer to her chest and found it utterly silly that she, who'd been prodded and poked, with every one of her sensibilities violated in that hospital bed, would react this way. Lark was a seasoned professional, wasn't she, used to every possible human frailty.

Lark grabbed another heated towel and placed it around Sheridan's shoulders before she removed the one Sheridan held on to so tightly. "Here, let me get that for you. It's got oil all over it."

The precious towel slipped away and Sheridan fumbled for the corners of the other one, only to feel it begin to slip as well. *Is the room really this hot?*

"Whoops!" Lark caught the errant towel and held it closed until Sheridan got her hands around it. "Got it? Good. Call me when you need help with your pants."

Without any further infliction, she left the room and Sheridan exhaled audibly, only then realizing she'd held her breath since the towel began to drop.

❖

Lark stopped outside the half-closed door to the massage room and wiped her hands on her sweatpants. It wasn't only the grape-seed oil that made them wet, and she frowned at the implications of this realization. Sheridan was an attractive, in fact, stunningly beautiful woman, even like this, pale and without a trace of makeup. Lark had had many female patients, but this was the first time she'd responded this way.

Ashamed at how her heart had raced when that towel slipped down one shoulder and began to fall off the other, she'd grabbed it and tugged it close around Sheridan's slender figure. It bothered Lark that she'd even noticed the fact that she glimpsed the outline of a breast. *Unprofessional. Beyond unprofessional.* Lark dragged her fingers through her hair twice as she tried by sheer willpower to calm down her thundering heart.

"Lark?" Sheridan's resonant voice called out. "You there?"

"Of course." Lark cleared her throat and rubbed a hand over her face before she entered the massage room. "Good job. You're fast."

"I've had some practice."

Lark took the sweatpants and knelt before Sheridan to push them up her legs. Rising, she wrapped a steady arm around Sheridan's waist while holding the lining of the pants with her free hand. "Hold on to me and rock slowly from side to side. With a little practice you can learn to do this yourself."

Sheridan's lower lip disappeared between her teeth, a habit that Lark was beginning to recognize as a sign of deep concentration. Wrapping her arm around Lark's shoulders, Sheridan and Lark swayed slowly back and forth together, as they both tugged her sweatpants up.

"Thank you. Very useful."

Lark managed to smile, still incredibly self-conscious. Was it her imagination, or did Sheridan seem shy? *Out of the question.*

"I know." Lark stepped back a little too quickly and almost tripped over her own feet. "Well, I think that's all you can muster today. Tomorrow morning, I'd like to start early and develop a good routine for you, if you don't object." She knew she was babbling. *I never babble like this, no matter what!* "And tomorrow afternoon we'll start the pool exercises too."

The thought of Sheridan in a swimsuit surfaced, but Lark slam-dunked it before it attached itself permanently to her mind's eye. As Lark left the room, she knew she had some soul-searching to do. Having lost her footing, she had to figure out what the hell was going on.

CHAPTER FOUR

Sheridan regarded the faint light of the rising sun with vehemence. She had been up, sitting in her study most of the night, with neural pain plaguing her legs and bitter thoughts shattering her mood. Mrs. D had looked in on her twice, probably roused by the night nurse, whom Sheridan chased away when she fussed too much. She grimaced at the thought of having to apologize to the woman yet again.

Lark had not fussed over her, Sheridan mused absentmindedly as she watched a flock of birds take off from the closest oak tree. She hadn't chastised Sheridan either, or admonished her for her admittedly lousy attitude, which was…refreshing. Sheridan gave a short bark of a laugh and turned the wheelchair back toward the desk. *She certainly is no doormat, though.* Instead, Lark had persevered with the calmness of someone sure of what she was doing and confident in her expertise. Lark had massaged her skillfully, and something in her unwavering touch had made Sheridan feel safe for a while.

Sheridan glanced at her watch. Quarter to seven. "Oh, well." She had begun to wheel toward the door when it suddenly opened, and the woman in her thoughts materialized on the threshold.

"Oh, my. I didn't think you were up yet. I mean, at least not in here already." Lark looked startled, but then smiled. "Erica gave me a copy of your schedule last night, so I could set up a program for you that you'll find convenient. I thought I'd put it on your desk—"

"Thank you. In the future, I suggest you knock before you enter." Sheridan uttered the harsh words almost as a reflex and regretted them instantly.

Lark looked down at her paper before she replied. "Naturally. I apologize." When she met Sheridan's eyes again, Sheridan was surprised that the enthusiastic gleam was still present, even if Lark's smile had vanished.

"Well," Sheridan said gruffly, "sometimes I'm conducting late night or early morning teleconferences, or long-distance phone calls, so…" She shrugged, uncertain what to say next. *God, when was I ever speechless before?*

"Don't apologize. I was wrong. Now that I know what crazy hours you keep, I'll be careful to knock in the future, okay? Have you had breakfast?"

Sheridan blinked at the sudden change of topic, and at how quickly Lark accepted the ground rules regarding her study. "Eh…no. I normally don't eat breakfast. Never have."

"That has to change. You're in a different situation now," Lark said. "Your body needs regular intakes of small meals, and to skip breakfast is to ask it to perform on nothing when it needs energy more than ever."

"It's never been a problem before."

"You weren't convalescing before. I've studied your medical history. You were fit and athletic before you succumbed to this virulent strain of meningitis." Lark leaned closer and placed a hand on Sheridan's arm. "There's nothing that says you can't be that way again. Perhaps not on your feet, but out of this chair."

Fury, fueled by sleeplessness and pain, surged through Sheridan. "You don't know what you're talking about. You didn't know me before this happened, but I will tell you, *I* know that I'm stuck in this chair. I'm not going to be *fit* ever again! So stop trying to blow smoke up my ass!" She wheeled out of Lark's reach and turned to face her head-on. "This is how it's going to be. I'll heed your little exercise schedule and give it a couple of weeks. If there's no progress, we'll call it quits."

"Wrong." To Sheridan's astonishment, Lark looked unfazed. "If you work with me, instead of against me, you *will* see progress, and you'll learn other ways to do things. I can't promise you that you'll walk again, but I can assure you that with your attitude you won't. It's time to go beyond self-pity and get to work."

Sheridan wanted to throttle Lark, slowly squeeze the life out of her for talking to her that way. "How dare you?" she asked, her voice a low snarl. "You presumptuous—"

"Yes, I've been called worse. But that doesn't matter." Lark stood and walked toward the door. "What really matters is that I do the job I'm hired to do. Help you help yourself feel better. See you in the gym in ten minutes." She smiled and left, quietly closing the door behind her.

Sheridan stared at the closed door, her eyes burning enough to scorch holes in the wood. She couldn't remember a single instant when her low, angry growl hadn't made people cower. And there Lark stood smiling, not bothered in the least. *Am I that predictable? Just another difficult patient of hers, probably.*

Disheartened at that possibility, Sheridan wheeled toward her room. One of the day nurses, new since two days ago, was waiting for her. Sheridan tried to remember her name—Anne, Anita something. Mrs. D hired the nurses, a chore Sheridan couldn't be bothered with, since they came and went every other week. Mrs. D had implied that Sheridan's mood sent them packing. Sheridan huffed and glared at the young woman waiting to assist her in the bathroom. "I'll let you know if I need you."

"Yes, ma'am."

Now this is the reaction my tone of voice always commands. But the fact remained, it hadn't affected Lark one little bit.

❖

Lark glanced up from her laptop, and seeing Sheridan was now in her gym clothes, she closed her e-mail software and tucked the computer away. "Good. That was quick."

"The sooner we begin, the sooner I can take care of business."

It was clear that Sheridan's mood hadn't improved.

"So true." Lark stood and approached Sheridan, deliberately not sounding too perky, but enthusiastic enough to get her attention. "I want to see how many low-impact exercises you can do."

Sheridan folded her arms over her chest, her eyes darkening. "Why?"

"Because we have to document where you are now, to be able to judge every week what progress you make."

Hesitating, Sheridan seemed to consider the indisputable logic in Lark's words. "How do we go about it? I thought Anne, Annie…eh, the new nurse would assist us."

"Annette. She had to go home early. Allergies, I believe," Lark lied. She had found the younger woman in tears in the corridor, and it didn't take a Nobel Prize winner to figure out who was the cause. "So, it's just us."

"Then how?" A worried frown appeared, like a crack in Sheridan's tough image.

"Like this." Lark knelt and pushed Sheridan's immobilized feet off the footrests. She folded the footrests out of the way before she got up and fetched the special walker and a harness from the back wall. "Here you go. Buckle this tightly around your waist. Tell me if you need help."

Sheridan fumbled with the belt, but managed to close it eventually. Lark wasn't about to step in and offer help when it was obvious that Sheridan would be able to figure it out.

"Good. Now, pay attention. This walker is special. It's taller than most, which means you can lean on it with all your strength. It may seem too tall for you to reach, but that's where the belt comes in. It has handles that I can hold on to, and together we'll raise you to your feet. I just have to put the braces on you, so your knees don't buckle."

"Sounds like a lot can go wrong."

"I can summon your head gardener, if you like." Lark had run into him, literally, when she completed her morning run.

"No. Let's do it."

Lark attached the braces, then took a position at a ninety-degree angle from Sheridan. She held on to the back of the belt with one hand and the walker with the other. "There we go. On three. One, two, *three.*"

Sheridan grabbed the handles and pulled, and the walker wobbled slightly. Lark tugged hard at the belt, and suddenly Sheridan was hanging with her arms fully supported on the tall walker. Wrapping her arm tightly around Sheridan's waist and holding on to the far handle, Lark stood pinned at Sheridan's side. "Good. Now walk over to that bench." A bench of queen-size-bed proportions stood about ten steps away.

"You could have told me we were doing it over there. I could've simply scooted over!" Sheridan was apparently still angry.

"No, you couldn't. The bench is at least nine inches too tall. This way you proved to yourself that you can rise into a standing position, with a little help." Lark kept her voice low and calm. "Now, I'm going to roll the walker. Try to imagine your feet walking. Try to move them."

The attempt turned out to be more than Sheridan was capable of, but they inched across the floor, and Sheridan put a lot of weight on her legs.

"You're doing great," Lark said. "This is so good for you. It prevents the risk of blood clots in your legs, as well as helps nutrition enter the cartilage in your joints. That can only happen when bones grind together from putting weight on them."

"All right. We're here. Now what?" Sheridan still sounded grumpy, but a little less so than earlier.

"You sit down. Hey, wait until I tell you to. This is all about collaboration. You'll notice that further on. You can't do this alone, and I can't do it for you." Lark helped Sheridan lower herself onto the bench. "There we go. Good."

"So we're joined at the hip until…?" Sheridan raised an elegant eyebrow, her face so close to Lark's, Lark felt tremors in her belly.

"Pretty much, at least during training. I'd also like to accompany you on typical things you do around your work, so I can fine-tune your training to suit your needs."

"I have a need right now," Sheridan groaned and looked unhappy. "I have a need for this to be over."

"This, as in this session, or this, the whole mess your illness left behind?"

"All of the above," Sheridan muttered.

Lark wondered if Sheridan knew how much she revealed of herself when she spoke like that. She meant to sound sarcastic, but the pain and exasperation shone through as clearly as if she wore it printed on her T-shirt.

"I won't keep you very long these first sessions. Now some push-ups. Try as hard as you can. I need a good number to start out with, so we can try to top your record twice a week."

"Very well." Sheridan tried to move over on her stomach, but kept slipping on the leather bench. "Damn!"

"Like this." Lark gently but insistently gripped Sheridan's hips. "A rocking motion. Feel it. You can do this. Rock or roll back and forth. Yes, like that. If the surface is hard enough, you'll be able to flip onto your stomach."

True enough, after a few attempts Sheridan twisted her body over, with only her left ankle still crossed across her right leg. Lark moved it for her, and without saying anything more, Sheridan forced her upper body up on straight arms.

Lark counted quietly to herself as Sheridan completed one push-up after another. After eight, her arms trembled so badly, she couldn't continue.

Cursing under her breath, Sheridan slumped onto her stomach, out of breath and sweating profusely. "How many?"

"Eight. Nearly nine."

"That has to be wrong. There were more. I'm beat, for heaven's sake!"

Lark bent down and stroked sweat-soaked bangs out of Sheridan's face without thinking. "No, Boss, you completed eight push-ups."

"But…Boss?" Sheridan's eyebrow went up again. "Are you sure you know how to count?"

Her new tone, with a slight teasing tinge to it, surprised Lark.

"Yeah, I know how to count. And you're my boss, aren't you?" She grinned at Sheridan, delighted that she still had a sense of humor.

"Then I have some work cut out for me." Sheridan grimaced and rolled over on her back. Placing her elbows behind her, she tried to sit up.

"Not like that. Here. Place that elbow like this. And the palm of your other hand like so. Now push." Lark smiled at the wondrous look on Sheridan's face as she quite easily maneuvered into a sitting position.

"Why haven't any of those other physical therapists showed me this?" Sheridan frowned.

"Did you listen to them?" Lark asked softly.

Sheridan's cheeks turned the faintest of pink. "Not really, I suppose. They infuriated me with their animated, overbearing ways. I didn't feel safe with them."

"And now?"

"You're more practical. Not so annoying. I appreciate that."

Lark coughed to hide a surprised laugh. *Thank goodness, I'm not so annoying. I suppose that's a compliment.* Looking at Sheridan when she tried the move she had just learned again was, however, reward enough.

❖

The men and women at Ward Industries headquarters, located not far from the Riverwalk Center, knew better than to gawk at their boss, Lark surmised. She had accompanied Sheridan in the limousine to the tall glass structure. Finished two years ago, the thirty-floor building hosted the headquarters, as well as the cutting-edge nanotechnology research center.

Sheridan wheeled past her employees with a rigid smile, not really acknowledging any particular person. Lark observed how she hesitated and tensed up even more for a few seconds before she entered the elevator, and made a mental note of the minor incident.

They exited on the top floor, and Lark had to look down to make sure her loafers didn't disappear into the thick carpet. An elegant woman in her early fifties, whose skirt actually matched the steel gray carpet, sat at the front desk.

"Ms. Ward! I wasn't sure you'd come in today. There was no message—"

"It's all right, Belinda. I'm taking the opportunity to show Lark around." Sheridan continued to formally introduce Lark and Belinda. "Lark's here to study my daily routine at the office. I think she'll be bored to tears very soon, when she realizes that all I do is sit by my desk and turn papers."

Belinda sent Lark an inquisitive glance, and Lark immediately picked up a possessive vibe from the other woman.

"Welcome," Belinda said politely and extended a hand. "I've worked for Sheridan for more than ten years now, so if you have any questions, I'm sure I can be of assistance."

Wow, if that's not marking your territory, I don't know what is.
"Thank you, Belinda. That's very kind of you." Lark smiled sweetly before she followed Sheridan into her corner office.

Inside, she nearly lost her manners and had to forcibly shut her dropped jaw. Sheridan's office was not what she'd expect from someone loaded with old money and traditions that stretched more than 150 years back. It was entirely ultra-modern. The Plexiglas desk was at least eight feet long where it stood angled from the window. Brushed metal shelves outlined an entire wall and were filled with books, awards, and collectibles of different types. The opposite wall held the mandatory diplomas and award plaques. In the middle, a large black-and-white family portrait caught Lark's attention. A man in his early forties sat on a leather couch with his arm around a stunning, yet frail-looking woman with long dark hair. On her lap, a little girl, perhaps six years old, sat, her eyes piercing.

"That has to be you," Lark said and pointed before she looked over her shoulder at Sheridan.

"Yes."

"Your mother was very beautiful. You look like her." Lark jerked when she heard her own words repeated in her head. *Damn! Talk about obvious.*

Sheridan didn't seem to notice. "Really? Most people say I'm a chip off the old block when it comes to my father."

Lark examined the photo again. "Nope. Sorry, but you're the spitting image of your mom. Look at the eyes, the facial structure. I think you have your father's nose though."

"And his sense for business, which is what really matters to the stockholders and the employees. I need to regain my strength, since it's sort of my trademark. I used to pull all-nighters all the time without a problem. Now it's impossible to stay awake after ten p.m." Sheridan spat the last words. "No matter what it takes, you have to come up with a way for me to accomplish that."

"All right. Sounds like you're giving me carte blanche." Lark grinned. "You might regret that."

Sheridan shrugged and wheeled over to the desk.

"If you give me a few seconds to examine how you utilize the equipment around your desk, then I'll be out of your hair and you can actually do some work, all right?"

"Sure." Sheridan sat motionless as Lark circled the desk.

"I'm going to start by taking some measurements. You see, in order to increase your level of energy, you need to be clever about how you use whatever energy you *do* have. Think of it like a bank account. You have only a certain amount of dollars put in, and if you constantly take out more than you deposit, you'll have to start to withdraw from other accounts, other resources, which creates a vicious cycle."

Sheridan seemed to consider Lark's analogy. "Makes sense."

"So that's why you should have your keyboard much lower. From your position, you need a shelf for it beneath desk level. See? Like this."

Lark reached around Sheridan to show her. "About one or two inches below your elbow level." Suddenly Lark realized that she virtually had her arms wrapped around Sheridan, and she forgot what she had meant to say.

Sheridan turned her head and her lips nearly touched Lark's cheek. "I guess I can have my decorator add…Lark?"

It was hard to breathe, and even more difficult to focus, but Lark did both. Smiling, she nodded. "Yes, that'd be great. Let's look at what else you do in here. You read and sign documents, right?"

A slight frown on Sheridan's forehead showed that she may well have picked up on Lark's temporary confusion. "Sure. I do that right here."

"Then that level needs to have plenty of leg-free space. No cords, bins, or anything like that." Lark heard herself speak faster than normal and willed her words to come out slower, more confidently. "Everything in here is glass and metal. As stylish as that look is, you need soothing things to look at. Your eyes are directly connected to the brain, via the optical nerve, and disturbing reflections in water, glass, or metal can trigger seizures such as the ones you suffered during the first months. The flickering image on TVs or video games can too."

"You mean I'll have to redecorate?" Frosty was a good way to describe Sheridan's tone.

"Yes. To stay healthy and as energized as possible, I think you do."

"I don't suppose you realize that I spent more than eight hundred thousand dollars hiring the best designer and buying the best materials in Texas to create this office?"

"I'm sure it's stunning and that it took a lot of—"

"Don't patronize me. I really could care less if you like it or not." The low growl, which was becoming familiar by now, was back in Sheridan's voice. "*I* like it. It stays."

"So you'd rather risk a seizure than change the décor?" Lark challenged Sheridan. "Is there any other office on this floor with a different design?"

"Any other room than the corner suite?" Sheridan commented disdainfully. "I think not."

"Well, I give you my opinions, and I'll argue them for a while, but ultimately the decision is yours, of course." Lark brushed Sheridan's annoyance away. "Now, the positioning of the desk...Yes?" Lark blinked and stopped talking as Sheridan rolled up to her.

"You want to move the desk too?"

"Not really, just move it a bit to the left to give you ample room to pivot with your chair to reach the printer and fax machine. That way you don't have to knock the footrests into the desk legs or the cabinets. Not only will it conserve energy, it will draw less attention to the fact that you're in a wheelchair. I find that this subterfuge means a lot to most of my patients."

"Really." Sheridan dragged a hand through her hair. "They did stare at me, didn't they? When we passed the people in the lobby?"

"Yes."

Tilting her head as she looked up at Lark, Sheridan smiled sadly. "You're the first one who's been honest about that situation. Other people mean well when they keep saying that people don't stare or aren't bothered by the fact that I'm this way."

"There's nothing wrong with the way you are. Don't define yourself by the disease. You aren't your disability."

"I know that. I'm a Ward, however, with all it entails. My great-great-grandfather came to this state from Boston with his parents. He became one of the first officers at Fort Sam. They were rich and became even richer, owning industries back on the East Coast, investing in several ranches in Texas; they were enterprising people who never rested. During WWII, my grandfather started what eventually became a virtual empire of companies. Ward Industries. This is who I am. This is the legacy I stand to lose if I don't get my act together!" Sheridan breathed hard after her outburst.

"Listen. You are who you are, and ultimately this experience will add to the person you are, but you won't know that until some time has passed." Without thinking how her gesture might seem, Lark knelt next to Sheridan and took her hand between her own. "You can't see that yet, which is okay. It's too soon. But, I promise you, this isn't the end of life as you knew it, not completely. I won't lie to you, ever. That's the worst thing anyone can do at this point. You need people to rely on, and it's counterproductive to embellish facts or hide them from you."

"Really." Sheridan's pale face seemed to color faintly. "You really are something. I suppose time will tell if you're all you say you are."

Lark laughed and let go of Sheridan's hand. Her own tingled in a telltale way. Unable to deny Sheridan's beauty, Lark struggled to keep her smile even and reassuring. "I'm a WYSIWYG kind of person, so you won't be surprised or disappointed, I hope."

A new spark of interest glimmered in Sheridan's eyes. "Wysi-what?"

"A what-you-see-is-what-you-get person."

For the first time since they met, Lark was treated to Sheridan's laughter. Throwing her head back, Sheridan guffawed, a contagious sound that sent Lark into a fit of laughter of her own. "I think you underestimate yourself," Sheridan said and smiled "It's been my experience that all of us have hidden depths, of good and bad."

Lark didn't miss a beat. "Then we'll tap into your hidden depths and your strengths. That's what you'll need to succeed."

"Touché." Sheridan gazed out the window where the city buzzed so far beneath them. "I believe you think you can apply your experience from previous patients to me, but I'm not so sure."

"Because you're special, and your brutal disease was unusual? I don't mean to diminish what happened to you, but the result was brain damage, which I'm very qualified to deal with."

Clearly angry again, Sheridan snapped her head back to nail Lark with her cool gray eyes. "For someone in my position, with the life I lead and the responsibilities I have, to sustain brain damage is devastating. I couldn't come any closer to a career-stopper than this!"

Lark spoke with emphasis, mildly exasperated. "Brain damage, *any* damage, to a person is devastating. Wouldn't you agree that a child who's in a car crash, or who develops a critical condition such as yours, no matter their social status, is in an even more heartbreaking position? A little person who'll never walk, who'll never know the joy of feeling fresh grass under his or her feet. A child who'll need assistance to do even the simplest things?"

Leaning forward, Lark wanted to get her point across so she could be sure they had crossed this bridge once and for all. "You can't compare your condition, your status, with anyone else's. You aren't worse off, nor are you helped by the fact that you're wealthy, when it comes to pain, anguish, and suffering. You're no more entitled to good health than anyone else."

"Don't you lecture me—"

"That's not what I'm doing. I come to this point with all my patients, sooner or later, where this needs to be said. We have to figure out this concept before we can really move on and expect progress."

"So you snap your fingers, and *voila*, I see the light and the errors of my ways, and we live happily every after?" Sheridan mocked Lark's words. "You really must be completely naïve, to strive for such principles."

Angry now, at having her whole philosophy for doing this job the right way thrown in her face, Lark rose to her feet. "Well, then. I have some business to take care of while I'm in town," she said, deliberately and slowly. She was fuming by now. *Of all the snobbish brats, she must feel that, with her status in society and business, she's above this whole mess. Damn it!* "See you back at the mansion for our five o'clock session."

"Unless work keeps me here."

Lark was afraid that her anger would show, so she stood with her back to Sheridan as she calmly replied, "Work can wait. I'll see you at five in the gym."

She would have liked to slam the door, but feared that the thin glass wouldn't survive.

CHAPTER FIVE

It was impossible to sleep. Sheridan shifted in bed, cold to the bone. Someone had set the air conditioner too high during the day, when the hot weather demanded it, and then forgot to turn it down in the evening. She tugged at the blankets, but found no warmth in them. She shivered, and for a moment she wondered if she would ever be warm again.

This was such a contrast from the afternoon when she'd been drenched with sweat from the physiotherapy session. Lark had been her professional, kind self when she worked with Sheridan, with no signs of any residual anger. Only the fact that Lark didn't even mention their altercation hinted that she hadn't quite put it behind her.

Sheridan was still upset at being called a hypocrite. Obviously Lark didn't see the big picture, the ramifications of Sheridan's disease. The company, the board of directors, the stockholders, the employees with their families; so many depended on her successful handling of Ward Industries. To compare her to any of Lark's previous patients was ludicrous!

A grinding ache between her shoulder blades began to seep down her spine. It changed into a cold, icy twinge, and she knew when it hit her hips that she was in for one of those hateful nights when nothing could ease the agony. Cold sweat ran down her temples and the back of her neck. Groaning out loud, Sheridan turned her head into the pillow to muffle the sound.

The rapping of fingernails against the door made Sheridan clench her teeth to try to contain the pain, but she couldn't answer. The door opened and Mrs. D poked her head in. At the sight of Sheridan, she hurried toward the bed.

"Honey." The soothing voice, so caring, made Sheridan lose her self-control. As flashes of pain shot through her legs, she flung an arm over her eyes and whimpered under her breath.

"Oh, Sheridan. It's that bad again, huh?"

Sheridan didn't want to meet Mrs. D's eyes, where she was certain the full extent of her pain—physical, emotional, all of it—would reflect and emphasize how trapped she was. Sheridan thought she heard several voices murmur next to her, but had to keep herself closed off, behind these self-inflicted bars, or the grinding ache would seep out, permeate everything, including the air she breathed, and there'd be no end to it. Some words filtered through despite Sheridan's best intentions to keep everything out.

"…found her this way. It's not the first time."

"The doctor's never seen her like this?"

"…won't allow me to call…"

"…medication…"

"None."

After a moment's silence, Sheridan had no idea how long, the mattress moved to her left, and she groaned as it made her body shift.

"Sorry, Sheridan. I brought something that will help. Please, let me help you through this."

Lark. The familiar voice, clear and soft, washed over Sheridan's senses and left her naked and raw for a fraction of time. Afraid that this vulnerability would allow the pain unrestricted access, Sheridan withdrew. "No, no. Quiet."

"Here. Let me try this. All you have to do is lie still. All right?"

"Hurts." Just uttering the word was almost more than Sheridan could manage.

"I know. But not for long."

"Go away."

"I can't. I was up late watching a movie and heard Mrs. D, when I was on my way to the kitchen for some juice."

"No. Make *it* go away." Sweat broke out on her back and chest as Sheridan tried to make herself understood. "Cold."

"All right. Mrs. D will turn down the air conditioner. It really is cold in here," Lark said. "Lie still, even if you feel a twitch or a little stick, okay?"

"No drugs. Nauseous."

"No drugs."

Small, warm hands poked Sheridan's skin and stuck her with something sharp every now and then. "It's acupuncture, Sheridan. Small, thin needles. Try to relax as much as you can. Good." Lark's voice, instructive, calm, was like water on a scorched piece of land.

"She always suffers the worst headaches when the neural pain's over," Mrs. D said worriedly.

"How do you handle that?"

"She has to lie in a dark room all day, and she still throws up constantly."

"Let's see if we can't prevent that, too."

Sheridan felt Lark move her sweat-soaked pillows out of the way.

"Let your head relax on my lap. I'm going to use acupressure here instead of the needles. I don't want to shock your system by using too many of them at once. So, here we go."

Fingers pressed into Sheridan's temples. "This isn't entirely orthodox, medically speaking," Lark continued. "My mother has suffered from migraines all her life, and this method works for her. I found out by mistake almost, when trying to massage her headache away as a physiotherapy student. She suffered through my efforts for a bit, and we were totally shocked when her headaches suddenly subsided and the nausea went away. Let me know if you feel any relief."

Sheridan had been focusing on Lark's beautiful voice, and was startled at how it in itself seemed to alleviate the discomfort. *Like hypnosis.* Slowly, the fire along her nerve endings mellowed, until it was back under control.

Taking a deep breath, Sheridan reluctantly opened her eyes, aware that she was sweaty, still freezing cold. She looked up at Lark with a silly sense of inferiority. "Thank you." It wasn't what she'd meant to say. Sheridan searched her throbbing head for familiar words of sarcasm or irony, but they seemed to have vanished, temporarily, she hoped, with the worst of the headache.

"You're welcome." Lark smiled down at her. "I'm glad I could help. Not all people respond to acupuncture."

"Now you tell me."

"And Mrs. D's description of how this normally plays out doesn't sound very appealing."

"I'd say so."

"Just relax against me a while longer. I think you've been under quite a bit of stress today, both going into work and dealing with a new health-care professional. We need to be careful in the future, so we don't make you sicker instead of better."

Sheridan eyed Lark closely, to see if she was being facetious, but ultimately decided that she was sincere. With a sigh, she let her head rest completely on Lark's lap. Gently now, Lark massaged her scalp and chased the last remnants of the headache away.

Down her hips and legs, she detected only a buzzing sensation now, a numbness that suggested her nerve endings had self-combusted from the attack and would need some time before they returned to what passed for normal these days.

The sensation of Lark's hands in her hair was pure bliss. The hovering migraine subsided, like a stormy sea coming to rest against an empty shore. The waves stopped crashing over her; instead they soothed her with their rocking motions. Dazed, Sheridan looked up at Lark, whose cinnamon eyes gazed softly back at her.

"Better?" Lark whispered.

"Yes. Thank you."

"You're welcome. Just relax. We'll change the sheets and help you settle a bit."

Sheridan frowned. She didn't like the sound of that statement. Too hospital-like. Too—fuzzy. She tried to pull back, away from a contact that had grown too close. "I'm okay. Really. Let go."

Lark's hand hovered above her for a second, and then Lark slipped out from beneath her. "All right. In that case, why don't you jump over into your wheelchair and go clean up a bit. You up for that, or do you need help?"

"I can manage." Sheridan tried to lessen the snarl in her voice. As soon as Lark had removed the acupuncture needles, Sheridan scooted over to her wheelchair, absentmindedly noticing how much easier this procedure had become. Her physical therapist was quickly placing her mark on a lot of things.

"Good. Mrs. D and I will remake the bed." Lark touched Sheridan's shoulder briefly. "Let me know if you change your mind. No shame in that, right?"

Sheridan heard her voice sink an octave. "Right."

Inside the bathroom, she ripped off her nightwear—a tank top and a pair of boxers. She reached for the knob to a top cabinet door, opened it, and as she rummaged around for the underwear, managed to spill all of its contents onto the counter and floor. *"Fuck,"* Sheridan muttered to herself. *"Damn, damn, damn."* She reached for a new set of underwear and placed it on the toilet lid. A glance at the shower made her press her lips together in a mock smile. There was no way she'd be able to shower on her own or pick up the stuff that she'd dropped on the floor.

The wheels couldn't turn among the scattered clothes, no matter how hard she tried. "Oh, wonderful." Sheridan glared at the closed door. *I don't want her to see me like this. Clumsy. Looking like an idiot.* Mrs. D was one thing, but what if Lark came in? Knowing she had no choice, unless she wanted to sit there the rest of the night, Sheridan rang the cordless buzzer attached to the armrest.

The sound of approaching steps announced that help was on the way. The door opened a crack and the golden-brown head made it impossible that it would be Mrs. D.

"You rang?" Lark grinned. "Need help? Oh, I see. No problem." Lark stepped inside, clearly unmindful of Sheridan's foul mood. "I do this all the time," Lark said. "I reach for one thing, and the way I chuck things into the cabinets, I manage to tear everything out at once. Garland says I'm a natural-born disaster."

"Garland?"

"My oldest sister. I have four. I'm a middle child."

"Four sisters," Sheridan said weakly as she watched Lark pick up the clothes and merely push them back into the cabinet. "I can tell you've done that before."

"What? Oh. You think I should've folded them?" Lark looked at the half-closed cabinet with two tank tops hanging out halfway.

"Yeah, well, I don't care. Mrs. D might have a small fit though. But don't worry about it." Sheridan shrugged.

"I'll rearrange them while you shower. I don't want Mrs. D to find out that I'm this sloppy. Not yet. I want to stay on her good side for as long as possible." Lark winked and walked over to Sheridan. "Now, I suppose you want a shower after having sweated bullets like that? And you're wondering how you'll be able to shower by yourself."

"Yes," Sheridan admitted through gritted teeth. In fact, she was hard-pressed not to smile at Lark's self-deprecating tone.

"Then, look at this. When I was here checking your facilities out—don't frown, you know that's my job—I noticed that your fancy tub comes with a chair. Did you know that?"

"We installed a lift," Sheridan said.

"Which was probably very useful when you were worse off than you are now. But this," Lark pulled out what looked like something made of plastic and pipes, "is better for you now. It'll give you what you need most right now."

"And what is that?" Sheridan eyed the chair that Lark attached to the tub. It glided on the bars, which meant that it could reach out to the middle of the tub.

"This is independence. Look, it even lowers into the water if you want to take a bath. You might need help raising it again until your arms are stronger, but you'll do fine just taking a shower on your own."

Sheridan had nearly stopped listening after the word "independence." Her heart thundered in her chest, and she gazed dimly up at Lark, who, lit up by the track lighting above her, looked almost angelic when she smiled at her. "Sounds fine," she managed.

"Okay. Do you feel comfortable trying to scoot over and handle the shower on your own, Sheridan? Or do you want me to stay and supervise this first time?"

Sheridan's first reaction was to ask Lark to leave. She was desperate for her first dive into independence after having to rely on other people all this time. But a warning voice inside her cautioned her to be smart. Sheridan hadn't reached her status as head of one of the most successful, and definitely fastest growing, conglomerates in Texas by being foolish. "What if you stay and fold the clothes and I handle the shower?" she suggested. "That way I can just ask for help if I need it."

"Brilliant idea. And it'll save me from Mrs. D's wrath as well. Cool." Lark winked and turned her back on Sheridan, then reached for the cabinet door.

The shower was heaven on earth. Hot, pulsating, and cleansing, it streamed down Sheridan's pale body, rinsing sweat and anxiety away. She washed her hair, taking her own good time, and cleaned her body's every crevice without having to think of anyone watching or waiting. Sure, Lark was waiting, but she was humming merrily behind the sliding door. At one point, Mrs. D. knocked discreetly, but Lark just said that they were fine, which seemed to be enough for the housekeeper.

When she was ready, Sheridan realized her mistake. She had

forgotten to bring towels close enough. "Lesson number one, make preparations," she muttered to herself.

"What? You okay?" Lark asked.

"Forgot the towels."

"No worries." The shower door opened a few inches, and two towels landed on Sheridan's lap. "I'm draping one over the wheelie too."

"Thanks." Sheridan had to laugh. So it was that easy. Like two friends helping each other out. Not the usual feeling of being the patient, not to be trusted to handle anything on her own. Instead, Lark seemed to assume that Sheridan could do just about anything, unless she asked for help.

It proved rather difficult to move from the shower seat with a towel wrapped around her, and yet another towel around her hair. She was so exhausted now that her hands trembled and her arms were very weak. "Lark?"

"Yes?"

"I—I need help getting back. I'm tangled in the towel." She cringed at how pathetic she sounded, but Lark seemed to take the request in stride as well.

"All right, hang in there." Lark opened the door and pulled at the towel. "There. Now come my way. Good."

Sheridan managed to move into the chair and sat slumped with fatigue, but with a sense of accomplishment that she hadn't felt in a long time. "I also need to get dressed," Sheridan confessed. "I'm exhausted." It wasn't hard to admit, for once; instead, she had a reason to be tired.

"Let me dry your hair first." Lark wrapped a robe around Sheridan's shoulders and began to brush it.

"This isn't really in your job description." Sheridan looked at Lark's reflection in the mirror, only now realizing that her physical therapist was dressed in silk pajamas under a terry-cloth robe. "And it's the middle of the night."

"Shh, never mind. It's in my contract to help you function, and this is one way of doing just that. I think we covered quite a bit of ground." Lark grabbed the hairdryer. "It means a lot to me to see you succeed." After that baffling statement, Lark switched on the hairdryer.

Lark's magic fingers were back in Sheridan's wet hair, brushing through it as she dried it, strand by strand. It didn't take long, but the process was hypnotizing, and Sheridan couldn't take her eyes from their reflection. She jumped, startled, when Lark switched off the hairdryer and placed it on the counter.

"There we go. Not bad, if I do say so myself."

"It looks fine." Nervous, suddenly, at how it would feel to have Lark help her dress without feeling utterly vulnerable, Sheridan withdrew, knowing full well how short she sounded. "If you give me the tank top and boxers, I'll ask Mrs. D for help."

"I think she went back to bed. I told her you were fine and that we could manage."

Great. Frustrated, Sheridan wanted to groan, but didn't object when Lark wheeled her back into the bedroom. The room was immaculate, and only a soft light burned. With Lark's help, Sheridan pulled herself over onto the bed. The towel slipped off completely in the process, but Lark merely tucked the robe closed around her.

"Are you able to put these on yourself?" Lark held out the tank top and boxers.

"The tank top. My feet are too far away to put on the boxers."

"Hmm. I need to introduce you to a couple of nifty tools that'll make you a lot more independent. Honestly, I'm surprised that you haven't had a visit from an occupational therapist from the rehab clinic you stayed at, to make sure you had everything you need."

Sheridan felt her cheeks go warm. *Not again.* What was it about this woman that flustered her so? "I think there was a woman here who tried." Sheridan shrugged and avoided Lark's eyes. "I wasn't ready for her." The truth was that Sheridan had run the poor woman off in a formidable explosion of anger. Regretfully, she now shook her head. "I'm afraid I was quite rude."

Lark was quiet for a moment, as if pondering what to say. "It was too soon, probably. I think you'd be more inclined to listen to her now. Or I can order a few items that I think you'd find useful, if you trust me to."

Sheridan opened her mouth to speak, then shut it just as quickly when an unexpected thought struck her. *Trust her?* It wasn't in her nature to be overly trusting. She found her natural habit of suspecting ulterior motives a lifesaver, professionally and privately. And still, Lark's golden brown eyes, darkened by an unreadable emotion, made

Sheridan almost trust her, no questions asked. *Dangerous.* Sheridan took a deep breath. "Sure. Order anything you want."

"Okay." Lark pulled the boxers over Sheridan's feet and up her calves. When she reached mid-thigh, she stopped and tipped her head back to look at her. Sounding breathless, she spoke quickly. "From here you know how to do it."

"Roll from side to side." Sheridan swallowed, feeling the dryness in her mouth as she gripped the lining of the boxers hard. "Not very dignified, but practical."

"Very practical." Lark's eyes grew even darker, and her hand covered Sheridan's for a moment.

"You can go back to your room. I've kept you up long enough," Sheridan murmured.

"No worries. I'll do a quick cleanup of the bathroom, then check on you. Only way I can sleep, you know."

"What do you mean?" Sheridan held on to the boxers under the robe, afraid they'd slip down her legs again. She needed to steer Lark out of the room, or she wouldn't be able to exhale.

"I sleep better if my client is safely tucked in, no matter her age." Lark winked, rose from the floor, and disappeared into the bathroom.

Sheridan eventually managed to haul the boxers up and over her hips. Shaking the robe off her shoulders, she eased on the tank top and felt much better for simply being covered. She wanted to lie down and pull the covers up, but stared gloomily at her dead legs. She had some feeling in them, but not all over. Unable to move them, she hated her legs, despised them some days. Now she studied them and tried for the first time since she came home from the rehab clinic to determine how she could perhaps drag them onto the bed by herself. *Thinking outside the box. That's my claim to fame in the business world.*

Sheridan began to push herself backward, until her calves rested on the edge of the bed. She lay down, then began to pivot and lie down on her pillow. Her legs were still at an awkward angle, but they were at least on the bed and she pulled the covers up, rather pleased with her first attempt.

Lark came back into the bedroom and stopped by the bed with a broad smile. "Hey, good job!" She slipped her hands under the covers and straightened Sheridan's legs. "Soon you'll get the hang of doing this yourself without a problem."

"If you say so." It was hard to believe, but Sheridan felt reluctantly optimistic.

"I do say so." Lark inspected the bedside table and moved the buzzer closer to Sheridan's bed. "You have everything here within reach. Time for all of us to sleep."

"Yes. Good night." Sheridan sank farther into the mattress and the pillows, exhausted.

Lark stood motionless for a while. "Good night, Sheridan. Sleep well."

The door closed behind her and Sheridan stared at it for long seconds. Was that the cause of the sudden darkness, or was it because Lark wasn't here? Grasping the corner of her pillow, she shut her eyes tightly and willed sleep to come. She was going to need all of her strength when it was time to face Lark in the morning.

CHAPTER SIX

L ark continued her interrupted stroll toward the kitchen to find
something to drink. Frowning, she thought a stiff whisky
would probably do her better than the juice she had originally planned.
Watching Sheridan in excruciating pain had affected her tremendously.
"To say the least," she murmured to herself. "What the hell's wrong
with me?"

The kitchen was deserted, with only a faint light coming from
the counter next to the refrigerator. She opened the door and picked
up a small juice carton. As she looked around, Lark tried to figure out
where the kitchen staff kept the glasses, but had to resort to opening the
cabinets one by one.

"Can I help you?"

Lark cried out and dropped the carton on the counter. She barely
registered that it didn't break before she whirled around. "Mrs. D!"

"I'm sorry. Didn't mean to startle you, Lark. Glasses are in that
cabinet." Mrs. D pointed to Lark's right. "Cook and the two boys that
serve keep a tight ship. Glad that thing didn't break. We'd be in here
scrubbing things spotless until daybreak."

The dry humor wasn't wasted on Lark, who laughed a little louder
than called for. "You took five years off my life."

"I hope not. That wouldn't sit well with Sheridan."

"What? Why?" Lark nearly dropped the glass she'd just pulled
out, and she glared at Mrs. D. "Stop *doing* that!"

"I can see you're going to be good for Sheridan. Let's not risk
your health by scaring you to death, eh?"

"Good idea." Carefully, in case Mrs. D caused her to flinch again,
Lark poured herself some orange juice. "Want some?"

"Don't mind if I do."

Lark filled another glass for Mrs. D, who took a seat by the stainless-steel kitchen island. "Join me for a little bit. I won't keep you long."

Lark sat down and sipped her drink. "You were saying about Sheridan?"

"She may not realize it yet, but you're just what and who she needs to push her toward healing. I think with time you'll see this as well. Sheridan isn't easy to get to know, it's true, and has been like that ever since she was a little girl. A tomboy at heart, she wore cute little dresses for her mother's sake. You have to understand that Sheridan idolized her father back then, but loved her mother even more. She would do anything, even things that were completely out of character, to make her mother happy. When Mrs. Ward passed away, Sheridan blamed her father, and they never quite reconciled."

"They never spoke? But she was so young?" Lark asked, horrified.

"Oh, of course they spoke. They both loved Ward Industries. But they never resolved the part that entailed Mrs. Ward."

"Why are you telling me this? I'd think you're the type who would never break a confidence even if someone dragged you over hot coals."

"True." Mrs. D smiled faintly. "But this is about Sheridan and her healing. She'd be on my case and string me up if she knew, but I've worked here long enough to love her like she was my own child. If I don't tell you things that might help you overlook her ways, she may end up firing you and…she can't afford to." The last words came out as a broken whisper.

Lark placed her hand on Mrs. D's. "I hear you. And as for that, Sheridan won't hear from *me* that you told me about her father. I know her mother died of cancer of the pancreas, it was mentioned in her medical file, but why did Sheridan blame her father?"

Mrs. D shook her head. "As much as I'd like to, I can't tell you that."

"All right."

"Not that I wouldn't if I could, since it would give you valuable insight into Sheridan's mind, but…even I don't know the full story. I have my theories, but since I'm not sure, I'd better keep them to myself."

"Smart thinking. Cheers, Mrs. D." Lark raised her glass. "Sheridan has a very good substitute for a mother in you."

"Don't tell her that." Mrs. D. clinked her glass against Lark's. "Sheridan cares for me like a family member, but to her, Mrs. Ward was as close to an angel as any human being can be."

They sat in silence for a moment before Mrs. D placed their glasses in the dishwasher and said good night. Lark padded back to her room and switched on her computer. It was obviously too late to call her family in Boerne or her friend in Austin, but she might have an e-mail.

To her dismay, her inbox only had spam, which Lark deleted with a curse. She went to her hotmail account, the one she used when she corresponded with people outside her immediate family and friends. A while back, she'd struck up a conversation with another woman, Debbie, who was a member of the physical therapist mailing list Lark belonged to.

Debbie was fun, lighthearted, and always ready to goof off in a chat room. Lark knew Debbie wanted more from her, she'd have to be blind not to see this, but she wasn't ready for any mindless flings in cyberspace. Or she hadn't been, at least. Her body's reactions these last few days indicated that perhaps she *was* ready to have a fling, no matter what kind.

Her youngest sister always accused Lark of being too serious about relationships. The family was well aware of Lark's sexual orientation, even if her mother wouldn't address it openly. This sister on the other hand constantly tried to hook her up with her lesbian friends, or encouraged Lark to approach someone.

Lark opened her chat software and Debbie's icon showed her status as online. Lark opened a chat window and typed a greeting.

Grey_bird: Hi Debbie. You around?
Sirensong: Lark! Why you up this late?
Grey_bird: Working late.
Sirensong: I'd say.
Grey_bird: And you?
Sirensong: Playing Scrabble with unsuspecting strangers
and trying to pick up a cute woman or two.
Grey_bird: Two???
Sirensong: Interested? *wink*

Grey_bird: LOL! Trying me too, huh? You must be
          desperate.
Sirensong: No, no. Just going for gold.

Lark frowned at the last comment from Debbie. What was that about?

Grey_bird: What are you talking about? What gold?

There was a brief pause and then Debbie typed a reply.

Sirensong: You're the gold.

Knowing full well she was in over her head, Lark rubbed the back of her neck as her mind raced.
Grey_bird: So what's the plan?

She held her breath. Apparently so did Debbie.

Sirensong: *gasp* For real?
Grey_bird: Like you, I'm just testing the waters.

Lark didn't know why she put it that way. Images of a naked, vulnerable Sheridan appeared in her mind, and Lark could feel the silken skin under her hands. She gripped the mouse and was about to just turn off the chat program and feign a computer crash, when Debbie wrote again.

Sirensong: Want to cyber hug a bit? No strings attached.

A hug. Apart from her family, Lark couldn't remember when she'd last held someone closely. Some of her patients had done so out of gratitude, but that was it.

Grey_bird: I like hugs. *squeeze*
Sirensong: Mmmm. Me too! *hugging back*
Grey_bird: If I close my eyes, I can feel you. Strange.
          Cool, but strange.

The truth was that Lark imagined Sheridan embracing her out of gratitude, probably since that was the only reason Ms. Ward would ever embrace her. "God, what am I thinking?" Lark moaned out loud. She refocused on the computer screen.

Sirensong: I feel it and then some.
Grey_bird: Describe "some."
Sirensong: I'm greedy and take my chances. I'm picturing you in a...let me see. A bikini. A black bikini.

Lark laughed and slapped her forehead.

Grey_bird: You horny devil. You're such a brat!
Sirensong: That does it. Off with the bikini.
Grey_bird: LOL!
Sirensong: *hugging again* Now that's more like it!
Grey_bird: Greedy is too mild a word. More like voracious!
Sirensong: Semantics. It feels good to hold you like this, in your birthday suit.

Suddenly Lark really did feel naked, no matter the tongue-in-cheek approach.

Grey_bird: Hey, we have to stop this. Feels a bit too real and I don't want to wreck the friendship. You're my best chat buddy.

Lark held her breath as she waited for Debbie to reply.

Sirensong: Oh, all right. Knew it was too good to be true. *pout*
Grey_bird: I'll make it up to you.
Sirensong: You will? Really? *hopeful*
Grey_bird: Really. You know you've bugged me for a picture. I'll send one later.
Sirensong: Pictures! *thud* Ow, I fell off the chair. Nudie pictures?

Grey_bird: Debbie!
Sirensong: Sorry, sorry. Force of habit. Really, I'd love a
picture. Will be nice to have a face to go with
the sexy character.

Lark rolled her eyes as she said good night to Debbie. She found a small head shot of herself in her pictures folder, which she sent to Debbie before she logged off. Just a little superficial fun. Nothing to be hung up about, so why did she feel guilty? She had gone further while chatting with other strange women and not suffered one single minute of remorse.

Lark put on her robe and crawled into bed. As usual she curled up on her left side and pulled the covers up to her nose. Safe and whole in her cocoon of bed linen, she allowed her thoughts to wander. It didn't take them many seconds to roam back to Sheridan. Lark frowned and turned on her other side, in order to try to shake them. She had a long day ahead of her. Three hours' sleep and then she was doing PT with Sheridan, before they went to the office where Sheridan had a meeting.

Sheridan. Lark's eyes began to close and she didn't fight sleep like she did some nights.

"Sheridan," she murmured, already dreaming. "Let me help, okay?"

❖

Sheridan sat at her Plexiglas desk, presiding over an impromptu meeting with a handful of her senior staff. Lark had literally taken the back seat by the wall to Sheridan's right, not about to get caught in the line of fire. She had asked if she should leave, but Sheridan had insisted that she stay, claiming she wanted Lark to know what a day at the office could be like. As Sheridan regarded the man who sat across the desk from her, Lark could sense Sheridan's anger simmer under a calm that was only skin deep.

"What are you saying, Dimitri?" Sheridan asked in a low voice, and Lark realized from studying the other people in the office that she wasn't the only one who found Sheridan's low register intimidating.

"Please, don't misunderstand, Ms. Ward," the CFO said, "but it's obvious that your, eh, illness has affected you. It's only human. Easy to make mistakes and lack judgment when you're not well." He coughed, probably to hide his awkwardness when Sheridan put him on the spot.

Sheridan seemed to ponder Dimitri's words. "So, you would argue that it's easy, *inevitable*, even, that a person who has recently suffered a serious illness would make mistakes?" she asked slowly.

"Yes, ma'am," Dimitri said, sounding relieved. "Completely human, of course."

"Of course." To Dimitri's left, two men covered their eyes, shaking their heads. Sheridan went in for the kill. "Well, considering I hired you for the job as CFO only two weeks after I came out of the coma, then might that prove to be the biggest mistake of all?" She raised an inquisitive eyebrow.

Dimitri was several shades paler now. "That wasn't what I was… I mean, I didn't…" He stopped talking, probably realizing that he'd painted himself into a corner. "Point taken, ma'am."

"Thank you." Sheridan relented. "So, we're in agreement, ladies and gentlemen? The stockowner festivities commence as usual in October?"

"Aye," the assembled group of people said in unison.

"Meeting adjourned." Sheridan released the brakes and backed the wheelchair away from the table. "See you in two weeks. Lark, come with me. I have a working lunch and you might as well tag along."

Lark sighed inwardly. "Nothing like a cordial invitation," she muttered and walked up to Sheridan's left side. She had learned the last few days that Sheridan was more comfortable with people standing on that side. Lark had filed the point for future reference, since it might be helpful information to factor into how she planned Sheridan's physiotherapy. "Where are we going?" she asked out loud.

"Hotel Valencia."

Lark had never been to the large, contemporary hotel on the famous Riverwalk. "Sounds nice. Posh."

"It is. I stayed there for a few months when my quarters at the mansion were being renovated. I enjoyed it. Great location."

A few months at the Valencia was bound to cost more than most people made in a year—before taxes. The casual tone in Sheridan's voice annoyed Lark. *To spend that amount of money so casually, just because you can't stand some hammering at your house…* Lark kept her facial expression neutral. It wasn't her place to criticize her employer.

"What?" Sheridan said when they sat in the luxurious minivan. "I can tell there's something."

"How could you possibly? You don't know me." Lark wasn't going to be baited like that Dimitri fellow. "I'm fine."

Sheridan looked at her from where she sat, strapped in, wheelchair and all. "One thing that the meningitis didn't take away was my inner radar," she insisted. "I can tell something's bothering you." Looking genuinely interested now, Sheridan leaned forward, obviously not about to drop this subject. "You were fine until I said…that we were going to the Valencia. What's the matter, not your kind of place?"

"The Valencia is a beautiful building."

"But?"

Pretty sure that Sheridan would pester her with questions until she screamed, Lark pursed her lips before responding. "Well, I just think places like the Valencia, expensive hotels, represent a life that most people never see, other than on TV."

"So you think it was a poor choice for me to stay there?"

"Poor isn't the word I'd choose." Lark wrinkled her nose, trying to make light of a conversation that was quickly turning into a Q&A session.

"What would you call it then? Did you have the same issues with all your wealthy employers? Your dossier indicates that you've mostly worked for the rich and sometimes even famous, although no names were mentioned."

"Am I being accused of anything here?" Lark asked, her voice sharp. She was angry now, for Sheridan to put her on the spot like this.

"Not at all, but you have to admit, if money is an issue with you, I have a valid reason to question if you're suitable for your position." Her dark gray eyes cold and calculating, Sheridan didn't look away once.

"You yourself deemed me suitable for your needs by examining the exact documents that you're quoting now. And surely you went by my well-documented expertise as a physical therapist?" Larked fumed, but fought to remain calm. "I have no problems with money as long as it's not in only one person's pocket."

"Then you ought to be happy that I take my business to the hotel and restaurants as often as I do, considering that many of the Hispanic citizens of San Antonio and its surroundings work there, at all levels."

Lark felt her cheeks color. *What was I thinking?* Going against a strategic thinker like Sheridan who had fought off much harder resistance. "I guess." She quieted and tried to sort her thoughts. Knowing better, she had to try again to get her point across. "The truth is also that nobody who works as maids, waitresses, or bellboys at these places can ever afford to stay there."

Sheridan looked oddly pleased. "True," she admitted. "I think the same goes for the ones who work as janitors, receptionists, etc. at Ward Industries. That's why I send my staff on cruises or vacations at the small chain of hotels I own in Puerto Rico, when possible. Like a bonus of sorts. God only knows how much I shell out to the brass in bonuses every Christmas."

Game, set, and match. Winner, Sheridan Ward. Lark realized that she should have checked her facts, since Sheridan hadn't stopped surprising her since the day she began this assignment.

"You're right, however," Sheridan continued. "Most people never see the inside of a hotel like the Valencia, unless there's a major discount or they work there. The question is, does the yearning for such glamour inspire people to excel, or does it leave them feeling hopelessly behind? Who knows?"

Reluctantly charmed by the way Sheridan, with unexpected grace, handed over an olive branch, Lark said, "My mother has said often enough that she wouldn't want to be caught dead in such a place. I guess she influenced my opinion."

"Where do your parents live?"

"My mother and stepfather live above their store in Boerne. We moved there from Houston when I was fifteen. Not a moment too soon. The neighborhood we lived in was more or less taken over by gangs back then. I don't know what it's like now."

"San Antonio has more than its share of gangs. It's a big problem, but our police force does a lot to keep track of them."

"Wish that had been the attitude in Houston twenty years ago." Lark pressed her lips together as she felt them tremble.

"What happened in Houston?" Sheridan asked mildly. "Did you get in trouble?"

"No, not me. My sister, Fiona, however—"

"We're here, Ms. Ward," the chauffeur's voice said over the intercom.

"Thank you, Ned." Sheridan said and smiled regretfully. "We'll finish this later."

"All right." Lark doubted Sheridan would even remember what they talked about ten minutes after she wheeled out of the car.

Sheridan stopped just below the ramp that allowed her to maneuver the wheelchair in and out of the minivan, looking apprehensive.

Lark slipped into her professional role. "What's up, Sheridan?"

"Nothing." Sheridan still didn't move.

"Want me to push you, ma'am?" Ned asked after rounding the vehicle.

"No!" Sheridan cleared her voice. "No."

Lark realized something and spoke quietly, so Ned wouldn't overhear. "This your first time here after the illness, Sheridan?"

"Yes."

"First time doing a lunch like this, too, perhaps?"

"Yes." The short word emerged through gritted teeth, and Sheridan's hands trembled where they rested on the hand rims of the wheels.

"You'll be fine. For what it's worth, I'll walk right next to you when we go inside."

At first it took so long for Sheridan to answer that Lark thought she was going to prevent herself from taking this step. *If I had memorized more from her charts, I might have realized this. Instead I let my pet peeve make her have to justify her actions, which are her business, not mine.*

"Thank you." Sheridan gripped the rims hard enough for her knuckles to grow whiter. "Let's go."

Lark strode next to her as Sheridan rolled in through the main doors.

CHAPTER SEVEN

Sheridan slumped back in her wheelchair, still on an emotional high after the lunch meeting. She knew she had pulled it off. Her success today was key to maintaining her image as *the* Sheridan Ward, corporate shark and indisputable financial tycoon of everything worth owning east of Austin. Her position among the industrial leaders in Texas was vulnerable right now, and she couldn't afford to slip, not for a second, while she dealt with the other wolves. It would be an unforgivable lack of judgment if she thought they'd cut her any slack for having been ill.

"You're trembling." Lark's soft voice reached Sheridan through her musings.

"What?" Distractedly, Sheridan looked at Lark, who rode across from her in the minivan.

"You're low on sugar. You didn't touch your food."

"What are you talking about?" Sheridan looked down at her hands. They *were* trembling, a faint, barely distinguishable tremor. *Trust Lark not to miss anything.* "Okay, I'll have a Mars bar at the office."

"At the office?" Lark frowned. "We have an appointment with the massage bench and then a relaxation exercise."

"Oh, that." Sheridan waved her shaking hand dismissively. "I thought I told Erica to change our plans. I have contracts to go through."

"Erica understood when I told her that you can't change anything about your schedule if you want to be in the best shape possible for the stockholders' meeting." Lark leaned back in her seat in the minivan, looking calmly at her.

"Erica understood?" Sheridan closed her hands into tight fists, willing them not to betray her anymore. "Erica is *my* assistant, and what she understands or not doesn't matter. I have a job to do and—"

"—and you won't be able to do it as well as you'd like if you don't give yourself time to heal by sticking to an exercise plan."

"You saw how well the luncheon went!" Furious at being questioned like this, Sheridan glowered at Lark who, to her dismay, didn't even blink.

"I did. You were fantastic and they were very impressed."

The immediate concurrence threw Sheridan off for a moment. "They were?" she asked, wanting Lark's honest opinion. Not quite sure why hearing it from Lark meant so much, Sheridan drilled her gaze into the other woman again.

"Yes, they were. That said, this fire and enthusiasm aren't going to last if you run yourself into the ground. If you ask me, your business contacts will find it more reassuring to deal with someone who knows how to take care of herself and create the best possible circumstances for them."

"And what do you base that on?" Sheridan heard herself snarl.

"You said it yourself. I've moved in the world of the rich and famous for a decade now. Italy, Crete, Russia, Sweden, Germany, and recently, Dubai and Abu Dhabi. You have no idea how much the staff, not just me, but also butlers, maids, housekeepers, and nannies, pick up. Just because I don't have a business degree, I'm not dense…or deaf."

Sheridan didn't detect any anger in Lark's voice, only a faint trace of resentment.

"I never said you were. But you haven't moved inside the boardrooms where big corporate sharks eat smaller baby sharks, as well as old, weak sharks."

"And you see yourself as an old, weakened shark?"

The challenge was out in the open. Lark had tossed the glove before Sheridan, who stared at Lark, speechless at her audacity. "What?"

"That's what you said." Lark didn't avert her gaze. Instead her eyes remained firm, and with something else hidden in them, something so excruciatingly tender, Sheridan had to look away. She tried to harness her temper and at the same time think of a defusing remark. "No. Not at all. Not yet. I mean, not ever."

"But you fear you've lost your edge, the same edge that kept you one step ahead in the game before."

Trapped, Sheridan swallowed repeatedly. "Yes. All right. Yes!"

Lark unbuckled her seatbelt and knelt beside the wheelchair. "You're wrong." She spoke tenderly, but with apparent conviction, and stroked Sheridan's arm down to her cold hand. "You have to allow yourself time. If you sell yourself short at this point, this early in your recovery, you set yourself up for failure. And for some reason," Lark added, a kind, crooked smile spreading over her face, "I think the word 'failure' has been deleted from the Ward family's dictionary."

"You've got that right." Sheridan spoke through clenched teeth. "I have no intention of failing at anything. That's why I can't stop, can't allow myself to cut back on the pace I have to keep to stay on top. You're a clever girl, Lark. Surely you realize that the nature of my business means that I have to unlock the brakes and go full steam ahead?"

"On the contrary," Lark said, clearly unfazed. "I think if you pace yourself, and actually trust the people you pay those fantastic salaries to do their job while you recover and regroup, *that* would be playing it smart."

Staring in disbelief at the woman who knelt next to her, Sheridan couldn't help but admire the strength and self-assurance reflected in Lark's eyes. Not many people dared to speak to her this way, or had the confidence to meet her gaze like Lark did.

A twitch in Sheridan's chest preceded a warm flood of feelings that took her off guard. Thundering and skipping occasional beats, Sheridan's heart nearly hurt as it pumped waves of heat to her face. She pulled her arm free from Lark's touch, which was scorching her skin underneath her suit jacket. "You're pretty stubborn," Sheridan murmured huskily.

"I believe every word I said. I wouldn't say them if I didn't." The honesty was obvious in Lark's voice. "Sheridan, I just want you to recover. I think we need to sit down and pinpoint your exact goals for your training, because you give me mixed signals. I don't know what you're aiming for, complete recovery or being back in the saddle when it comes to your businesses."

"All. Both." *Wasn't that the same thing?*

Lark frowned. "That's what I mean. We need to talk. Perhaps involve your physician. I've read your medical file, but as far as I could tell, you haven't been evaluated by a neurologist in a while. Did you miss the appointments?"

Sheridan was not going to be interrogated, especially since she wasn't quite sure why she'd rescheduled the appointment in question three times. "Very well. Call the neurology clinic and schedule for me then." Her response was curt, but she wasn't going to sound apologetic. She simply didn't believe in apologies and rarely resorted to one. Mostly they were a waste of time.

Lark nodded, looking thoughtful as she rose and sat down again. "All right. I hope they can fit you in soon. We need to know that we're on the right track."

"Fine."

Silence grew between them and Sheridan gazed out the window, knowing full well if she looked at Lark, she would see herself measured by those mesmerizing golden eyes. Lark had a way of scrutinizing her that made her feel vulnerable and far too exposed.

"Sheridan?" Lark said quietly.

"Yes?" Sheridan kept her eyes on the impressive exteriors of the buildings they passed.

"You do believe that I merely want you to become independent, don't you?"

Sheridan knew not looking at Lark was immature, but she simply couldn't do so right now. She felt raw, skinless, even, and Lark's soft voice engulfed her and threatened to lure her into a false sense of caring. Lark was an employee, paid by the vast Ward fortune that paid the salaries for all the people that lived under her roof. Sheridan didn't think anyone but Mrs. D could really be bothered with her on a personal level.

"I think you mean well," Sheridan conceded, trying to keep Lark at a distance.

"But?"

"I'm...Look, let's just drop it, huh?" Sheridan finally turned her head and met Lark's eyes. "It's not like we're going to solve everything right here and now."

"Not if you're not open to discussing it." Lark sighed and smiled in a halfhearted way. "But we'll have to talk about this sooner or later."

"Let's make it later." Sheridan knew the finality in her voice effectively ended the discussion. She also knew from the angle of Lark's chin that they had a lot more to say.

❖

"I can't work with her!" Sheridan sighed and glowered at Mrs. D. They were in Sheridan's living room and she had just called for someone to turn up the air-conditioning. The heat from outside seemed to seep indoors and Sheridan was sweating profusely, which didn't exactly calm her down. "She's too presumptuous and she thinks she knows exactly what I need, when, in fact, she really doesn't know me at all!" Her voice climbed with her anger. "Damn it, she talks to me like I'm in this wheelchair to stay. She says I have to learn all these things to become independent, and I say it's a waste of time. This is a temporary solution until my body heals, and *that's* what she's paid to do. She's supposed to work with my body, train it, and help the healing process, not make it convenient for me to live like this!" She slammed her palms onto the armrests, indicating the hateful wheelchair. "If she insists on treating me like this, she can't stay on."

"Sheridan, listen to yourself." Mrs. D spoke calmly and sat next to her after adjusting the AC controls on the wall. "You speak of yourself as 'the body,' as if you think Lark can train your body without you actually in it. You're a smart woman. You know that the only way you two can make progress toward a common goal is to work together. Lark's a good person, and what's more, honey, she's very good at what she does. You gave me her résumé to read, remember? Lark has had tremendous success and her recommendations are flawless. You can't hope to find anyone better."

"It's not only a matter of skill. If she doesn't understand the nature of my problems, then how can she possibly help me?" Sheridan folded her arms across her chest.

"Oh, Sheridan," Mrs. D said softly. She coaxed one of Sheridan's hands out and held it between both of hers. "I'd say, from your reaction, that Lark understands you only too well. Now listen to me. Lark's not afraid of you, nor is she overly impressed with your social status, and that's exactly what you need. Do you really think you could ever work with a yea-sayer, who never dares to challenge you? You've never surrounded yourself with such people!"

Sheridan glared at Mrs. D, aware of the love beneath her austere appearance. "You're living proof of that," Sheridan huffed, a reluctant grin forcing its way across her lips.

"There. My point exactly." Mrs. D. nodded regally. "You're smarter than that. If you weren't, you wouldn't have brought the family business into the top five in its field."

"I suppose." It was still hard to acknowledge the logic in Mrs. D's words, but Sheridan knew she was right. *Damn it, she always is.*

"Sleep on it, Sheridan."

"That's your standard response to everything." It was true. Ever since Sheridan was a little girl, Mrs. D had offered that advice when something bothered her.

"It works, doesn't it?" Mrs. D raised an eyebrow.

"Sometimes." Sheridan had to laugh at the mock-offended expression on Mrs. D's face. "All right, all right. Often enough."

"Good. Remember that, and sleep well. Who's working tonight? Leila?"

"Yes. I think so."

"You know where to find me."

"I do. 'Night."

Mrs. D began to walk toward the door, but stopped halfway and came back. She leaned down and cupped Sheridan's face with both hands. "Good night, honey. Trust in Lark. Please." She kissed Sheridan's forehead and left the room.

Sheridan knew she was fortunate to have Mrs. D in her life, someone to care for her much like a mother or an older sister. Mrs. D had never acted judgmental toward her, never chastised Sheridan for being a lesbian, or for her way of dealing with her sexuality or life in general.

For her to side with Lark…Curling her fingers around the armrests, Sheridan fought to stay true to herself. Mrs. D wasn't siding with anyone, she just wanted what was best for Sheridan. So, Lark, despite her apparent misconception of what Sheridan's needs and goals were, was the best for her? Mrs. D's arguments made annoying sense, and Sheridan knew she would have to try to work things out. It was going to be difficult, if not impossible.

Flashbacks of Lark's velvet voice and her nearly magical touch when she reduced the onslaught of a migraine flickered by. Sheridan's lack of awkwardness when Lark helped her after the shower amazed her. Why was it so hard to accept the other side of Lark or what she had to say?

Sheridan began to wheel toward her bedroom, where Leila was waiting for her. Even if the young nurse was most professional and skilled, she lacked something, something that made it painfully obvious that she didn't have Lark's touch.

Get a grip. Focus, damn it. Sheridan tried to tell herself she didn't require any special touch or treatment. *I just need to get through the day.*

❖

Lark walked into the large library at the end of her hallway. Built-in shelves made of dark wood held thousands of books. Mrs. D had told her that Sheridan had a part-time librarian on her payroll who was in charge of buying books and archiving them. Along the far wall sat three stationary computers with flat-screen monitors blinking at her. Lark approached them and touched the mouse belonging to the first one. Mrs. D. had given her a username and password for a guest account, and Lark logged in without a problem.

She did a quick search of what she had access to and discovered that she could reach practically any e-book, movie, or music via the Ward Intranet and that the computer system had enough software licenses to cover the needs of everyone who worked at the mansion. Thinking she might find Debbie online, Lark opened a chat program. The software was preset to someone called "Sheri_star," obviously Sheridan's username, and asked for a password. Lark chose "new user" and entered her own data. To her dismay, none of her online friends was active and she logged out again. Lark then closed the window, not entirely comfortable with having spotted Sheridan's online nickname.

She rose and walked around the room, exploring the titles along the shelves. A large section contained books about anthropology. Intrigued, Lark climbed the narrow ladder to the top section and let her fingers dance along the backs of the closest books, only to stop in mid-air when she found a book by a familiar author. It didn't take long for her to realize that the entire top shelf held lesbian romances, mysteries, science fiction, and even some horror. *Oh, God, can it be? Is she gay?*

Since Mrs. D had said it was all right for her to borrow any book in the library as long as she left a note for the librarian, Lark pulled out two mystery novels by her favorite author and left a brief message about them.

Back in her room, Lark put the books down on her nightstand, then took a quick shower. She sat on the bed with her laptop, logged into the Ward Mansion network, and checked her e-mail. Apart from some work-related messages, one of her sisters had sent her a humorous e-card with a loony alligator that made Lark chuckle. She opened her chat program again, and this time she found a message waiting for her.

Sirensong: When you see this, ping me. Have some news for you. Hope your day is going better than mine.

Lark frowned, worried and curious as she read Debbie's short lines. She hit "reply" right away.

Grey_bird: You there? What's up?

There was no reply at first, but just as Lark was about to log off, the laptop pinged and Debbie replied.

Sirensong: There you are! Great! Just what I needed.
Grey_bird: You OK?
Sirensong: Not really. Got fired today.
Grey_bird: What??? Why?

Shocked at this piece of news, more serious than Lark had thought, she tried to think of something helpful to say, but nothing came to mind.

Sirensong: My own fault, really. I finally told the old fool to keep his hands to himself, and he apparently wasn't too happy with my choice of words. He fired me. That's it for me. Never a private home ever again.
Grey_bird: I understand. I really do. I had promised myself never to work like this again. But my patient really does need me, even if she thinks she doesn't.

Sirensong: Ah, that type of patient, huh? Stubborn and in denial.

Not entirely comfortable discussing her patient, even in this faceless, anonymous way, Lark felt an instant sense of protectiveness. She didn't want Debbie to criticize Sheridan.

Grey_bird: It's denial and fear.

Sirensong: And since you usually work with the "Richie Rich", she's annoyed that she can't buy herself good health, no doubt. One of my patient's grandkids wondered if her grandfather was "playing poor" when he was in a wheelchair at the dinner table.

Grey_bird: OMG! That's both funny and rather sad, you know.

Sirensong: Yeah. Exactly. The kid probably thought if a person's rich enough, they could buy their way out of the wheelchair.

Grey_bird: So what's your plan now?

Sirensong: Going to apply for a position at my local hospital. Just a small unit, but they have some vacancies, I think.

Grey_bird: I hope you get it, Debs.

Sirensong: Me too.

Tired, Lark said good-bye to Debbie, preoccupied by finding the books that waited for her on the nightstand. She glanced from the books to the chat software on her laptop, as her mind raced. It wasn't hard to tell that Sheridan was determined to shut her out. Lark recognized an emotional brick wall when she sensed one. Something about Sheridan penetrated Lark's professionalism, and she couldn't remember ever having felt this adamant about any patient before.

Sheridan's attitude was equally frustrating, but Lark sometimes glimpsed a vulnerable woman who seemed utterly lost. Lark wanted nothing more than to ease the pain that Sheridan so bravely, and stubbornly, tried to cover up. The way Sheridan jutted her chin out and donned a faint smirk did not intimidate Lark, though she was certain

Sheridan intended to achieve just that effect. Instead, Lark was prepared to do almost anything to help Sheridan.

Lark pulled the laptop closer. After a brief hesitation, she typed "Sheri_star" into her chat window, asking for permission to contact the person behind this username. Most likely Sheridan would dismiss this too-forward individual and block her. That was what any sane person should do, but Lark hoped Sheridan would cooperate. If she could learn more about Sheridan, really get to know her, Lark would use this information only to help her. This method was questionable, at best, but it hurt to think about failing Sheridan. This proud woman deserved every chance to improve her condition, and Lark knew in her heart that she was the right person to make that happen. If she had to resort to these covert ways to go about it, so be it.

Lark briefly acknowledged the question that prodded the back of her mind: why Sheridan's well-being meant so much to her. She knew that her concern suggested something more than professional consideration, and this awareness made her derail that train of thought. Sheridan needed her, no matter what. Since they might possibly be able to really communicate, like new—anonymous—friends, Lark would take the chance. *I will debate this with my conscience later. Nothing matters but Sheridan.*

Lark took a deep breath. All she could do now was wait.

CHAPTER EIGHT

H i, there, gorgeous. What's going on? Something wrong with your phone?"

Sheridan gripped the cell phone tighter. Against her better judgment, she had charged and opened her personal cell phone, the one she used for times when she wanted to keep her identity private. The small screen had flickered to life and informed her that she had more than two hundred missed calls. Her voice mail was full, and listening through a few of the messages, Sheridan realized that all she had to do was call Liz, Fergie, or Drew to have a good time, as they put it. Unable to deal with that part of her existence till now, perhaps even now, Sheridan had tucked the Motorola into her nightstand drawer after she came home from the hospital. *Why did I decide to pull it out now?*

"It's me, Fergie. Where are you, Sheri? I waited at Bianca's for hours, and I don't take too kindly to being stood up. If I don't hear from you in a few days, we might as well call it quits."

Sheridan sighed and placed an arm over her eyes. Fergie was a headstrong, quite self-centered woman, who preferred to dress in narrow black jeans and white shirts. Thin and tall, even towering over Sheridan, she wore her blond hair short and spiky. Fergie was sexy as hell, but a bit overwhelming with her intensity, and Sheridan could only handle being with her for a few hours at a time, or one night at the most. That, however, was all in the past. The days of sneaking off to Austin for a bit of fun in her favorite bars, Bianca's or Cowgirls & She-Devils, were over. For now, at least.

Sheridan hated the fact that she was unable to do any of those things, slip into casual jeans and a T-shirt, drive the Bronco to Austin where nobody connected her with Ward Industries. In San Antonio, she was a well-known face around town, even if she dressed down.

Austin, with all its students and youthful population, was a much more anonymous place, despite the fact that it was little more than an hour away by car.

Sheridan pressed the button for the next voice mail. Somehow it was comforting to hear the voices from Austin, even if they became increasingly concerned with each call.

"Sheri, Drew here," a soft, light voice said. *Drew. Oh, God.* Sheridan was about to press the skip button, but relented as Drew really sounded worried. "I think something's happened to you. You're never gone this long, and you never treat people rudely. Fergie's mad at you, but that's just because she feels neglected. I worry about you. Please, let us know that you're all right."

Now feeling guilty for taking the easy route, Sheridan hesitated over the reply button. She wasn't ready to talk to any of her friends, or former lovers, so she opted for the text-messaging feature and sent a group message.

> *Sheri here. Sorry for being out of commission. Will get back*
> *in touch when I'm up to it. Thank you for understanding.*

The message felt short and inadequate, but it was the best she could manage at the moment. It was as if she were addressing strangers, or people she had known in a previous life. She felt as if she'd been reborn into another reality, one where she was helpless in ways she'd have thought impossible only a few months ago. If anyone had told her then that she'd have to depend on strangers to perform the most private of functions, Sheridan would have claimed she'd rather die.

Startled, Sheridan pressed the phone to her chest. *Would I, really?* Would she really rather be dead than struggle like this? Golden-brown eyes under a shock of light brown hair appeared in her mind without warning. Sheridan gasped and the cell phone fell out of her hand. Lark's features were as clear as if she were there in the room with Sheridan, and she couldn't possibly think of death, of escape, any longer. *God.* Lark's presence, whether in the flesh or as a thought, was clearly enough to chase such dark thoughts away. *Is she that annoying, or what do these lingering thoughts mean?*

Sheridan hit "send" and let the text message go out to four of the women from Austin she had hooked up with on occasion. She surmised that they would spread the word to the others that had called her cell phone.

Still unable to sleep, Sheridan pushed herself higher against the pillows. She was not entirely comfortable, but she was still reluctant to ring for assistance. She felt raw at the moment, as if the messages had peeled her skin off and left her bare to the world in the harshest of ways. She reached for the laptop that was always available on a special shelf attached to the wall so that she was able to type comfortably.

As soon as she booted the computer, her chat software appeared, with many messages much like her cell phone and, to her surprise, with a request to chat. The short message that went with the application said, "Hi Sheri_star, my online handle is Grey_bird, and I would like to chat if you are interested. I'm facing some challenges and could use the insight of a total stranger, as opposed to the people around me that are pretty rigid in their beliefs. No strings attached. What do you say?"

Stunned, Sheridan tried to figure out whom she might have given her online handle to before she became ill. No face came to mind, and Sheridan decided to delete the contact unseen. But just as she held the cursor above Grey_bird's avatar, something spiked her curiosity. There was something special in the way the person expressed herself—like a woman would. Changing her mind, Sheridan clicked on the icon to approve Grey_bird's request. She could always block this person later if she turned out to be a complete idiot or, worse, a stalker.

Sheridan had been surfing the Internet for a few minutes, reading a couple of news articles on CNN, when a blinking banner alerted her.

Grey_bird: Glad you approved me, Sheri_star. Nice to "meet" you.

Sheridan stared at the screen for a few seconds before she moved her hands to the keyboard.

Sheri_star: Hi Grey_bird. How did you find me? Do I know you?
Grey_bird: So many questions!
Sheri_star: Do I?
Grey_bird: Not really.

Sheridan's heart pounded wildly in her chest as she tried to figure out who this woman was and where they could have met. She wasn't that generous with her chat-room nickname. And talk about being evasive! Annoyed, but mostly intrigued, Sheridan kept typing.

❖

Sheri_star: So you're going to keep me guessing?

Lark's mouth was dry and she licked her lips in vain. She hadn't counted on Sheridan coming online at this point. Thinking of several ways her spontaneous idea might backfire, Lark groaned as she replied.

Grey_bird: That's the point of this faceless media. We can take things slow. Get to know each other at a nice pace, without any of society's rules or stamps hanging over us. I like the idea of a clean slate.

Sheri_star: Like a fresh start? Sounds like utopia to me.

Grey_bird: It doesn't have to be. It could really mean something.

Sheri_star: Like what? Life-altering bliss?

Grey_bird: Not like that. New beginnings, well, don't we all want them and deserve them?

Sheri_star: Are you for real? Life's not exactly fair, you know.

Grey_bird: I know that firsthand. I still think things can change for the better. I've seen that happen too.

Sheri_star: Really?

Grey_bird: Yes.

Sheri_star: So you claim that miracles can happen?

Grey_bird: Absolutely.

There was a brief pause, and Lark feared that her assertiveness had deterred Sheridan from answering. She was afraid that she had sounded too much like herself, like the Lark that her older sisters used to call "our Pollyanna" with a teasing expression.

Sheri_star: I will remember you said so, if only to

prove you wrong one day. IMHO there is
no such thing as a miracle. Only fluke and
happenstance.

Grey_bird: You're on!

Sheri_star: On what?

Grey_bird: It was a bet, right?

Sheri_star: I see. Yes. What should we wager then?

Grey_bird: Oh, the possibilities are endless.

Sheri_star: I know. If you can prove that a miracle's taken
place, you can ask me a favor.

Grey_bird: What? Any favor? Are you crazy? You don't
know me!

Sheri_star: But that's quickly changing, right?

Grey_bird: Eh…yes…

Sheri_star: Then are we on, as you put it?

Lark swallowed repeatedly at the innocent words. Surely they
were innocent? Or was Sheridan onto her and suggesting that she knew
what was going on and trying to trap her? Or worse, was this the first
stirrings of something flirtatious?

Grey_bird: Sure!

Sheri_star: All right. How about another chat session
tomorrow some time?

Grey_bird: Look forward to it!

Sheri_star: Me too. See you then

Sheri_star has left the conversation.

A bit taken aback at the sudden departure, Lark drew a trembling
breath. A strange mix of regret and excitement burned just beneath
her rib cage, and she closed the laptop. Normally, she dutifully went
through the logout procedure, but now she felt as if she needed to
physically break off the contact with Sheridan. *This is so not like me.*
Lark barely grazed the idea that her instant, forbidden physical reaction
in Sheridan's presence might have anything to do with her unorthodox
measures. She sighed again. *If this doesn't backfire, nothing will.*

❖

When Sheridan came into the gym the following day, Lark busied herself with a pile of towels. "Morning," she said over her shoulder, half expecting Sheridan to give her a knowing, contemptuous glance. When this didn't happen, Lark welcomed the fact that Sheridan looked her regular aloof self. Introverted and distant, she raised an inquisitive eyebrow toward Lark.

"Good morning. We ready to start? I have a ton of work to do today. I'm only here because Mrs. D promised to chain me to the bench if I didn't volunteer."

"Now there's a thought," Lark teased, eager to keep their conversation light. "We're going to stretch you out a bit today, but we need to warm up first."

"I'm sure 'we' do."

Lark sighed at the sardonic undertone in Sheridan's voice. "No kidding. This is hard work for me too."

Sheridan looked doubtful. "I see."

After a warm-up session that left them both a bit breathless, Lark guided Sheridan onto a large mattress. "Here we go. We're going to stretch your muscles and tendons, create resistance for you to work against, even if it has to be a passive motion." Lark continued to educate Sheridan on the importance of their exercises, hoping the matter-of-fact approach would lighten the mood enough for her to accept the necessity of it all.

Pulling and stretching Sheridan's legs were what took most of Lark's strength. Every tendon and muscle tended to contract, and she forced them to loosen up, ever mindful not to overdo it. Sheridan moaned under her hands, breaking into a sweat as Lark pulled her leg sideways and up, bending it at the knee.

Lark ended up standing between Sheridan's wide-spread legs, looking down at her pale face as she gently circled Sheridan's hip joint, feeling for any tension that might betray spasticity. The intimacy of the position had never bothered her before, but now, while watching the gasping Sheridan, Lark had to hold back an unprofessional moan and she shivered inside. She clung to Sheridan's leg, trying hard to refocus on her job.

"Lark!" Mrs. D poked her head into the gym where Lark had just helped Sheridan back into the wheelchair. "You have a phone call."

"I'm pretty busy. Can you take a message, please?" Lark, just as sweaty as Sheridan was after the exhausting session, pushed her damp bangs out of her eyes.

"I've already asked if I could, but it's your father and it seems urgent."

"Daddy?" Lark quickly made sure Sheridan was comfortable before she accepted the phone. "Daddy? What's wrong?" Out of the corner of her eye, Lark noticed Sheridan wheeling toward the showers, followed by Mrs. D.

"Hi, sweetheart. Don't worry now, but it's Fiona."

Lark closed her eyes. Fiona was two years younger than she, and Lark was very close to her. "What is it this time?"

"We've just come home from the hospital. She's had another episode, but she's doing better now."

"The hospital? Why didn't y'all call me?"

"She wouldn't let us, sweetie."

It hurt to swallow, and Lark sat down on a bench by the wall, her knees suddenly weak. "Why did you have to go to the hospital?"

"The anxiety hit her bad this time, Lark. She couldn't breathe properly, even after she took her medication. You know what it was like for her the first couple of years."

Lark knew only too well, having shared a room with Fiona after they moved to Boerne. "I know."

"Well, we've been happy that she's done so well the last year. Our guard was down, and when she panicked, your mother and I panicked right with her."

"And?"

"And when she turned blue around her lips and earlobes, we called the paramedics, just like you told us to. Your mother had to go to bed when we came home. It scared all three of us."

"I bet it did. Well, I'll just let my employer know, and then I'm coming home."

"No, no. That's not why I called, Lark. You don't have to stop what you're doing."

Lark frowned and reached for a towel to wrap around her neck. The drying perspiration was cooling her skin and making her shiver. "Why did you call, then?"

"Your mother insisted that we tell you. But Fiona doesn't want you to jeopardize your new job."

"What if they need me? Mom especially. She counts on me being there for Fiona."

"Your mother is stronger than you realize. I know she's relied a lot on you over the years, sweetie, but trust me, she's capable of handling this."

"Does *she* know that?" Lark tried to not be sarcastic, but she'd lived through several years when her mother clung to her, needing reassurance and sympathy at every turn. Her mother wasn't weak by any means, but fear could sometimes make her act like a frightened child.

"Listen, sweetie. She's come a long way too."

Lark wasn't so sure, but then again, before she came home to Texas two months ago it had been a long time since she'd lived with her parents. The room that she'd shared with Fiona still remained the same girly haven as it had been ten years ago, but now Fiona resided there alone. "All right, so you called me like you promised Mom. You know me, Daddy. I'm not going to be able to relax until I see Fiona for myself. Or Mom."

"I know, Lark. I tried telling your mother exactly that. Fiona was upset when she heard your mom insisted I call you because she knew you'd feel left out and worried."

"She's right. I do." Lark closed her eyes again and pinched the bridge of her nose to prevent the stupid tears that burned at the corners of her eyelids. "Tell you what. I'll finish early today and come home."

"Lark…" Arthur's voice sounded tired, but not unkind. "All right. Come for dinner tomorrow evening. It might actually be a good thing. If your mother can home in on you, it'll take the pressure off of Fiona."

"Yes, and if I bring up my pet peeve, that'll really liven up the get-together." Lark pursed her lips. "Mom doesn't like it when I talk about Fiona being on her own."

"Please. Just come and we'll take it from there. Your mother needs you. You've been her anchor for so long."

"You're that person these days, Daddy. But all right, I'll be home for a few hours tomorrow."

Lark said good-bye to Arthur and held onto the phone with both hands after she pressed the disconnect button. Fiona was so fragile and insecure, but also the most beautiful and talented woman Lark had ever met. *What a waste. She needs to find herself a place of her own.* Lark knew this could be done, with the proper planning.

"Lark? Everything okay?" Sheridan wheeled toward her from the showers, her hair glistening almost black where she'd combed it back from her face.

"Yes. Thanks for asking. I have to go home to Boerne for a few hours tomorrow evening."

Sheridan frowned. "You look pale. Something the matter at home?"

"My sister's been a bit under the weather. I need to check on her. We're getting together for dinner. This is the first time I've worked this close to my hometown in quite a while. I imagine my parents are just figuring out that I can pop in without too much hassle."

"I thought your hometown was Houston." Sheridan tugged the towel around her neck tighter.

"It was, but none of us liked it much. We moved to Boerne when I was fifteen. We love it there."

"Boerne is picturesque, and if I didn't live here, I wouldn't mind having a house there, although Lake Travis is my escape." Sheridan smiled faintly. "Guess we all need a space to call our own. Where do you go when you need time out?"

Taken aback by the question, Lark gazed down at the phone in her hands. "I...I don't suppose I have a place where I can be alone, unless I'm off to a park, or go for a drive." She tried to figure out when she'd had time to be alone. After her last assignment, she'd made herself useful at the store in Boerne. She'd never gone on her long overdue vacation to the Florida Keys. The days simply seemed to rush by with no brakes. "You're right, of course. We all need a refuge. Lake Travis sounds great. It's beautiful there."

Sheridan looked at her with a puzzled expression. "I'll have to show you the summer house one day." Silence filled the space between them, then Sheridan stroked her palms against her sweatpants. "I better go and get ready. See you tonight." She didn't wait for a reply but wheeled out of the room.

Lark, still hugging the phone to her chest, stared after her, trying to read something, anything, into Sheridan's abrupt words. It was impossible.

CHAPTER NINE

Sheridan placed the binder on her lap and rolled toward the desk. The office block was almost deserted save for the duty nurse and the ever-present guards. In the labs on the floors below her, the night shift was already working, and she could barely sense the faint hum of their equipment through the thick-carpeted floor.

It had been a long day, longer than she had originally planned. Sheridan had taken advantage of the unexpected break in her physical therapy schedule and pushed on with work that had accumulated during her absence. She couldn't catch up, and at times she figured Dimitri's misgivings were not entirely unfounded. To push herself this way and to work normal ten- to twelve-hour workdays had taken a toll on her lately. It hadn't always been this hard. In her position, an eighty-hour work week was what it took to remain on top and in power. Sheridan knew she had to regain that energy level again soon if she was to take back full, hands-on control of her empire.

Sheridan reached out to flip the off switch, but stopped her hand in midair. Curiosity and a slight feeling of dread coursed through her. She placed the binder on her desk and maneuvered her wheelchair into place. Logging on to her private account, she started the chat software, but to her dismay, or was it relief, Grey_bird's icon wasn't highlighted. Several of her other contacts were online, but Sheridan made sure she was invisible to them. She didn't want to talk to anyone really, but she still felt empty when she opened her Web browser and her favorites folder.

She clicked on *resources*, and a list of links to various Web pages appeared. Sheridan picked a link that led to another chat Web site, where she typed her username and password. She browsed the list of usernames and saw several she had struck up conversations with, even flirted with, but now, when she saw them playing the field, she wasn't tempted at all. Sheridan waited, anxious at her strong feeling of apprehension. Finally she logged off and closed her laptop.

Granted, this was the first time that she'd been back at the special chat forum since she became ill, but her reaction was still disconcerting. On more than one occasion, Sheridan had found relief and a moment's relaxation and fun at this site. Membership was by invitation, and Sheridan missed the friends she'd made there, as well as the casual cyber sex. She had used it as a clever outlet for her emotions when her career seemed to weigh on her personal choices more than she could stand.

It wasn't as if she hadn't had her fair share of lovers. They'd been anonymous trysts, usually in Austin, in the bachelor apartment she kept in the university neighborhood, far from any of the places her peers normally visited.

Sheridan liked her little getaway a lot, but she loved the estate at Lake Travis. The hacienda-style house had been in the family for more than seventy years. Sheridan wasn't a sailor; in fact, she wasn't comfortable around water, which made it even more remarkable that she enjoyed the Lake Travis house so much. She liked to walk the four-mile private beach, usually accompanied by her Irish setter, Frank. Frank never came back to San Antonio with her. She knew the dog was happier by the lake so she left him there with the Johnsons, the married couple who took care of the estate for her. She hadn't been there since her illness. She missed Frank, but it pained her to think she'd never walk with him along the beach again, never run and play with him like she used to. Better this way. Better not to confuse the dog by showing up in a wheelchair that would no doubt startle him.

"Ma'am?"

"Yes…eh…Lisa?" *Damn, I hope that's her name.*

"Karen." Karen only grinned at Sheridan, apparently not offended in the least. "You told me to remind you when it's 9 p.m. I'm sorry. I got carried away by the book I was reading." She waved a paperback in the air. "It's 9:30."

"Let's go then. There shouldn't be much traffic, though."

"Yeah, at this hour, for sure."

Sheridan rolled to the door and as she passed Karen, she stole a glance at the book. "What are you reading, by the way, that had you so engrossed?"

"A self-help book."

"Self-help? About what?" Sheridan raised an eyebrow.

Karen colored faintly. "The book's called *The Ten-Step Program to 'Fessing Up*."

Sheridan was intrigued. "Confess what?"

"Eh, to whatever you need confessing to…well, different people." Karen was now crimson, and she fiddled with the well-thumbed book. "You know."

Sheridan found it immensely tempting to ask what in the world this otherwise-so-cheerful young woman would have to confess, but she resisted. It was obviously not any of her business. However, she felt she should say something, which in itself was mind-boggling. The old Sheridan wouldn't have had the time or cared what any of her staff had to confess. "Just don't force the issue," Sheridan said, a bit awkwardly. "Confess to things in your own time."

Brightening, Karen's expression softened and she smiled warmly at Sheridan. "Thanks, ma'am. I'll take that into consideration."

"Good. Come on. It's time to go home."

Karen laughed, a very pleasant sound, and Sheridan knew that she wouldn't forget this employee's name again.

❖

The house was quiet and Sheridan rolled through the corridor after assuring Karen that she could manage on her own. Her suite was prepared just as she liked it. The lights were dim, her medication on the nightstand, and her bed turned down. Still the emptiness of the room got to her, and she completed her evening routine as fast as she could, wanting to go to bed and sleep away the loneliness.

The mirror told of too many hours at the office, and Sheridan groaned at how grayish pale she looked. *If Lark didn't push me so hard in the gym, I wouldn't look like I'm falling apart.* Sheridan thought how she used to be able to pull all-nighters twice a week without a problem. Now it seemed as if she was barely able to stick to her physiotherapy routine and do her work at the same time. This situation was disconcerting, since this was why she'd hired Lark in the first place. She needed to be in shape for the stockholders' convention, and her plan wasn't working.

It's only been a few days. A small inner voice tried to reason with Sheridan that she was rushing things, but she pushed the annoying thoughts away. Results were what counted in her world, and quick results even more so. Sheridan had learned from her father that in the corporate world you planned for the future by wielding your sword today. You chopped off the pieces that didn't fit, cultivated the pieces you wanted to keep, and ended up with a thriving empire.

She wasn't sure how this analogy fit in with her training program, but she was annoyed, and she knew if Lark had taken an approach more doable from a business point of view, she wouldn't feel so lousy right now. *Damn it! The only difference between Lark and the other useless health pros is that she's cuter. Same idealistic, unrealistic approach—*

Sheridan stopped. She looked up at her reflection and put the washcloth down. Cute? She thought Lark was *cute*? Sure, Lark had a pretty face and the biggest, dreamy golden eyes Sheridan had ever seen, but cute?

Sheridan put on a long T-shirt and grabbed her briefcase on her way to bed. One thing that Lark had shown her was how to maneuver from the chair onto the bed, and feeling slightly more good-humored toward her physical therapist, she practiced her new skills and scooted in under the covers. With a few more exhausting moves, she was finally able to pull the covers up. Sheridan flipped open her laptop, and as soon as she was online, a chat window appeared.

Grey_bird: Hello! Good to see you online again.

Sheridan stared at the screen, her stomach suddenly trembling.

Sheri_star: Hi you. Been working overtime.
Grey_bird: Ah. That sucks. Demanding boss?
Sheri_star: The worst! How about you?

Grinning, Sheridan began to relax.

Grey_bird: Have one that's quite challenging. She'll end up giving me grey hair, or firing me.

Sheri_star: Can't you talk to her about what's wrong?
Grey_bird: I try. I may just reach her one of these days.
Sheri_star: Well, I wouldn't want you to work for my boss. She's got to be worse.
Grey_bird: Give me an example.
Sheri_star: Hmm. Let me see. She can never keep track of any employee's name.
Grey_bird: Really? Well, perhaps she has too many employees.

Sheridan read Grey_bird's response with surprise. She had expected her chat counterpart to mock Sheri_star's "employer" and come up with a few suggestions on how to deal with such a rude person.

Sheri_star: It's not like she deals with all of them personally. You'd think she'd be able to memorize just a few, at least.
Grey_bird: True. How long have you worked for her?
Sheri_star: Too long. Almost quit not long ago.

There was a brief pause.

Grey_bird: What stopped you?
Sheri_star: I guess you can say I saw the light.

Grey_bird paused again.

Grey_bird: Sounds kinda good, Sheri_star.
Sheri_star: It was. Actually.
Grey_bird: And now? You back in the same situation?
Sheri_star: Yes. And no. Some things changed.
Grey_bird: Not your working hours!
Sheri_star: *grin* For sure.
Grey_bird: You tired?
Sheri_star: Like you could never believe. But don't leave. Great chatting with someone.
Grey_bird: Glad you think so. I was kinda waiting for you.

Sheridan jerked her hands off the keyboard and reread the last sentence from Grey_bird.

Sheri_star: Oh yeah?
Grey_bird: Yes. I was bored and somehow felt connected to you the other day. Hoped you felt the same way.
Sheri_star: In a strange way I did. You're easy to chat with.

And refreshingly friendly, not just after a fast cyber fuck. Sheridan felt a rather silly grin form on her lips and blushed at her own reaction.

Grey_bird: Thank you. So are you. We just might become friends.

Sheridan couldn't make herself type at first. Her fingers suddenly trembled so badly, she almost feared she'd come down with yet another new symptom. Trying to control the tremors, she placed her fingers on the keyboard and saw text move on her screen.

Grey_bird: Sheri_star? You still there?
Sheri_star: Yeah, I'm here. Sorry. And yes. I would like to get to know you.
Grey_bird: Whew! What a relief. For some reason I thought I might have offended you.
Sheri_star: No way.
Grey_bird: I think it's time for me to go to bed. Stern boss expects me to pull miracles out of my hat tomorrow as usual.
Sheri_star: Just stand your ground, Grey_bird.
Grey_bird: Will do my best. You too, though. Don't let that boss of yours get away with acting badly.
Sheri_star: And how do you suppose I do that?
Grey_bird: *smile* Lead by example!

Sheridan burst out laughing. Grey_bird's comment was funnier than she could possibly guess.

Sheri_star: I'll do just that. Night, night, Grey_bird.
Grey_bird: Good night. Sleep tight.

Sheridan logged off and placed the laptop on her nightstand. Karen had already put her medication next to her water bottle, and Sheridan swallowed it with an impatient grimace. She shifted impatiently until she finally tucked a small pillow between her knees and hugged another one against her chest. Thinking of Grey_bird, she wondered what her chat partner did for a living. For some reason, Grey_bird struck her as a genuinely warmhearted person. They had shared only a few words, and Sheridan still speculated about which ones of her cyber buddies had given her username to Grey_bird. But even considering that puzzle, Sheridan instinctively liked her. She could almost hear the soft voice and look into the velvety brown eyes—

Sheridan stopped her train of thought. Why did she associate Lark's features with a stranger's persona? Sure, Lark was also very sweet, and her touch was the gentlest Sheridan had ever received. When she spoke, her voice caressed Sheridan and made her want to care for her, protect her.

But I don't know her any more than I know this Grey_bird person. Startled, Sheridan backtracked. She had just listed a lot of very positive, and highly personal, traits regarding Lark and concluded by expressing concern for her. As if Lark were some vulnerable young flower, in need of protection from…what? Her?

Clenching her teeth, Sheridan willed her mind to empty itself. It was a technique she'd perfected after her mother died. If she didn't think of anything, nothing hurt. It was as simple as that.

Successful, and pleased, Sheridan felt sleep begin to overcome her. Annoyingly enough, a last conscious thought snuck in just before the dreams took over. *Why did I stay late, despite my promise to Lark? What am I up to?*

❖

Next morning, Lark stood in the gym waiting for Sheridan. She checked her watch against the clock on the wall, and they both showed

9:30. Frowning and stewing, she tapped her foot as she browsed the CD rack on the wall. She worked a lot with music as she helped her patients heal. Research showed the undeniable success stories with this method, and Lark knew if she used music Sheridan liked, preferably up-tempo to help keep the pace moving during strenuous workouts, the exercise would impact her system much more.

"I'm here."

No "sorry I'm late" or "did I keep you waiting."

"You're late." Up till now, Lark had been prepared to show Sheridan the benefit of the doubt, but the stubborn look on her face, tinged with condescension, made it impossible.

"I was tired this morning."

"You stayed late at work even after you promised you'd prioritize your exercises. No wonder you're tired. If you'd been home in time, you wouldn't be." Lark knew she sounded like a nagging mother, but she had to make sure Sheridan knew that *she* knew.

"Honestly, Lark. I have no obligation to report my comings and goings to you. I employ you, not the other way around."

"True. But just keep in mind why you employ me. You're wasting my time and your money by doing this."

"I don't see how half an hour here or there can matter so much." Sheridan folded her arms over her chest.

Lark sighed and placed the CD she was holding on the table. She tempered her movements, quite an accomplishment when she really wanted to slam the innocent object onto the pile of CDs there. "That just proves my point. All those little moments add up to a lot of lost time that can make all the difference to our tight schedule. You want so much to happen in a few months. That makes every minute of treatment important."

"Well, we just have to speed the gym session up, then." Sheridan waved a hand in the air, looking as if she already had her mind on today's business. The fact that she had dark circles after a most likely tough night should have made Lark back off a bit, but it didn't. Instead she thought of the chat last night, and how she'd thought she was finally starting to understand Sheridan and even hoped to get under her skin. *Apparently not.*

Sheridan was one person when she fooled around on the Internet and a completely different person in real life. What would it take to reach her?

"You can't speed it up. It doesn't work that way." Lark tried to remain polite. "If you rush through the different exercises, you might damage yourself. Besides, they won't have the desired effect."

With her gray eyes crystal clear, Sheridan blasted Lark with her gaze. "I thought I made it clear that I needed you to design the exercises to fit my schedule. If you can't be realistic and work with me under these circumstances, your high recommendations are false advertising."

"What?" Lark's normally calm nature boiled over. "Nothing can alter the fact that I'm one of the best in my field in San Antonio. I'm sure if you settled for someone easier to manipulate, you could find just such a person from an inferior agency. But let me tell you this, that person won't help you be fit for the stockholders' conference!"

"That's my choice." Sheridan's voice was cold now and her features rigid. "You are not making this easy for me, and you are not paying attention to my requirements."

"You hired me for my expertise, to help you be in the best possible shape before the fall." Lark took a deep breath. "Sheridan, I want you to regain as much of your good health as possible and become independent of others. But I can't work well under these circumstances. Your attitude is key, and frankly…your attitude sucks."

Sheridan rolled close to Lark, her lips white as she pressed them in a thin line before she spoke. "If that's your opinion, why are you still here? Why would you want to work with me?"

"Valid questions," Lark agreed. "But this is what I do. Some of your reluctance is about fear, and I understand that. And part of it is simply the repercussions of the illness talking. It's not unheard of that—"

"Don't you dare suggest that I don't know what I'm saying!" Sheridan's voice dropped an octave.

"That's not what I—"

"It's what you said. You just proved my point. You're not right for this job if you insist that I'm brain damaged!"

"I didn't say that, but if you push the issue…well…you *are* brain damaged." As Lark tried to reason with the furious, almost panic-stricken woman, she felt as if she'd stepped into a nest of burning fuses. "Listen, Sheridan," she began and reached out. Shocked, she felt Sheridan force her hand away.

"No. I don't have to listen to you." Intense anger burned in Sheridan's gray eyes. "That's my prerogative as boss. You're merely an employee and can be replaced. You're fired!"

Lark stared at Sheridan, afraid to blink even once since the movement might dislodge the tears that stung threateningly where they lay hidden. Not sure if they stemmed from fury or remorse, Lark stepped back, unsettled at the sight of a chalk-white Sheridan. "Wait just a damn minute here," she said slowly. "I took this job because my agent practically begged. It's been *hard* to find a PT that was ready to work with you. I came here prepared to do my best, to really help you the way you needed to be helped, rather than indulge your unreasonable ideas of a quick fix."

Sheridan gasped. "Well, that won't be your problem any longer. From this moment you're relieved of any duty in this household. I'll have Mrs. D and Erica take care of everything." Barely audible, Sheridan continued. "I had high hopes for our collaboration, Lark. Apparently I was wrong. Very disappointing."

"So did I." The anger left as quickly as it came and Lark slumped back against the table. The edge cut into her hip, but she didn't care about the pain. "I had high hopes as well."

Sheridan's pale face was now blank and devoid of emotions. "Too bad then."

Lark straightened up, thrust her shoulders back, and elevated her chin like her stepfather had taught her when she was a teenager. "I'll vacate my room then." She hesitated for a moment but then thought better of extending a hand. She just couldn't. "Good-bye, Sheridan. I wish you the best of luck, and I hope things work out better for you with your next PT." It was hard to utter these words; her senses felt like they had been scalded by boiling water.

"Farewell, Lark," Sheridan said quietly, suddenly not seeming angry at all. Rather, the thickness in her voice spoke of other, unexplained emotions.

In fact, Lark thought as she left the gym, it seemed as if both of them had hidden something entirely different behind all that anger. What had just happened? She tried to examine her whirling emotions, but it was no use. Lark drew a trembling breath. She simply didn't know.

CHAPTER TEN

G oodness, child, you don't look well at all!" Doris Hirsh rose from the kitchen table where she sat with Lark's stepfather, having lunch. "Come here."

"I'm fine, Mom." Lark sighed, but enjoyed the firm embrace just the same.

"What's up?" Arthur asked. "I'll find you something to eat while you fill us in. It's clear that something's happened."

Lark smiled faintly. "I can get a bowl myself, Dad. Stay where you are." She grabbed a bowl from the counter and filled it with her mother's chili. Sitting down next to Doris, she took a spoon full of food and savored it as she gathered her thoughts. "Okay, folks. I was fired today."

"Why?" Doris asked. "What happened?"

Lark looked at her parents. Doris was obviously stunned, and a dark edge ringed Arthur's irises, a surefire sign of concern on his part.

"My patient wasn't pleased with my work."

"That's ridiculous!" Doris slammed her palm onto the table, making her glass of iced tea jump. "You're the best at what you do."

"Thank you for your vote of confidence, but she obviously doesn't agree. To be truthful, I wasn't quite my usual diplomatic self."

"That says a lot," Arthur said. "You were always the diplomat among you five girls. What can your patient have said or done to mess with that?" He tilted his head.

Lark had always admired Arthur's astute way of reading the situation and aiming for the core of the matter. "I questioned her judgment." Lark sighed again. "I guess I should have made my point more delicately, but she's so direct that I fell into the trap of thinking she could handle the truth."

"And she couldn't."

"Nope." Lark frowned and had to swallow twice to force the next spoonful of food down. "I think she panicked. I mean, I know she did and then, when she reacted by insulting me, I couldn't see past her words. So, I'm fired."

"Poor darling," Doris said loyally and put an arm around her. "Well, you can stay here until you know what you want to do next. Actually, that might be good for Fiona."

Lark stopped eating. "She okay?"

"Yes." Doris patted Lark's shoulder. "But of course she's still upset that she had a setback like this. It takes her so long to bounce back emotionally, you know."

"Yeah, I know." Lark looked up as if she could penetrate the ceiling and look at her sister. "I'll go up to her. I can finish this upstairs." She grabbed her bowl and kissed the top of her mother's head. "Delicious as always, Mom."

"Thank you, darling."

"Hey, Lark," Arthur called out as she reached the doorway. "If anyone calls, I mean about this, what should we tell them?"

Lark glanced back over her shoulder. "They won't. But if I'm wrong, just tell them I'm not home."

"Okay. Will do."

Lark ascended the stairs to the second floor, with its four bedrooms and three bathrooms. The downstairs consisted of the kitchen, living room, guest bathroom, and her parents' gallery and gift shop. Arthur and Doris had bought this house shortly after they were married. When Lark had moved with her mother and sisters to live with Arthur in Boerne, she had loved the place from day one. The house with the gift shop and gallery held such ambience; coming home was like swaddling her heart in a bowl of cotton.

The door was half open to her old room where Fiona now stayed alone. Lark rapped her fingernails on the door frame and heard a muffled, "Enter." She pushed the door open and stood motionless on the threshold.

Fiona sat in an electric wheelchair, her upper body strapped tight to the backrest and her legs resting in cushioned indentations, equally strapped into place. Fiona turned her head, and as usual, the sight of the stunning woman tore at Lark's heart. Only able to move her head and her right arm, Fiona had an ethereal beauty that made everyone forget about her disability. Dark brown hair, kept in a simple, low ponytail, framed a delicately chiseled face with large blue eyes. Her lips, usually soft and luscious, were today pressed to a thin line, and the eyes were nearly black.

"Hello, sweetie," Lark greeted Fiona. "Heard you had a bit of a rough time."

"You could say that." Fiona spoke tightly, clenching her right fist. "I'm okay now."

"Sure you are. You're the okayest person I know," Lark joked, knowing Fiona had a soft spot for her silliness. As she hugged her sister she could feel the stiffness in Fiona's neck and wondered how much was because she was upset, and how much of it was spasticity. "I'm back home for a bit."

"You have a vacation already?" Fiona's thin, black eyebrows knitted in disbelief.

"Nope. Got fired."

The statement seemed to reach Fiona. Her features mellowed and she touched Lark's face. "What kind of idiots are you working for, sis?"

"Thanks for the vote of confidence. And no, they're not idiots. Just someone who's scared and lashes out at everyone, especially those who try to help."

"Sounds familiar." Fiona made a face. "So your patient sacked you because you got too close, huh?"

"You're an astute young woman, that's what I've always said." Lark pushed a few errant strands from Fiona's forehead. "And yes, you're probably very right."

"Been there, done that, burned the T-shirt." Fiona operated the joystick on the right armrest and pivoted the chair to face Lark fully. "Sit down. You make my neck ache when you stand so close."

"All right, all right." Lark sat on Fiona's bed and placed the bowl of chili on the nightstand as she picked up Mr. Gogo, her old teddy bear that had found a new home there. "I'm exhausted, but I still want to hear about what happened the other day."

"It was tough on Mom. She wanted to call in the cavalry, but the thought of all four of you dropping everything just because I… stumbled, so to speak, was too much. I'm twenty-seven years old, for heaven's sake!" Fiona gestured impatiently. "I also wanted to move on, go home and get back to work."

"I don't blame you. Just tell me that you're *really* doing better and I'll back off," Lark said gently, not wanting to antagonize Fiona.

"I promise. I was pretty bad off when the flashbacks hit, and I totally freaked out. It's been so long since last time. I woke up and heard the gunshots all over again. And I swear, I felt the bullets hit me. They drilled…into me…and…and…" Fiona began to breathe faster, her lower lip trembling. "I mean, it's been almost fifteen years! And still, it was like it happened last week."

"But you handled it. You rode the demon until he gave up and you won. Take pride in that, sweetie." Lark took Fiona's motionless hand. She knew Fiona allowed very few people to touch her paralyzed limbs, and Lark was one of them. Caressing the hand, she knew Fiona could sense her touch even if she had very little feeling left. "You're a champ, sis. A true winner."

"Yeah, well, I don't feel like that sometimes. There are days…" She quieted and her gaze strayed to the window, as if she longed to be somewhere else. "You know."

"I do. I really do." Lark knew that her parents had built in every possible helpful solution for Fiona's sake, including an elevator between the floors and ramps everywhere. The bathroom was better equipped than even Sheridan's. Lark winced at the thought of Sheridan, images of the furious woman flickering in her mind.

"What?" Fiona tilted her head, looking as inquisitive as only she knew how to.

"Nothing. I just thought of something." Lark knew this explanation wouldn't fly with Fiona, but it was worth a try.

"What?" Fiona repeated, a little smile playing at the corners of her mouth.

"You're like a dog with a bone, you know that?" Lark couldn't help but smile back, genuinely happy and relieved to see the new light in Fiona's eyes.

"I have to be. Nobody tells me anything if I don't nag." Fiona blinked and suddenly Lark felt as if they had been transported through time and were teenagers again, sharing a much smaller room in their house in Houston.

"Well, but you nag so well. Wouldn't want to keep you from

showing off your talent, would I?"

"And you're changing the subject."

"And you prove my point!"

Fiona raised an eyebrow and Lark saw something so strong about the ethereal features that she relented, knowing she'd cave in sooner or later. She always did when it came to Fiona.

"I don't know, sis. I have a hard time thinking professionally with this patient. She…she gets under my skin with just a few words, you know. There's something about her, no matter how annoying and arrogant she can act."

"Act. As in it's a front?"

"Yeah or, well, I'd like to think so."

"You attracted to her?" Fiona's tone wasn't judgmental, and her eyes were kind but unwavering while she waited for Lark's response.

"As I said," Lark sighed, "I've never had this reaction to a patient. Ever. She's not even my type!"

"You mean she's not short, blond, and timid?" Fiona's eyes sparkled as she summed up Lark's first long-term girlfriend Tina perfectly.

"Funny. And no. She's not anything like the women I've usually found interesting. She's out of my league in all sorts of ways, and the fact that she's my patient…well, hearing myself talk now, her firing me was probably clever. I could have ended up being reported for unprofessional, unethical, and generally lewd behavior."

"You?" Fiona's eyes glittered. "Surely you would've been able to control any untoward lusts and desires? Or would you have jumped the poor defenseless creature's bones at the first possible opportunity?"

Lark burst out laughing, feeling altogether cheered up being teased by this fragile-looking woman, who had the will of a thousand mules and a greater sense of humor than anyone meeting her for the first time would ever credit her with.

"You're crazy! Me jump *anybody*?" Lark giggled, but recalled her body's unmistakable reaction to Sheridan's presence. How Sheridan's silken skin had felt under her touch, and how her massage could have easily turned into caresses.

"Lark, honey. What are you thinking about? I was only joking, you know." Fiona looked remorseful.

"Oh, no, no. I know you were, Fee. I know. I'm okay."

"No, you're not. Why not tell me the rest?"

Lark hesitated, her cheeks burning. "One night she was hurting badly and needed lots of help." She stopped talking and scrutinized Fiona's expression.

"I know what that's like. Go on."

"I held her in my arms, well, on my lap really, and gave her that massage I give Mom when her migraines hit. And she relaxed against me. It really helped her."

"And how did you feel?"

"I...I don't know. I ached with her when she hurt, more than I normally do with a patient. And I ached for holding her, when the pain went away. It's odd. I can't describe it, and I sure as hell can't understand it."

"Come closer." Fiona motioned.

Lark obeyed and Fiona touched her cheek again, much like their mother had done when she wanted to convey something very important to them. The gesture fit Fiona, Lark reflected absentmindedly as she focused on her sister.

"Listen," Fiona said. "Don't sell yourself short. You're only human, and the fact that you found your patient attractive isn't the end of the world. Who knows, she might find you drop-dead gorgeous too! You know what's right and what's wrong, and I assume from what you've told me that she's an adult?"

"Yes. Yes, of course," Lark answered, startled.

"Then, since nothing really happened, you're fine. Ask yourself if you ever contemplated crossing the line and seducing Ms. Arrogant and Dazzling."

"No! But just the thought that I—"

"But nothing," Fiona said with finality in her voice. "You're beating yourself up for nothing. And look at me, you have me all rallied to defend you for actions you never committed. Just look how much you've brought me back into the real world."

It was true. Fiona's eyes sparkled and her skin had a new, healthy tone, rather than the earlier paleness, which had emphasized her brooding, haunted eyes.

"Trust me to bring you into my world and then not be considerate while doing so." Lark grimaced, only half joking.

"Good God, woman. Don't you think I need more real world in my life instead of old ghosts that really need to be put to bed?"

"Yeah. I understand. And I agree." Lark stood, suddenly restless. "How about we go down the street to The Daily Grind for some java? You up for it?"

Fiona hesitated only two seconds. "Sure. We need some latte, or something. I just need to powder my nose. Lend a hand?"

"No problemo, my dear."

Lark followed Fiona into the spacious bathroom designed to fit her needs. At times like these, when Fiona needed help with the most basic things in life, her face seemed to soften until she looked thirteen again. *Perhaps she regresses in her mind to when she was a child and this handicap wasn't as invasive for her.*

But that wasn't true either. Even at thirteen, Fiona had hated having to accept help with such private matters. *But what choice does she have?* Putting on her cheeriest face, Lark went about the task in a way that she hoped Fiona would interpret as both casual and loving, because it was.

❖

"Fuck!" Sheridan looked at a shocked Erica. "You mean they have only these two to offer?"

"Yes, and Mr. Vogel was most apologetic, but on such short notice, this was the best he could do."

Sheridan stared at the folders before her. "One woman in her fifties who only recently came back to practicing physiotherapy after having stayed home and raised her children. How old were they when she let them out of the nest? Thirty? And this, a guy, attending his last year at the university. He's not even qualified yet! What the hell is this? Aren't there any other agencies in this city?"

Erica stepped back as if the strength of Sheridan's voice forced her to. "The Vogel Agency is the best, ma'am. I called two others and they're going to fax me resumes of their available personnel."

"Let me know as soon as they arrive. They can't be worse than this!" Sheridan pushed the files off her desk and into the bin. "Where's that nurse, eh, Brenda-something?"

"Mary Ann."

"What happened to Brenda?" Sheridan frowned, disgusted with herself and the entire situation.

"Brenda quit a month ago, ma'am."

"Oh. Is Karen on tonight?"

"Yes."

"Good." Sheridan found Karen refreshing, and in a way she reminded her of Lark. Sheridan winced. She didn't want to even think about the last, disastrous meeting with Lark. For some unfathomable reason, Lark's brown eyes seemed to regard her from a distance wherever she was, no matter what she did. Knowing deep inside that she had screwed up, Sheridan wasn't prepared to confess the fact out loud.

Surely there were a dozen, at least, equally competent physical therapists in San Antonio. Or, if not in the city, then in the great state of Texas. Sheridan ignored the small voice that tried to tell her that if these people were as good as Lark, they'd make the same demands on her that she had.

"Eh, ma'am?" Erica cleared her throat.

Sheridan looked up and felt a twitch of remorse at the sight of the uncertainty on Erica's face. When even her long-term employees tiptoed around her, the situation was bad. "Yes? What else?" she said, nearly slapping herself over the head at how pesky she sounded. "Sorry, Erica. What's up?" That was as close to the heartfelt apology that Sheridan meant to give, but Erica smiled faintly, which was a good sign.

"Your two o'clock meeting is here. The Granger Conglomerate's president."

"Oh, God. I forgot." Sheridan felt her cheeks flush. What the hell was going on? She never used to forget anything. Lark would have been able to explain this memory lapse in terms that gave her hope for the future. *Damn, I wasn't going to go there. Unproductive.*

"Give me five minutes to freshen up. Page me before you send them in. And treat them to that wonderful coffee you make, all right?"

"Sure thing, boss," Erica said, her normal humor back in her voice, which made Sheridan feel a little better. At least she hadn't been so bad toward Erica that she'd threaten to leave too. These thoughts startled Sheridan into action and she wheeled toward her en suite bathroom.

When there, she examined her reflection, not at all surprised to see herself look just as haggard and haunted as she felt. The words "emotionally incontinent" from the hateful brochure the hospital counselor had brought her came to mind, but she disregarded them with a disdainful huff. Lark would never have described her reactions anything like that. Lark would have told her that it was normal to feel out of sorts, lose footing and all, when you'd nearly died just a few months ago and had your entire life turned upside down.

Sheridan ran the faucet and washed her hands. Lark would have reassured her on this issue and many other things. *And I, like a prize fool, chased her away by being totally out of control. How's that for emotional incontinence?*

CHAPTER ELEVEN

Y ou've got to be kidding!" Sheridan huffed and glowered at the woman standing next to her. Sweat poured down Sheridan's face as she used all her strength to not plummet to the floor between the bars. "Did you say swing?"

"Yes, ma'am." Lydia—or was it Gladys?—beamed. "Just *swing* forward. Use your arms. They look quite sturdy." She patted Sheridan's left biceps encouragingly. "There. Hop to it."

Sheridan swallowed a growl. This woman was the best person Erica could scare up on such short notice, or so her assistant claimed. She had arrived from yet another agency, claiming to be eager to work for the esteemed Sheridan Ward and that this was a God-sent opportunity, since she was able to start the very same afternoon.

God-sent, Sheridan huffed to herself. *I wish.* "I don't have any strength left to remain standing, let alone swing."

"Ah, but it is through pain that we learn, Ms. Ward."

That's it! "I find your presence here painful enough," Sheridan said, her voice low and menacing, which seemed to have zero effect on the new physical therapist.

"You won't succeed with a negative attitude." The woman smiled cheerfully. "When life sends us hurdles, we learn how to jump, and—"

"You're fired."

"What?" The first look of uncertainty flickered over Lydia, or Gladys's, face.

"You—are—fired."

"But I've only been here a couple of hours."

Sheridan managed to drop relatively gracefully into the wheelchair. She unbuckled her leg braces before she returned her attention to the stunned woman who still stood next to her. Lydia-Gladys seemed utterly confused by the turn of events and stood with her hands hanging by her sides.

Suddenly remorseful at her tone of voice, Sheridan relented. "You will get three months' pay. That way you can find another job and be paid double for a while."

"But I've already told everyone I know that I'd be working with a high-profile patient."

Sheridan wanted to groan out loud and throw something. *At least she didn't indulge in name-dropping. I hope.* "Well, that's too bad," she said between clenched teeth. "I don't see how we can work together. We have very different ideas about what my training should be."

"Everything I do is by the book."

"What book? A history of the Spanish Inquisition?" Sheridan snapped. "Listen, Lydia—"

"It's Gloria."

Damn, close, but not quite. "Gloria." Sheridan conscientiously adjusted her tone of voice not to agitate Gloria anymore. "Follow your own advice."

"What?" Looking desolate, Gloria pressed her hands together in a gesture that reminded Sheridan of the von Trapp family singing "So Long, Farewell." *How appropriate.*

"See this as just another hurdle to jump." Sheridan was prepared to duck at the sight of Gloria's reaction to her own advice.

Now the woman looked like she was ready to throw something.

❖

Lark glanced around the attic. Her mother had turned the bare space into a cozy den with plaid curtains for the small windows, warm colors on pillows and bedspreads. Converting what had been a storage area into an additional guest room was a brilliant idea on Doris's part. Lark's sisters and their families would use the guest room frequently.

"You got everything you need, honey?" Doris poked her head up just above the banister.

"Yes, Mom. I'm fine."

"I know everyone has asked you this a million times, but are you sure?"

"Yes. I'm sure."

"Your father said he thought you looked...desolate." Doris ascended one more step and folded her arms as she leaned on the railing.

"Desolate?" Lark cringed. "That's taking things a little far. Of course I'm not happy that I lost my job. And I'm mad at myself for letting Roy talk me into taking the job in the first place. I'd promised myself not to work in a private home anymore. Well, at least not for a long time. It's a lonely job, really."

"I can understand that."

"I missed not having workmates and...well, backup."

"Understandable too."

"And now, when I really had begun to care about my patient... Mom, this has never happened to me before. I mean, I've had issues with my patients' family members interfering and stuff, but like this? Never."

"Maybe you'll see it differently in a day or two."

Lark doubted it. She missed Sheridan on a whole different level, and not to be around her, not hear that smooth, husky voice, was painful. "Yeah, I hope so," Lark said for her mother's benefit. "Things change."

"They do. I'm not sure you believe that right now, but you will, honey."

"Okay."

"Get some sleep. I heard you and Fiona giggle after the movie you took her to."

"She seems better."

"She does. After you came today, she seemed to turn over a new leaf. That's one good thing about having you here."

Lark knew her mother was right. No matter why she was back again so quickly, the difference it made to Fiona was undeniable. "Yes. And I'm glad to be here, no matter what."

"Good. Sleep tight, child. See you tomorrow." Doris smiled, the familiar broad smile that had always comforted Lark while she was growing up, and walked back downstairs.

Only when Fiona was injured had Doris stopped smiling for quite some time. And only when they knew Fiona would live had she relaxed and ever so cautiously regained her easy-going warmth. Lark had long struggled with the notion that the assault on Fiona had forever changed all of them.

Arthur's introduction into the traumatized family had been yet another turning point. Arthur possessed a soothing calm that could inspire a person to excel. It hadn't taken Lark long to find out that she wanted to impress him, to make him as proud of her as her mother was. Arthur had never once given her reason to doubt his love for his new family.

At first, Lark's youngest sister had tested Arthur, compared him to the fragmented memories she had of their biological father who died when she was five years old. Arthur had probably banged his head against the wall when it came to the younger Mitchell sister. Over the years, however, he'd won her over, and today she openly stated that Arthur was her daddy and nobody should ever try to argue this fact.

Lark sighed. Being the mediator in the family sometimes took a toll on her, and now, when the conflict was her own, and not something she could help someone else with, she was at a loss. "It's what I do," Lark murmured. "I care, I help, and I solve. What else is my purpose?"

She glanced toward the half-open window. The special scent of Boerne, fresh, sometimes a bit dusty, and always so much cleaner than the big city, made her feel safe, at home. Once Lark had started junior high, Houston had been a nightmare. It had never been home the way Boerne was.

After Lark plugged her air card into a slot on her laptop's left side, she flipped it open, booted it, and connected to the Internet. Lark logged into her e-mail, and when she found nothing of interest, she opened her chat software. Her heart stopped for a moment when she saw Sheridan on line. Time to confess a sin. Lark was rehearsing the words when the chat program suddenly pinged, making her jump.

Sheri_star: Well it's official.

Lark frowned, uncertain what to expect. She began to type.

Grey_bird: What are you talking about?
Sheri_star: I'm a prize fool.
Grey_bird: How's that?
Sheri_star: I fired someone today.

What the...That was very honest of Sheridan, to admit it up front to Grey_bird.

> *Sheri_star:* And to make matters even worse, I did a repeat performance this evening.
> *Grey_bird:* Wait a minute here. You fired people? What does your boss say?
> *Sheri_star:* That's just it. I am the boss. Sorry that I didn't tell you.
> *Grey_bird:* Wow.
> *Sheri_star:* Yeah. The buck stops here, as they say. With me.
> *Grey_bird:* That makes me feel a bit dumb.
> *Sheri_star:* Don't. I didn't mean to lie. I don't know what I was thinking.
> *Grey_bird:* Were you lowering yourself to my level?
> *Sheri_star:* No, no! I don't see you as inferior. I don't. Do you believe me, Bird?

The way Sheridan used part of Lark's nickname felt almost like a term of endearment, which was of course crazy. Lark berated herself. They were casual chat buddies and nothing else.

> *Grey_bird:* I suppose. This is the nature of online chats, after all.
> *Sheri_star:* I don't like deliberate lies or have any patience for people who use smokescreens to cover their true agenda.

Lark inhaled sharply and scratched her scalp as it prickled with shame. *How can I criticize her for being dishonest when I'm the one who started this?* Disgusted, Lark was prepared to tell Sheridan the truth, but Sheridan was already typing.

> *Sheri_star:* Hey, let's change the topic. How's your boss doing? Any progress?
> *Grey_bird:* Not really. I've been having problems and have to stay with my parents for a while.

Sheri_star: Ouch. Sounds painful.

Grey_bird: Actually, my parents are the least of my problems. They're no problem at all.

Sheri_star: Then what's up?

Grey_bird: It's work related, but I can't break confidentiality.

Sheridan clearly hesitated before answering.

Sheri_star: I see. What do you do for a living?

Grey_bird: I work closely with my clients, which I enjoy, normally.

Sheri_star: But not at the moment?

Grey_bird: Let's just say that it's wearing a bit thin. Hey, how did this switch to being about me?

Sheri_star: You are so much more interesting. A bit of a mystery, actually. I still don't know who set us up chatting with each other.

Stunned and speechless, literally, Lark stared at Sheridan's last message. It was as if she was talking to another woman, and yet she could hear Sheridan's voice as clear as if she'd been sitting next to her on the bed. Lark gasped. On the bed...

Grey_bird: She wanted to be anonymous in case we didn't hit it off. Apparently you're quite intimidating? *smile*

Sheri_star: Anonymous, huh? And as for intimidating, yeah, I've heard that before.

Grey_bird: I'll figure things out. Now tell me, why did you fire these people? What did they do?

Sheri_star: Nothing. That's just it.

Grey_bird: Surely they must have misbehaved somehow, or not pulled their weight?

Sheri_star: Nope. There was a difference of opinion today, but that in itself wasn't grounds for firing anyone.

Grey_bird: Then what?

Sheri_star: Compatibility problems combined with my temper, I think.

Grey_bird: Ouch. Bad combo?

Sheri_star: You bet.

Grey_bird: I've got a bit of a temper too, even if I try not to show it most of the time.

Sheri_star: Anything else you're hiding? You're not a bearded guy, are you?

This question made Lark laugh and feel better for some reason. She was, after all, pulling more wool over Sheridan's eyes than vice versa.

Grey_bird: LOL! No, I'm all woman.

There was a brief pause and Lark wondered if Sheridan had lost her Internet connection.

Sheri_star: Good to hear. I have no problem with men, usually, but I like women better.

Grey_bird: Like as in *really* like?

Sheri_star: Yup.

Oh, God. She actually is gay. And so out of my league, and out of reach, for that matter. Lark pressed her fingertips to her temples for a moment before she began to type again

Grey_bird: Me too.

Sheri_star: You out to your family and friends?

Grey_bird: Yes. To the ones that matter. You?

Sheri_star: No. My job prevents it. I used to go to another town where I have an apartment and... *socialize.*

Grey_bird: Sounds like you got lucky once in a while.

Sheri_star: I made some friends. But you know this, right? From our mutual friend?

Grey_bird: Some, but not very much.

Sheri_star: So you go out a lot?

Grey_bird: Not really. I don't have time either. But I've
           had a couple of girlfriends. Been a while
           though.
Sheri_star: So nobody right now?

Heat seeped up from Lark's neck to her cheeks.

Grey_bird: No. You?

Another pause.

Sheri_star: No. Sometimes I think my ship has left for
           good.
Grey_bird: How so?
Sheri_star: I've been ill. Still not well.

There! Lark sat up so fast her back ached. Sheridan's unexpected
trust nearly numbed her fingers, and she had to erase several times to
manage the next two words.

Grey_bird: What happened?
Sheri_star: Let's just say, life threw a wrench, or a
           complete tool set, into the works. I'm still
           recuperating.
Grey_bird: Slow progress?
Sheri_star: Yes.
Grey_bird: What do the pros say?

This time the break was so long that Lark was certain that Sheridan
had pulled the cord to the computer.

❖

Sheridan pulled herself up farther on the pillows. Her fingertips
were cold, and she struggled to type as she chatted with Grey_bird.

Sheri_star: That's just it. My neurologist is really
           pessimistic, and…the caregivers do what they

can to help, but it's not enough.
Grey_bird: You have help at home?
Sheri_star: A fully staffed house, actually.
Grey_bird: A group home?

Sheridan laughed huskily, feeling her cheeks warm with embarrassment.

Sheri_star: No, not like that. I'm pretty privileged. I employ ten, twelve people around the house.
Grey_bird: Wow. Sounds like you have every chance of working this out, from a financial point of view.
Sheri_star: Yeah, you'd think so. I'm afraid I'm not easy to get along with. I'm demanding.
Grey_bird: Autocratic? *helpful suggestion*

Sheridan laughed, and some of the tension left her shoulders, which she had pulled up tight by her neck without realizing it.

Sheri_star: Yeah. Tyrannical, pesky, and self-absorbed. Just look at this chat. Mostly about me. What about you?
Grey_bird: I lead a common, everyday kinda life. Nothing exciting.

Somehow Sheridan guessed this wasn't entirely true.

Sheri_star: Hey. I spilled my guts. Share.
Grey_bird: Trust me. Nothing much to share.
Sheri_star: Indulge me.

The chat program indicated that Grey_bird was typing, and Sheridan prepared herself to remain patient as she waited for her chat friend to finish.

Grey_bird: My former boss, well, the one I had before my current one…I just couldn't work there. I tried,

I really did, but talk about miscommunication. I feel like I compromised over and over, but it wasn't enough. I dunno. I might have been too set in my ways, since my method has always worked before. I could have listened more, paid more attention. Now I feel like I not only failed big-time, but also that I left my boss high and dry, ya know. It kinda hurts.

Sheridan read Grey_bird's comments and something in her loosened up, while something else knotted tighter and made her ache. She stroked her sweaty palms against the blankets, but she felt suddenly cold as well. It had never quite occurred to her, no matter how progressive and sensitive she would like to believe she was, just how much being fired devastated a person.

Sheri_star: How are you coping? Is your current employer paying you enough?
Grey_bird: Yes. I'm well provided for. No complaints there. The pay is great.
Sheri_star: I can tell that isn't enough.
Grey_bird: You sound surprised. And concerned?
Sheri_star: I can't help it. I feel I know you. Weird, huh?
Grey_bird: Not really. I feel the same way. You seem like a friend.

Sheridan's palms tingled as she typed the question that had burned in the back of her head ever since she started chatting with Grey_bird.

Sheri_star: Is that all?
Grey_bird: What do you mean?
Sheri_star: You know what I mean.
Grey_bird: I guess so.
Sheri_star: What?
Grey_bird: I guess that I think there's more. Something in what you say and how you say it.
Sheri_star: Oh.
Grey_bird: And you, then?

Sheridan swallowed hastily, then coughed. This situation was nerve-wracking, to say the least, and she was sure she wasn't being very clever to make herself vulnerable to a faceless individual whom she'd met online. Still, she couldn't stop herself. Images of women she'd met over the years flickered by, but one image was clearer than any of the others. Lark's soft features, the heart-shaped face with the slightly upturned nose and her smooth complexion—they all fit so well with the words the woman on the other end wrote.

Sheri_star: I only know that I don't want you to just disappear. It means something to me that you might be here when I log on. If you knew me, you'd know that I don't say this casually. I really mean it. You've gotten under my skin, somehow.

Grey_bird: Oh, God. I never meant for this to happen, but you've touched me too. Perhaps we need to put a damper on things before it goes too far.

Sheri_star: What do you mean?

Grey_bird: You don't know. You're not the only one who struggles with guilt, ya know. I'm not exactly Snow White.

Sheri_star: Well, neither am I. Think I'm more the evil Queen.

Grey_bird: Sounds more interesting, if you ask me. *grin*

Sheridan smiled broadly.

Sheri_star: So if I serve you an apple, or something, then you'd take a bite?

Grey_bird: You bet. I'd feast on…the apple. *wink*

Losing her breath for a moment, Sheridan hurried to type.

Sheri_star: I think I might enjoy experiencing your feast. You sound voracious.

Grey_bird: What can I say? I love apples.

Sheri_star: Sounds delicious.
Grey_bird: This is getting out of hand, Sheri.
Sheri_star: I know.
Grey_bird: You have an unexpected effect on me.
Sheri_star: Tell me about it.
Grey_bird: You too?

Sheridan touched her right breast and wasn't surprised to feel a hard nipple spear her palm, her body's response to the increasingly sexy chat. Even if she couldn't move her legs, she still had some feeling, and right now it was painfully obvious how aroused she could still become—and how wet.

Sheri_star: Yes. Me too.
Grey_bird: Too fast. Too soon. I have to go.

Sheridan flinched.

Sheri_star: No. Please.
Grey_bird: See you tomorrow. If you want.

Sheridan moaned and closed her eyes briefly. This couldn't be happening. Hot and cold at the same time, depending on which body part she considered, Sheridan trembled as she typed.

Sheri_star: I look forward to it. Also, just so you know,
            Bird, you leave me in agony.
Grey_bird: I do?
Sheri_star: Yes. And you know it. Your reaction tells me
            that you're in the same frame of mind.
Grey_bird: So that's fair then.
Sheri_star: Tomorrow?
Grey_bird: Tomorrow.

Sheridan closed the chat window, before she made a fool of herself by begging Grey_bird to stay, to…do what? Sheridan was always careful online. She had engaged in occasional flirtation but had never been affected like this. It was as if Grey_bird could actually see her, and Sheridan's hand on her breast only strengthened the feeling that Lark... Grey_bird, Sheridan corrected herself, more than a little annoyed.

She pushed the laptop over onto the nightstand and managed to wriggle into a comfortable position. Sleep eluded her at first, and she began to pull her boxers down a bit. She was tempted to touch herself, but didn't dare after the illness. Her body felt completely alien, and she feared she would discover she was incapable of feeling anything, of ever being able to enjoy sex again. As long as she didn't try, she could convince herself that she was fine, merely exercising abstinence for the time being. Until she was better, stronger and more self-confident.

Now, however, she reached the wetness that covered her engorged folds, and it was blatantly clear that this part still worked. Amazed at how drenched she was from just talking to Grey_bird, Sheridan pushed a fingertip against her clitoris, slipped, tried again, but it was impossible to establish the rhythm she normally required to be able to come. Frustrated, Sheridan knew she wouldn't be able to grind her thighs together, another surefire way to push her toward orgasm.

"Fuck." She sighed and pressed her palm firmly against her sex. She had been so close, and now she was rapidly cooling off, since both Grey_bird's words and the image of Lark seemed very distant. Wincing at where her thoughts relentlessly wandered, Sheridan closed her eyes firmly and tried to will sleep to come. Deep down she knew it was a fruitless attempt.

CHAPTER TWELVE

I can only work between five and eight in the evening."

Sheridan looked with tired and careful optimism at the tall man in front of her. "Sounds doable, Mr. Henderson. May I ask why?"

"I have five children under the age of eight, and my wife is pregnant again. This means she needs me at home." Henderson nodded thoughtfully, as if he'd just stated a profound truth.

"So, I assume that you have your hands full?"

"Yes, I do. It's exhausting to keep up with the kids." Another nod.

Ever heard of condoms, man? "Which doesn't sound good from my perspective. I need someone who isn't more tired than I am."

"I'm not tired, exactly."

"No. Merely exhausted. I don't think you'd be the right one for this position."

"You won't even give me a chance?"

Henderson scrunched up his face, and for a moment Sheridan feared he would actually burst into tears.

You really must be exhausted. "No, I'm sorry, but I need the position filled right away. I don't have time for temporary or tryout solutions."

"I came more than a hundred miles for this interview." Henderson began to look annoyed, rather than weepy, which was better, but not entirely good.

"I'm sorry."

"I need to be reimbursed for gas."

Sheridan barely refrained from groaning. She wasn't sure whether to laugh or chew the guy off at the ankles. "I'm afraid that's not company policy. You have to take that up with your agency."

"Hey, you lure me to drive this far by dangling a coveted position in front of my nose—"

"*Mr.* Henderson." Sheridan let her voice boom. "This interview is over."

"But—"

"Thank you." Sheridan wished she could have risen to her feet and met the man's eyes at his level, but apparently her glare had a pretty good effect.

Henderson muttered what sounded like a curse and stomped out. A concerned Erica quickly appeared in his place.

"I heard shouting, ma'am. Are you all right?"

"I'm fine. And Erica, you've worked here for almost ten years. Please call me Sheridan when we're alone. I know you like to keep our relationship formal, but indulge me." Sheridan had asked Erica to be on a first-name basis from day one, but the young woman adamantly reiterated that formalities were invented for a purpose.

Erica studied the floor for a few seconds before she met Sheridan's eyes. "I've been stubborn, haven't I? Actually, I've thought about it since Lark was on a first-name basis with you right away. So, why not?"

"Mark the calendar," Sheridan muttered good-naturedly. "Perhaps I should have called in witnesses? Speaking of that, any more interviews? I mean, interviews *not* like this one."

"Only one more this afternoon. You have a teleconference, then a meeting with two of your regional directors."

"Which regions again?" Sheridan was suddenly irritated. Once she had known all these things, remembered a full week of appointments without a problem.

"San Francisco and Oregon."

"Very well. Give me a copy of their reports half an hour before the meeting."

"Already on your desk, ma'am—Sheridan."

"You'll get used to it. I'm not always a dragon, you know."

"I have never regarded you as a dragon."

"What then?"

"A mule?" Erica winked and smiled broadly.

Sheridan had to laugh. The unexpected comment relaxed her, strangely enough, and she also enjoyed how her firm gaze always seemed to rattle Erica. This was the case now, when Sheridan deliberately drilled into her. "Mule, huh? Hm. You're suddenly very bold. Perhaps it was a mistake to suggest a first-name basis."

"Too late." Erica grinned. "Now all bets are off."

Sheridan shook her head as Erica left the room. She had never imagined that she had such a brazen personality. *Then again, I keep everyone at arm's length. Except Lark. With her, I—* Sheridan broke off the unproductive thoughts and reached for her laptop. She switched on the teleconference software and browsed through the documents containing the information she needed to prepare. Beginning to read, she heard a small voice in the back of her mind continually insist that it would take much more effort than this to shove Lark out of her mind.

❖

"Six thousand dollars?" Lark stared at the price tag on the painting that hung center stage in her parents' gallery. "Wow, Fee, that's not bad."

"It's not my most expensive artwork." Fiona pointed toward a set of two paintings farther along the wall. "That combo is set at eight thousand dollars. But that's two for the price of one, of course." She wrinkled her nose and shrugged her shoulder.

"Sho' me da money." Lark grinned. "I couldn't be happier for you. And for the buyers of your art. I read that art magazine of yours when I couldn't sleep last night, and you were mentioned among the year's groundbreaking artists."

"You couldn't sleep?" Fiona ignored the comment about her own success.

"Yeah. I was thinking. All sorts of thoughts tangoed in my head."

"Tell me."

Lark looked around the gallery. A dozen customers wandered among the paintings. "Not here. I don't want to broadcast my inner feelings to half of Boerne."

"I understand. If Mr. Bloomberg down at the grocery store finds out anything, *all* of Boerne knows it within seconds. He's like a switchboard on legs."

"Remember when he caught onto who Callie was seeing when she was barely eighteen?"

"Oh, yeah. Exciting times," Fiona said gleefully. "At least until Mom and Dad found out, probably last of all, that Rick Ferris had spent more than one night in our garage."

"I don't think anyone else in Boerne has been grounded that long. Relentlessly."

"She couldn't even call her friends. She had to rely on her beloved sisters to tell her what was happening around here."

"And since she was Callie, Ms. Good and Proper, that must've sucked." Fiona laughed and Lark joined her. It was impossible not to when Fiona's laughter was so incredibly catchy. "But when Rick substituted another girl for her, Mom and Dad—especially Dad— comforted her. She was still grounded though!"

"Poor Callie. She thought she'd never get over him, and then she met Burke."

"We're all happy she met Burke. I can't imagine her with anybody else."

"That's putting it mildly." Lark motioned with her head toward the door. "How about some coffee? I saw some of Mom's brownies in the kitchen."

"No coffee for me. Reached my limit of six cups already. The doctor will have my head on a platter if I'm naughty."

"Okay. I'll make us some hot chocolate if you want."

Fiona nodded eagerly. "Yes, please. Mom has the air-conditioning on so high that it feels like December."

Lark walked behind Fiona into the kitchen and began to heat some milk.

"So, are you going to share with me why you couldn't sleep? I mean, what you were thinking about?" Fiona parked her chair in her customary spot by the short end of the table.

"You have to keep it to yourself," Lark said, looking at Fiona over her shoulder. "I won't tell you any patient-PT confidential stuff, but still...it's important."

"You know I'm no gossip."

"Yeah, I do." Lark kept her attention on the milk simmering in the pot. "I had this dream that my patient fired me and regretted it immensely. It felt so real. And when I woke up, you know, with a jerk in the middle of the night, I couldn't help but wonder if she was in trouble."

"Medically, or—?"

"Well, that too. But also because…and here's the deal. You may lose all respect for me when I tell you this, but I'm chatting with her."

"What? You mean online?"

"Yeah."

"Why would she want to chat with you if she fired you? That doesn't make sense…" Fiona sounded baffled, but then her tone changed. "Oh, no. Lark."

"Yeah, she doesn't know it's me. She only knows me as Grey_bird online."

"You realize if she puts her mind to it, she can find out who Grey_bird is?"

Lark shuddered. "I do, but I suppose I'm in denial about that possibility." Lark proceeded to tell Fiona about her initial motives for going against every one of her principles.

"And now things have changed?"

"Yes." Lark pulled the pot off the stove and poured it onto the cocoa-and-sugar mix. She stirred longer than necessary, stalling, before she turned around and handed Fiona her mug. "It's hot."

"The way you chat with her?" Fiona asked.

"The chocolate's hot, genius." Lark shook her head. "No, well, yes, in a way, that's what's happened. There's a new tone, an element of attraction when we chat, even if we're dancing on burning twigs, sort of. She asked me some pretty interesting questions last night, and even if she was merely flirting—"

"What did she say?"

"She was being silly, you know, double entendres, that sort of thing. Then she said, between the lines, so to speak, that she regretted firing a person, but she didn't say what the person she fired did wrong or anything like that."

"So," Fiona said slowly, "she enjoys the privacy of a faceless chat, where she can pretend to be well and able to do anything. Can't say I don't find such a thing tempting, but I'd never do it. At the end of the day it would hurt more than it gave pleasure. I'd always know that it was make-believe, even more so, I think, than a healthy person."

"I understand what you're saying, Fee. I do. But my deception is worse than hers. She's living a dream, in a way, and who could blame her? I'm deceiving her in a much more callous way. I'm lying for completely different reasons."

"Your intentions were good. And here's the breaking news, Lark. You're not infallible. You make mistakes out of the goodness of your heart, like the rest of us."

"It's not like I've pulled off anything like this before."

"I know."

"And I'll call it quits next time I see her online."

Fiona frowned. "What do you mean?"

"I'm going to tell her we can't chat anymore." Lark stared down into her mug and twirled the spoon between her fingers.

"Are you going to tell her who you really are?"

"Eh, no. I don't want to cause her that type of grief."

"Lark."

"Yes?"

"You're being a chicken, which is *not* like you." Fiona placed her hand on Lark's. "I think you should go to her. Tell her everything face-to-face."

Lark shuddered again. "Oh, God, Fee. That takes more courage than I can scare up. You don't know her. She may be physically challenged and use a wheelchair, but she can chop your head off with one word."

"Your head? What on earth did you do that made her that angry?"

"You tell me. I'm not quite sure myself." Lark rubbed her forehead. "I was pushing her to stick to a certain schedule, and when she wouldn't make the effort to even be on time, if she showed up at all, I got a little pesky."

"Pesky? You?"

"Yeah. I suppose."

"That's even more enlightening," Fiona said, her smile frustratingly all-knowing. "So you challenged her, demanded too much of her time, in her opinion, and there was no doubt an attraction was going on already." She placed her right hand under her chin and mimicked stroking a goatee. "I see, I see, dear child."

"Very funny, Fiona."

Fiona's laughter was not without kindness. "Oh, Lark, welcome to us humans. All the years you lived at home, we went to you when we needed to 'fess up or confide a deep dark secret. Now it's you who needs support. It's all right, sis. I promise. We'll figure something out."

Fiona's last statement brought tears to Lark's eyes, but she refused to let them run down her cheeks. She didn't do well crying in front of anyone. She even kept away from mirrors and other reflections if she was overwhelmed with tears.

"Fee," she murmured and reached for a paper towel. She blew her nose and coughed a few times for good measure. "The cedars," she wheezed and nodded toward the window. "They bother me every year."

"I know. Me too. But the cedar pollen isn't very high now."

Lark glared at Fiona, but had to smile at the same time at the sparkling light in her eyes. Focusing on someone other than herself had obviously been good for her sister. Lark couldn't detect any trace of the haunted expression that had been written across Fiona's eyes the day before. "So what do you suggest I do?"

"Go to her. Don't tell her in a chat session. Tell her in person. What do you have to lose?"

"My license to practice?"

"I don't think you have to worry about that, do you?"

"You never know."

Fiona rubbed her chin again. "Hmm. Then let me think about it. I should be able to come up with something. Are you going to chat with her again tonight?"

"I really shouldn't. If she's online, I can always change the chat settings to 'invisible.'"

"A coward's method. Chat with her tonight, and try to keep off the topic of identities and so on."

"What are you plotting?" Lark knew plenty about her sister and was justifiably suspicious.

"It's called stalling. We need time to figure this out."

"Oh, God." Lark covered her eyes, but Fiona's shrewd tone of voice was impossible to shut out. "You scare me sometimes."

Fiona merely laughed. "Ah, ye of little faith…I'm at your service, dear sister. Never fear, Fiona is here, when troubles appear."

Lark groaned. "You still use that supergirl saying? God almighty."

"It's never failed me before."

"Really."

"Doubter."

Lark huffed. "I call myself a realist."

"Same shit, different name," Fiona said with aplomb. "There. I win."

❖

Sheridan wheeled into her living room and noticed that Mrs. D had lit tea lights on the side tables and put a tray of fresh fruit and orange juice on the coffee table. All furniture that used to be fashionably low now had extended legs to fit her needs. The clumsy extenders were meant to be temporary, and Sheridan intended to make sure they were.

"Sheridan? Want me to take your coat?" Mrs. D showed up as if she had materialized simply because Sheridan thought of her.

"Yes, please."

Mrs. D skillfully pulled Sheridan's trench coat off with no effort. "You see the tray?"

"Yes. Thank you. That'll be all. Oh, wait. Who's on duty tonight?"

"Karen. She's relieving Sandra right now."

Sheridan clenched her teeth around a "who is Sandra?" and only nodded.

"Anything you want me to pass on to her?"

"No. Nothing yet. She can report to me as usual in an hour or so. I'll be in here, reading."

"Good. There's a stack of new books from your book club. I put them on the shelf next to the couch."

"Thank you."

"Good night, Sheridan."

After Mrs. D left, Sheridan pivoted her chair to head over to the small table on the other side of the room. The books could wait. She took her laptop out of her bag and flipped it open. A couple of minutes later, she logged onto the chat, scanning her list of contacts for Grey_bird.

She wasn't online. The disappointment shot through Sheridan with a surprising force. It was silly, she thought, to feel so intensely about a complete stranger. She had anticipated coming home and spending some time with Grey_bird, eagerly reading her messages before bedtime. *I thought it would see me through tomorrow, with work and doing PT on my own.*

Fighting for self-control, Sheridan instead opened her e-mail program and started a new document. She was going to use her Hotmail account, which was more difficult to trace back to her. Grey_bird's personal introduction on the chat program's Web site showed her e-mail, which helped. Chewing on her lower lip, an old habit that had resurfaced since her illness, Sheridan began to type.

From: *Sheri_star@hotmail.com*
To: *Grey_bird@msn.com*
Subject: *Being the boss sucks!*

Hi Bird,
I suppose this e-mail strikes you as surprising, since so far we've only used chat to communicate. I like chatting and prefer it to e-mail, because I'm by nature quite impatient. But some things are better said in an e-mail where you have time to gather your thoughts and phrase what you mean to say.
You can exhale. I don't have anything world-altering to confess, and I don't expect you to. I suppose I was just less than thrilled to find you absent from the chat window. I had hoped to talk to you before tomorrow, and this is the second-best thing. Well, not counting the phone. But I think it's far too soon for that. I'm guessing that you're deep down a shy girl, and even I can be that, especially these days.
To tell the truth, I struggle with some health issues that demand my full attention. I hope this piece of information doesn't completely turn you off. Not everyone is equipped to deal with disease, and I used to be one of them. Still am, in a way. I have a hard time dealing with my own situation. I think that pain was what lay behind me firing my PT the other day.
There you have it. I fired my PT because she wouldn't conform to my needs, my decisions, and the way things work around here. She disliked me personally. I'm sure of that because I felt the evasiveness in her touch several times. One time when she massaged my head

when I had a migraine is memorable. I've never had anyone do that to me, with such immediate results. She's an amazing person, and I let my haughty nature get the better of me. Wish I could turn back time and be more open-minded.

I interviewed two people for the position today. I had one over yesterday, on recommendation from an agency, and I'll never hire anyone "unseen" again. The woman who worked with me in the gym damn near killed me. She was perkier than a group of girls going after the Ms. Universe title. The guy I interviewed this morning demanded to be reimbursed for wasting his time, and the third PT wannabe was so indifferent that she could have sat through her time chewing gum and watching Bonanza *reruns.*

I never thought I'd say it, but I let the best one go. Damn it, it hurts to be honest. Guess it's easier in an e-mail like this, but I'm also worried what you might think of me now. For some reason it matters, Bird. I'm usually known as a maverick of sorts, and I'm not always well liked, even if I'm usually respected and on occasion even admired.

This egocentric e-mail has been all about me, and I haven't even asked how you're doing. See what I mean? To make up for that, how are you, dear Bird? Did your boss at least have the decency to make amends? If not, let me know and I'll chew them out for you. I suck at some social skills, but not that.

I'll check the chat later this evening to see if you're around. Would be nice to able to say good night to you.

Sheri

❖

Lark stood by her window in the attic. She'd helped tuck Fiona in, which was normally her mother's job. Fiona insisted on paying her mother, which Doris had found appalling at first, but accepted when she realized that it did wonders for Fiona's self-esteem. The money went into a joint college fund for Doris's grandchildren, a plan Fiona and everyone else thoroughly approved of.

Placing a hand on the cool glass, Lark sighed. She had stood by the closed laptop for a few moments, but chickened out for the third time that evening. She knew Fiona would ask her tomorrow how everything went, but it seemed impossible to talk to Sheridan right now.

Lark opened the window and let in some of the humid evening air. Her mother traditionally made their teeth clatter by lowering the air-conditioning to "arctic." However, on hot summer evenings, when the velvet sky offered bright, shimmering stars, Lark loved to let the scent of this part of Texas fill her room. When she worked in Dubai, she thought it might smell like home, but it was so much dryer, it reminded her more of Arizona.

Eventually, Lark became disgusted with her own hesitation and closed the window. She pulled the laptop onto her thighs and started it, her blood racing through her veins. Stalling, she checked her regular e-mail program and noticed a lit icon in the bottom right corner of her screen that showed she had new mail in her "junk account," as she referred to her Web mail. She clicked on the icon and opened the mail site. Ten spam mails hit the bin without hesitation, and only one was left that looked genuine. She checked the sender. Sheri_star@hotmail. com. *Oh, my God.*

Lark read the e-mail so fast that she had to reread it, twice, to make sure she hadn't misunderstood. Sheridan regretted firing her? Surely that was what it said? Lark guided her eyes with her index finger, occasionally stopping at words like "Bird...shy girl...wouldn't conform... disliked me...felt it in her touch...memorable massage... amazing person...nice to say good night" and they hit home, every single one of them.

"This changes things," Lark whispered to herself. She couldn't possibly pull the rug out from under Sheridan now. She regretted firing Lark, and she was reaching out to the stranger she knew as Bird, another sign that she was opening up. If nothing else, Lark would, as Bird, be able to guide Sheridan when it was time to hire another physical therapist, keep her on track and help her not to fire the next one. *She thinks I disliked her.* Lark realized that Sheridan had misinterpreted her attempt to keep her professional decorum when she was close to her.

Lark ached inside at the thought of someone else literally handling Sheridan. Now tomorrow morning she had to face the next problem—explaining this turn of events to Fiona.

CHAPTER THIRTEEN

What do you suggest I do?" Sheridan muttered. "I've been working out alone and it's going pretty well."

"That's a lie," Mrs. D said. "I know you've tried, but if I hadn't poked my head in yesterday, you could have injured yourself badly trying to do the bars exercise by yourself."

"I was handling it." Sheridan knew Mrs. D was right but wasn't ready to admit it. In fact, her entire body hurt, and the headache that had plagued her through the night hadn't let up.

"And as for what I suggest, I think you know the answer."

"Nope."

"Sheridan." Mrs. D shook her head. "You need to find Lark and bring her back. She was the right person for the job, and you let your pride and your ability to be such a know-it-all get in the way. You made a mistake by firing her, and you know it."

Sheridan was used to Mrs. D's frankness, but this time she was almost too blunt. Blinking at a burning sensation under her eyelids, Sheridan tried to muster enough strength to stand her ground. "I hire and fire whom I damn well please."

"Yes, you do, but you have to live with the consequences." Mrs. D's voice was soft, but her words cut like a knife. "Now, consider what matters most to you—becoming better in time for the meeting or being determined not to lose face."

"I'm not worried about losing face. I could care less what people think of me."

"Normally I'd agree with you, but in this case, I'd say you're full of it. It does matter to you what Lark thinks. And it matters to you that you fired her."

It was painful to breathe, and Sheridan felt deflated since she knew

Mrs. D was right. "All right. Give Roy Vogel a call—"

"No. *You* give Lark a call. Or better yet, go visit her in person."

"What?" Cornered by Mrs. D's stern blue eyes, Sheridan pressed against the backrest of her wheelchair. "I wouldn't have a clue where to find her. She could've gotten a new job instantly. With her qualifications, it should be easy."

"Something tells me that she needed a break after your rather brusque dismissal. Her parents live in Boerne and that's her billing address. Do the math, Sheridan. It's not hard."

"Don't patronize me, *Glenda Drew*," Sheridan snapped, deliberately using Mrs. D's hated first name. "You're pushing your luck."

"I'm not pushing anything. You need to climb down from that high horse of yours. You're not doing yourself any favors, you know."

It was impossible to resist Mrs. D when she sounded so sure and tender. "All right. You win." The fire went out of her, and she slumped sideways. "I'll go see her. Happy now?"

"Very." Mrs. D rose and kissed Sheridan gently on the forehead. "Don't worry. If you're honest and speak from your heart, Lark will understand. I don't think that girl has a vengeful or spiteful bone in her body."

"I know she doesn't. I did slam her pretty good, though."

"I didn't mean she was meek, just forgiving. Do your best, honey."

Though Mrs. D was close to Sheridan, she didn't commonly use terms of endearment. To hear one, right now, was amazingly soothing.

"Okay. Will do," Sheridan said with a sigh. *Why shouldn't I expect the worst? It's been life's MO for quite some time now.*

❖

Sheridan wheeled out of the minivan using the automatically extending ramps and looked at the house where Lark's parents lived. Located at the far end of North Main Street, it was a big stone house with a store in the front.

"Catch!" a young boy shouted, drawing Sheridan's attention to the lawn to the right of the house. He grinned at a smaller boy standing next to him before he smacked the baseball twice into his glove, then assumed the classic pitcher's position.

"Just don't break my arm, kid!" Lark, just coming into view, shouted back. "You and your brother, y'all will be the death of me."

The child threw a curve ball that threatened to sail right by Lark, who ran backward, her gloved hand raised above her head, but the ball continued on its trajectory toward Sheridan. Just as Sheridan caught the ball, Lark's foot slipped off the limestone garden path, and she stumbled while trying to regain her balance. She toppled over and landed on her butt with a resounding thud. "Ow!"

Sheridan wheeled forward again and stopped next to Lark on the garden pathway. "Hello, Lark. Are you all right?"

Lark's head snapped back as she stared up at Sheridan. "Sheridan," Lark squeaked. "What are you doing here?" Lark's racing pulse was clearly visible on her exposed neck, and Sheridan wondered if her unexpected presence or playing ball with the boy had caused its activity. Lark remained on the ground, staring up at Sheridan. "I mean, hello."

Sheridan reached out. "Here. Let me help you. That looked painful." She gazed over at the boy. "Good arm there, kid."

"Thanks. My name's Sean. This is Michael. Are you a friend of my aunt?"

"Aunt? Oh, I see. Yes, I am. My name is Sheridan."

Sean shook Sheridan's hand. "I can help her up." He tugged at a flustered Lark. "Six-one, Aunt Lark."

"Embarrassing." Lark brushed some grass off her jeans. "Run along now. Grandma's making ice cream."

"Cool!" the boys said in chorus. Sean waved his fingers at Sheridan in a funny little gesture before they disappeared through the front door.

"Sean seems like a really nice boy," Sheridan said, feeling a bit awkward, so she fiddled with her fingers, lacing and unlacing them over and over.

"He is. Sean's one of District 19's best pitchers, and as you just saw, he has a mean arm. His three siblings are great too, but a handful, as you can imagine."

"Goodness, I'd think so. Four kids." Sheridan was impressed.

"You didn't answer my question," Lark reminded her.

"I need to talk to you."

"Why?" Lark's eyes were expressionless, but her frown showed she wasn't going to just accommodate Sheridan.

"Please." Sheridan felt her cheeks warm slightly. "In private. Anywhere we can go?"

"Sure. The living room is usually off-limits for the kids. Follow me."

"I meant outdoors. This chair—" Sheridan gestured down to her wheels.

"Won't be a problem. We've got ramps."

Sheridan raised her eyebrows, but didn't ask the question she wanted to. "All right."

Lark guided Sheridan around the corner to the side entrance next to the garage where a ramp led up to a small deck by the door.

"Very clever," Sheridan said. "But why?"

"You'll see."

As if on cue, Fiona wheeled toward them in her electric chair. "Lark, I—oh, we've got company. I didn't know." She regarded Sheridan with open curiosity. "I'm Fiona Mitchell, Lark's sister." A paper plane swooshed by. "And I might add that this brat pack doesn't belong to me."

"Nice to meet you. I'm Sheridan Ward." Sheridan felt shell-shocked as she leaned forward to shake Fiona's hand. She quickly glanced at Fiona's motionless left hand, positioned around what looked like rolled-up bandages. *God. What's happened to her?*

"If y'all want to chat—I mean talk," Fiona corrected herself, "the living room door is locked to keep the twins out. They were about to watercolor on Mom's best linen tablecloth."

"God," Lark muttered. "The key in the usual place?"

"Yup." Fiona did the same wave with her fingers as Sean had done. "See you around then, Sheridan." She pivoted her chair and left the two of them alone.

"Fiona is two years younger than me." Lark guided Sheridan to two glass doors and fished out a set of keys from behind a flower pot. "She's the beauty of the family. The rest of us look more like our dad than our mom."

"You look fine to me." Sheridan spoke without thinking, absorbed by the house filled with children laughing, adults talking, and the scent of cooking food.

"Thank you. You look nice also," Lark said politely. Unlocking the door, she motioned for Sheridan to enter. She sat down in an easy chair and pulled a leg up beneath her, seemingly calm and unaffected. "Why are you here, Sheridan?"

"To ask you to forgive me and to come back." Sheridan spoke quickly. The words came out staccato and not as together and smooth as she would have liked.

"Why?"

"Why what?" Sheridan asked, confused.

"Even if I forgive you, which I already have by the way, why should I come back? What has changed?" Lark's voice, on the other hand, was indeed as smooth and calm as Sheridan would've preferred her own to be.

"I won't lie. I tried several other PTs after you left. One tried to kill me, and the other two only made it as far as the interview. Mrs. D talked some sense into me, and everything she said was something I already knew." Sheridan felt sweat bead on her forehead. The room faced the street and sunlight streamed in through the windows. "Please, Lark."

Lark sat in silence for a moment, looking down at her loosely folded hands. "Things would have to be very different, and I don't think you can manage that."

"Won't you even let me try?"

"I know you mean what you say—now. But back at the mansion when business calls, you'll have tons of excuses not to stay committed to your schedule. Then you won't reach your goal, and both our lives will be miserable." Lark cleared her throat. "I care too much to watch you do that to yourself."

The words hung between them, as if suspended in the rays of the sun. Sheridan knew then that if she let Lark slip through her fingers, in whatever capacity, she'd regret it for a long time, perhaps forever. "Listen," she said and wheeled close enough to Lark to take her hand. "I had an idea. What if we spend the upcoming weeks at Lake Travis? All we have to consider is being back in San Antonio two weeks before the stockholders' meeting. Would that do it?"

"Lake Travis. Didn't you tell me y'all have a summer house or something there?" Lark spoke slowly.

"Yes." Sheridan smiled cautiously. "It has four bedrooms, six baths, a kitchen, a library that doubles as a study, and a living room. Very manageable. The Johnsons live in a bungalow on the property and tend to the house when I'm away. I haven't used the house at all since I came home from the hospital."

"Why not?"

"I used to feel so free there. I'd spend time with Frank, and we'd just do what we want."

"Frank?" Lark frowned. "Who's Frank?"

"My Irish setter, who lives there permanently." Sheridan thought she saw relief on Lark's face.

"Oh, I see." Lark smiled carefully. "If you're prepared to leave San Antonio for a while, that shows me what I need to know. I'll come back to work for you, but this time, if you fire me again, or if you go back to ignoring your schedule...I just don't want to go through this again. I mean, investing my time and efforts in caring about...I mean *for* your rehabilitation." Lark sounded solemn, despite her smile. "You understand that?"

"Yes, Lark. I do." Sheridan began to relax, loosening her clasped hands. "Thank you. I just can't risk failure and, what's more, I missed you."

"What? For real?"

"For real," Sheridan said and had to laugh at Lark's obvious surprise. "You're interesting to talk to, and you challenge me. I never know what you're going to say next, which is a rare quality."

"Too many yea-sayers?" Lark winked.

"You could say that." Sheridan dragged a hand through her hair to mask how much her hand was shaking. She hadn't eaten since that morning, and the anxiety of making herself vulnerable was also taking its toll.

"Well, I go under many names here at home, but the resident yea-sayer isn't one of them."

They heard a knock on the door and a voice asked from behind it, "Can I tempt y'all with some coffee or tea? Arthur's baking his famous cinnamon rolls."

"Sheridan?" Lark asked.

"I don't want to impose—"

Doris opened the door and greeted Sheridan. "You're not imposing, child. I'm Doris Mitchell Hirsh, Lark's mother. We have coffee and enough cinnamon rolls to feed an army. Please stay and help eat some of them. Honestly, we need help."

"Mom, you make Daddy sound like a cinnamon-roll terrorist or something." Lark laughed. "I agree, though. It would be blasphemous if she left without having any of his rolls. By the way, this is Sheridan Ward, my...my, eh..." Lark seemed at a loss, and Sheridan realized that she was trying to maintain patient confidentiality.

"I'm Lark's patient."

"You *are*, as in the present tense?" Lark's mother asked, looking back and forth between them.

"Yes. She's agreed to come back, and I know better now than to make the same mistake again."

"I'm very glad to hear that." Sheridan could hear a mother's pride, and protection, in Doris's voice.

"And I'd love some coffee. I just need to tell my driver—"

"Oh, you mean that nice young man, Dave?" Doris asked with a bright smile. "He's already in the kitchen chatting with Fiona and one of my other daughters, Garland. Having his second coffee and third roll, I believe."

"He is?" Sheridan was stunned. "That's very hospitable of you, Mrs. Hirsh."

"Doris."

"Then please call me Sheridan."

Sheridan followed as Doris guided her toward the spacious kitchen. Cherrywood cabinets and black marble countertops, coupled with the happy banter around the table, made for a cozy atmosphere. Fiona, who sat at one end of the table, looked up and waved them over. "Better come quick, y'all. The rolls are disappearing at lightning speed."

"Hey, don't worry about that," a bulky man at the stove said as he pulled out another baking tray crowded with enormous cinnamon rolls. "There's more where they came from."

"Good, Pop, because I can eat twenty more," Michael bragged.

"If anybody else had said that, I wouldn't have believed them, son." Arthur put the tray down and approached Sheridan. "Welcome to our home, Sheridan. I'm Arthur, Lark's second father. And if you wonder how I know who you are, my wife's method for delivering family intel is amazing."

"Sounds like a good method. Excuse me, did you say second father?"

"Yes. Harold Mitchell was Lark's first father. He passed away more than twenty years ago. I was lucky to inherit them all, so to speak, about thirteen years ago when they moved here to Boerne."

"And he really is a dad," Fiona said and sipped her coffee. "We simply informed him that we weren't interested in a *step*dad, but as a real daddy he was welcome."

"Our youngest sister was only ten at the time. She really needed a daddy. Well, we all did."

Sheridan hesitated, not sure where she would fit in at the table. Her uneasiness must have been obvious, because one of the boys scooted his chair closer to his brother's and patted the table between him and Fiona. Sheridan glanced at Lark, who only smiled. Wheeling around Fiona, Sheridan parked her wheelchair, and the boy—*Michael, was it?*—smiled broadly at her.

"Is your name really Sheridan?" he asked.

"Yes, it is. Why do you ask?"

"I thought it was a boy's name. A boy in Sean's class is called Sheridan, and he's *really* a boy."

"I know. Some kids teased me when I was little that I looked like a girl. They were really surprised when it turned out I actually *was* a girl."

Sean and Michael burst out laughing, sputtering small pieces of cinnamon rolls over the table. Their behavior broke any ice that might have lingered, and soon Sheridan found herself the center of attention and the subject of the friendliest interrogation she'd ever been part of.

The children began asking personal questions.

"Do you have a boyfriend?"

"No?"

"A girlfriend then?"

Before Sheridan could answer, Lark interrupted. "She has a dog called Frank."

Sheridan pulled out her wallet and showed them a picture of Frank retrieving a stick out of the lake. After that, the boys grew bored and were excused.

Sheridan knew she had to make sure she didn't fall into this trap of coziness. Granted, Lark's family seemed genuinely nice and welcoming, but they weren't *her* family. *I mustn't forget that.*

An hour later, Sheridan signaled her driver that it was time for them to say good-bye. Dave seemed reluctant to leave, and who could blame him? He had had Fiona's undivided attention for the last fifteen minutes and kissed her hand gallantly before he helped Sheridan out the door. Lark walked her to the car and placed a hand on her shoulder before she rode the lift into the minivan.

"Do you want me to come back with you now?"

"No, Lark. Spend tonight at your parents and enjoy your sister. You have a lovely family. Fiona, your parents, the boys. Everyone made me feel very welcome."

"They're great. But they love homing in on new blood, as you could tell."

"Yeah, the boys were very curious."

"And a bit too forward." Lark made a funny face and wrinkled her nose. "Sorry 'bout that."

"No problem. I just find it curious that they'd ask me if I had a girlfriend."

"Ah. Well. They are, how do you say, a modern family. The boys…" Lark blushed and faltered, which paved the way for speculation on Sheridan's part.

"…are politically correct?"

Lark coughed. "Something like that."

"See you tomorrow. Don't forget to pack more sweats and shorts. It's very informal at the lake."

"I look forward to it. Is there a pool?"

"Yes. I'll have Mrs. D call ahead so Mr. Johnson can fill it."

"Is it heated?"

"Yes. And in this weather we've been having, it doesn't take much."

"Great. We'll make good use of it."

Sheridan stopped inside the minivan and turned around to look at Lark. "Just so you know, I'm not very thrilled about water."

"Don't worry. I won't let anything happen to you."

Too late, Lark. I fear something already has. "Sounds good to me. Just no diving, all right?"

"All right. I'll remember that."

"See you tomorrow, around ten?"

"I'll be there."

Sheridan let Dave secure the wheelchair and leaned back as he pulled out into the sparse traffic. When she looked at the house, she saw Lark still standing on the sidewalk, her hands pushed deep into her jeans pockets.

CHAPTER FOURTEEN

L ark stood on the patio at the Ward summerhouse. Constructed right on the shoreline, it had a spectacular view.

The ride to the lake had taken place in comfortable silence. Sheridan had worked on her laptop, after apologizing to Lark that she couldn't stay away from her business completely. Lark assured her that she didn't have to ask permission to do anything as long as they were communicating. Sheridan looked surprised, as if Lark had said something unexpected.

During the rest of the drive, Lark had dozed off and on, though very aware of Sheridan's presence. Several times when she looked up, she found Sheridan watching her. Lark felt her cheeks warm slightly every time, and she squirmed; it was impossible to be still.

Now, the refreshing breeze from the lake cleared Lark's mind, and she raised both arms and stretched.

"Beautiful, isn't it?" Sheridan said from behind, causing Lark to lower her arms quickly.

"You okay?" Sheridan asked.

"Fine. I'm fine." Lark faced Sheridan. "Are you settled in yet? Need any help?"

"Yes, and no, thank you. Mrs. Johnson put everything away for me, and she's probably doing that for you as we speak. So if you packed something very personal…but I should have told you this before we came, right?"

"What do you mean, personal? All my stuff is personal." Lark had no clue what Sheridan was talking about.

"Nah, I mean something *personal*."

Lark blinked. "Now you've lost me."

"Apparently. Which is kind of reassuring in this case."

Lark groaned. "You're being too cryptic. Sheridan."

Sheridan colored slightly. "Eh, well, if you'd packed something to cozy up with, something you wouldn't want Mrs. Johnson or anybody else to find." Sheridan grinned. "An electronic companion?"

"An electronic com—" Lark laughed. "Oh, you mean a vibrator?"

"Or something." Sheridan fiddled with the armrests of her wheelchair. "I just thought that...well, I was trying to be funny, really."

Lark laughed at the pink tinge to Sheridan's cheeks. "And I just didn't get it?"

"At first I thought you were just as innocent as you look, but apparently I was wrong."

"I look innocent?" Lark tilted her head and watched Sheridan's expression alter yet again. This time she definitely looked as if she wanted to slap her forehead, and Lark couldn't hold back a giggle.

"I meant, you have an innocent way about you, and I felt I was being too—"

"Straightforward? Personal? Inquisitive?" Lark said helpfully.

"Yeah. Well. Something like that," Sheridan muttered.

"Ah, the *something* again." Lark relented, even if teasing Sheridan was exquisitely delicious. She turned toward the water again. "Yes, to answer your first question, it *is* beautiful. I can see why your family's maintained a house here."

"I just wish I had time to come here more often."

"I can't see how you couldn't work from here at times. It really shouldn't be difficult, with today's technology. As far as I know, several of your companies are at the forefront of the computer business. They should be able to hook you up as if you were there. That way, you'd heal faster and could ultimately be more independent."

"There's that magic word again. Independent. You hold it in front of me like the proverbial carrot."

"And isn't independence what you're after?"

"Yes. But to reach that, I need to regain the use of my legs! That's where you come in."

Lark stared at Sheridan, willing her mouth not to fall open. How could she have missed this point? How could she have surmised that Sheridan was accepting medical facts when she was in denial regarding just about everything else. This wasn't the time or the place to bring the facts up, not when Sheridan was about to give everything her best when it came to the physiotherapy.

She arranged her features in what she hoped was an encouraging expression. "One step at a time. First we need you to get in shape for the stockholders' meeting. Then we'll set up new goals."

"All right," Sheridan agreed, not showing any signs that she'd picked up on Lark's moment of truth. "I know it takes time and patience, but it'll happen."

It was so different to hear the confidence in Sheridan's voice and see the glitter in her eyes; it nearly broke Lark's heart. "I have every faith in your stubbornness," she joked so she wouldn't become mushy or teary eyed. It wasn't like her to become this emotional over her patients, not the adults anyway, and Lark knew Sheridan was perceptive enough to realize what was going on if she wasn't careful.

Sitting in her wheelchair dressed in a black linen suit, looking the epitome of casual elegance, Sheridan was the most stunningly gorgeous woman Lark had ever seen. The setting sun tinted her pale skin golden, and the breeze blew her wavy hair into slight disarray, making Lark want to stroke it back from Sheridan's forehead. Her long, slender hands lay loosely folded on her lap, and she looked happy. The ache in Lark's belly turned almost acidic when desire drowned out the tenderness.

"How about we go inside and have something to eat?" Sheridan asked. "I think Mrs. Johnson has cooked something for us in advance. She and her husband go home after she takes care of the evening dishes, unless we need them for anything more."

"We shouldn't keep them waiting, then." It was hard to speak as if nothing was amiss or out of the ordinary.

Sheridan led the way inside, and Lark followed as she tried to persuade her poor heart to stop acting like a racehorse on speed.

❖

Mrs. Johnson lit a group of five block candles in the fireplace, just enough to set the mood since the evening was humid and warm. Lark had helped a tired Sheridan onto the couch and lifted her legs so she lay half reclined. Mrs. Johnson made sure "the girls" were properly set for the evening, reminding them that she'd made midnight snacks for them.

Lark sat down on the floor with her back against the couch. Leaning her head against the cushion behind her, she tried to relax. She was tired, she could feel it in her stinging eyes, but her body acted as if she was high on too much caffeine.

"This is cozy," Sheridan said from above.

"Yes, it is. Are you tired?"

"A little. It's been a long day. Someone pushed me to outdo myself during PT." Sheridan laughed, a lazy, thoroughly sexy sound.

Lark gasped quietly, not daring to look at Sheridan. "You did great. Tomorrow we'll take it up a notch."

"What happened to slowly and surely?" Sheridan snickered.

"That went out the window when I saw how well you did this afternoon. And with Mrs. Johnson's cooking, we'll both need the exercise."

"That's true." Sheridan sighed, and sounded more blissful than exasperated.

"Lovely couple, the Johnsons. They obviously care for you a lot."

"It's mutual."

"Now, what's with Frank the dog?" Mrs. Johnson had taken the Irish setter with her to the bungalow.

"What do you mean?"

"He greeted me, a person he'd never met, like a long-lost friend, but took wide circles around you?" It was true. The dog had acted strangely, giving Sheridan dark looks and barely accepting her pats.

"I don't know. I've probably been away from him too long." Sadness crept into Sheridan's voice. "He may feel like I've abandoned him."

"That doesn't make sense. It was something else. Could be the chair, you know."

"The chair?" Sheridan shifted behind Lark. "You think so?"

"It's the only thing I can think of. Dogs don't hold grudges. They live in the moment. He looked like he *wanted* to approach you."

"I hope you're right. Maybe we could teach him not to be afraid of the chair."

"I bet we can do that easily." Lark looked at Sheridan, wanting to reassure her. "One of my patients used an electric scooter. Turned out that her dog was frantic around her and the scooter because he wanted to *ride* it!"

Sheridan burst out laughing. "Oh, my God. How did that end?"

"She let him. I'm sure the neighbors had a field day watching this German shepherd sit between her legs, his tail trailing alongside the scooter as they rode down the street to the store."

"I wish I could have seen that."

"I have pictures on my computer somewhere, I think." The thought of her laptop made Lark think of their chats, and her guilty conscience surfaced, banishing her good mood.

"What? What's wrong?"

Damn it! Lark knew that having an open-book kind of face wasn't always in her favor. "Nothing," she said, stalling. "Just tired, I guess. The weekend was pretty crazy."

"A full house at your parents' place," Sheridan agreed. "I haven't been the subject of such friendly interrogation in a long time."

"Did it bother you?" Lark frowned. "I'm sorry. They can be pretty overwhelming."

"No, no, not at all," Sheridan said and pulled herself up. She touched Lark's temple with quick, light fingers. "They're wonderful. Don't apologize. I'm just not used to the normal, disorganized chatter among family members. It wasn't like that in my family even when my mother was alive. She was ill for most of my life..." Sheridan shrugged. "I dreamed a lot about having siblings and a more 'normal' home. Instead I resented my father for being in denial about my mother's illness, and for having to live in the mausoleum."

"The mausoleum? You call it that?"

"I used to."

"So, did you feel like you were the only one who understood how ill your mother was?"

"Close. I overheard my parents countless times discussing it. She would try to tell him how she felt, that she wasn't well, and he would call her weak, say she wasn't living up to the Ward standard. Mom wasn't weak. She stood up to him and sought help, the best care the hospitals could provide back then, but even if she did live longer than they anticipated, she still lost the fight eventually."

Sheridan's voice was slow, almost dreamy, as she recounted her childhood memories. "Daddy was devastated. He blamed himself for losing her. I couldn't reach him or comfort him, and to tell the truth, I was very, very angry with him for not making her last years easier.

Even after her diagnosis, he was in denial. He could have made her last months so much better. The doctors told us it was fruitless to subject Mom to any more chemo, yet he nagged her to try. She refused and he was furious, of course. He didn't relent even on the day she died. I think that's what killed him in the end. His behavior ate at him, and I didn't help."

"What makes you say that?" Lark leaned her chin on her hand on the couch. Her temple still tingled from Sheridan's unexpected little caress, and she could hardly believe that Sheridan had confided in her rather than the faceless Grey_bird.

"Because as soon as Mom was gone, I packed my bags and left for Boston. I loved life there and didn't return to assume my position until my father had his first signs of heart problems."

"Did the two of you reconcile?" Lark hoped so.

"I suppose we did, but as true Wards, we didn't acknowledge our truce openly. That would have been the same as admitting we had a problem, which my father never did. In business, he could find and diagnose a problem instantly, but in his personal life? Never."

"I'm glad that you were on good terms before he passed away."

"Yeah. Me too."

The sky outside was black, and Lark realized it was getting late. "How about if we turn in, so I can PT the living daylights out of you tomorrow?" she joked.

"Good idea. I'm rather sleepy."

"All right. Come on, then." Lark stood up and pulled the wheelchair close to the couch. Sheridan dislodged the armrest and moved over as if it was second nature. Lark didn't have to help her but refrained from saying so. She wanted Sheridan to gradually discover her abilities in a natural way.

"What do you need help with?" Lark asked as they moved toward the bedrooms. Sheridan had the master bedroom while Lark used Sheridan's old room.

"Just to undress and put on my sleepwear."

"No problem."

Lark pushed her own feelings aside and stepped into full caregiver mode as she helped Sheridan change. In order to help Sheridan, she would have to work hard on not blurring the lines when it came to these duties. A person who needed help with such intimate activities was entirely vulnerable. Lark waited while Sheridan used the bathroom, then helped her into bed.

"If I wasn't so tired, I could've shown you how much better I am at doing this."

"I believe you."

"Good." Sheridan yawned as she took Lark's hand. "Thank you for coming back. And for coming to Lake Travis with me."

"I'm glad to be back. Really."

Sheridan's face lit up, her sleepy eyes a soft, dark gray. "Good night, Lark."

"'Night, Sheridan. I'll leave the doors open so you can just call if you need me. I sleep lightly."

"Me...too."

Lark was certain Sheridan was already asleep before she had left the room.

Lark sat up in bed, rubbing her eyes. Had Sheridan called her? The house was dark, except for the night-lights that Mr. Johnson had installed to guide anyone who got up in the middle of the night. Noticing that it was a bit brighter in one spot, Lark flipped the covers back and rose to investigate. She poked her head out into the corridor and saw a faint light around Sheridan's half-open door. Curious, and a bit worried, Lark tiptoed across the hallway, the floor cool against her naked feet. She made sure she stood out of sight and peeked inside.

Sheridan was awake and working on something on her laptop. Lark frowned, since this was not what she wanted Sheridan to do. She wanted her to get a good night's sleep, but also knew if Sheridan couldn't sleep, she'd go stir-crazy if she simply stared into the darkness. Lark was the same way.

"Damn it, Grey_bird, where are you when I need you?"

Lark's mouth fell open and she stumbled backward, barely avoiding a bad fall. She held her breath as she listened for signs that Sheridan had noticed anything. When she heard only the sound of quick typing, she drew a silent breath of relief and snuck back into her room. She grabbed her laptop and logged on, knowing that she couldn't stay away when Sheridan needed her, no matter in what capacity. Fortunately, the air card she'd just invested in allowed her to be online no matter her location, and she opened her chat window. It only took a second for Sheridan's nickname to appear.

> *Sheri_star:* There you are. Just in the nick of time.
> *Grey_bird:* Hello to you too.
> *Sheri_star:* Sorry. Can't sleep.
> *Grey_bird:* As you can see, I'm awake too.
> *Sheri_star:* You OK?
> *Grey_bird:* I'm fine. How about you?
> *Sheri_star:* I'm fine too. Just can't sleep. I didn't have any problem falling asleep, actually, but I woke up and that was it. Wide awake.
> *Grey_bird:* Any news?
> *Sheri_star:* Actually, yes. I rehired my physical therapist.
> *Grey_bird:* Oh, you did? That's great! I hope?

Lark knew she was fishing, but she needed to know.

> *Sheri_star:* Yes. Best thing I've done in a long time. I was just lucky she forgave me. But that's just her, somehow. She understands.
> *Grey_bird:* Sounds good. I'm glad for you.
> *Sheri_star:* Me too. I just wish that your employer would see the light.
> *Grey_bird:* Actually, that was my news. I've got a new job.
> *Sheri_star:* Great! Doing what?

Lark thought quickly.

> *Grey_bird:* Teaching.

It wasn't entirely a lie. She was teaching Sheridan how to train and practice. Lark ignored the small voice that claimed she still wasn't telling the truth.

> *Sheri_star:* Sounds like your thing.
> *Grey_bird:* How do you mean?
> *Sheri_star:* You have tremendous patience.

Grey_bird: :-) How could you possibly know?
Sheri_star: You chat with *me*!
Grey_bird: LOL! So true. That takes more than patience!

Lark smiled broadly, afraid she might actually burst out laughing in the quiet house.

Sheri_star: Told you. So, what should we do to pass the time?
Grey_bird: If I was there, I could've sung you a lullaby.
Sheri_star: I can think of other things to put me to sleep.
Grey_bird: Sheri! We've talked about this. Behave! *smile*
Sheri_star: I am behaving. This is as good as it gets, Bird.
Grey_bird: Well, that says a lot, I suppose. I, on the other hand, was brought up to be a demure girl.
Sheri_star: I think I'm gonna be sick. LOL! What bull!
Grey_bird: Such language!
Sheri_star: Hah! Don't you think I don't recognize a hot chick when I see her?
Grey_bird: I'm sure you do, but as you can't actually see me...that proves my point. Demure. *giggle*

Lark could actually hear Sheridan chuckle through their open doors, which made her smile grow wider. It was as if they were really talking, she tried to tell herself.

Sheri_star: If you were within sight, I could show you how I react when I find someone sexy.
Grey_bird: I bet you could. Now, perhaps I should warn that physical therapist of yours. She may have to watch out, if you're that foxy.
Sheri_star: Actually, she's very cute.

Cute? Innocent looking and cute. Lark's thoughts shimmied in her head. "Oh, my," she whispered.

Grey_bird: Cute, huh?

Sheri_star: She looks at me sometimes with this expression
that just doesn't make sense.

Lark waited for Sheridan to continue, her heart hammering slow, hard beats against her ribs, as if it couldn't power up to race like before.

Grey_bird: In what way?

Sheri_star: Damned if I know. She has the most beautiful
golden-brown eyes, which I'd swear could
glow in the night if I didn't know better.

Grey_bird: So, is she really helping you? I mean, do you
think you can stick to a schedule? I'm sorry I
haven't answered your e-mail, but I have read
it several times.

Sheri_star: It's OK. And yes, I'm going to prove myself
to her. She came back because I promised. If I
let her down, I'll let myself down, and then I
think she'll leave for good. I don't want that.

Lark stared at the last sentence, her mouth parched when she tried to wet her lips.

Grey_bird: She sounds like she's devoted to her job. She
probably wants to give you her best, which
she can't if you don't let her.

Sheri_star: That's something she'd say, so I think you've
got her pegged.

Lark yanked her hands off the keyboard and pressed one to her chest. Her heart had no problems racing now, and she wanted to close the chat, certain that Sheridan was onto the truth.

Sheri_star: You there?

Grey_bird: Sure. Just had a sip of water.

Sheri_star: You must be sleepy by now. I should let you
go.

Grey_bird: How about you, then? Don't want to leave
you hanging.

Lark groaned inaudibly at her choice of words.

Sheri_star: I could take that the wrong way if I wasn't just
as demure as you.
Grey_bird: *groan*
Sheri_star: A problem, there, Bird?
Grey_bird: What makes you think that? *rolling eyes*
Sheri_star: You'll give yourself a headache doing that.
Actually, I think I can try for some more sleep
now, after I get something to drink.
Grey_bird: OK. Sleep tight, then. See you around later.
Sheri_star: Hey, Bird?
Grey_bird: Yeah?
Sheri_star: Thanks for listening.
Grey_bird: No problem. Any time.
Sheri_star: Good night. Sleep well.

Lark signed off and closed her laptop. Just as she put it on her
nightstand, she heard a muted thud from Sheridan's room and a low
curse. "Damn it!"

Lark rose, but realized that Sheridan hadn't called her and halted,
uncertain what to do.

"Lark? You awake?"

"Yes. Be right there." Lark hurried across the hallway. "I heard a
noise. What's...oh."

The pitcher that had been sitting on Sheridan's nightstand was
now on the floor in a large puddle of water. "I'll grab a towel. You're
thirsty, I assume?"

"You assume correctly," Sheridan muttered. "Why am I so clumsy?
It's as if I have no sense of distance."

"You and me both. My mother says I can walk into anything that's
within a three-foot radius, no matter the size."

"Glad I'm not the only klutz."

Lark found a towel in the hamper in Sheridan's bathroom and wiped
off the floor. Then she padded to the kitchen and filled another pitcher

with water. Returning to the bedroom, she poured a glass for Sheridan and sat down on the side of the bed while she drank. "Better?"

"Much."

Lark saw the computer wasn't tucked away yet. "Think you can go back to sleep now?"

"Yes, it shouldn't be impossible." Sheridan moved and suddenly had a pained expression on her face. "Ow. Damn." She wriggled under the covers. "Can you help me? I really am a super-klutz today. I think my foot's stuck in the pajama leg."

"What are you talking about, stuck?" Lark pulled back the covers all the way. "Ah. I see." Lark untangled Sheridan's toes from the hem of the silk pajama bottoms. "There you go." She replaced the covers and tucked them in around Sheridan. When she began to leave, Sheridan grabbed her wrists gently.

"Thank you," she said and looked at Lark intently. "You take such good care of me, and you do it so I don't feel...awkward."

Lark turned her hands under Sheridan's and returned the soft squeeze. "Hey, that's how it's supposed to be. You're meant to feel at ease. If I ever do or say anything to make you feel awkward or upset, you have to tell me."

"I will."

Sheridan seemed reluctant to let go, and their touches were entirely innocent, so Lark remained where she was. She felt Sheridan's grip loosen, and as her eyelids began to close, Lark stroked Sheridan's lower arms, up and down, over and over.

"Feels good," Sheridan whispered, half asleep. "Thanks—"

"Shh. Just go to sleep. I'll be here when you wake up."

"Mmm."

When Sheridan's breath became deep and even, Lark reluctantly let go and rose. She stood and watched Sheridan sleep for a few moments before she returned to her own bed. It took her a while before she relaxed enough to feel sleepy. Her last thoughts were of how Sheridan had reached for her, almost instinctively. It had to mean something, didn't it?

CHAPTER FIFTEEN

At the end of their first week at Lake Travis, Lark had finally worn Sheridan down and made her at least consider working in the pool. The last few days and nights had been hot and humid, and the hot weather constantly warmed the pool.

Sheridan now sat next to the enclosed sixty- by thirty-foot pool. Her father had built it when Sheridan moved back to San Antonio, hoping it would help her overcome her fear of water. She had used it only a few times, more than she had ever swum in the lake. She couldn't explain her fear of water; she only knew it had always existed.

"Mr. Johnson is going to join us," Lark said from behind her.

Sheridan felt her palms grow sweaty at the sight of Lark, dressed in a black swimsuit like elite swimmers used. Lark looked fantastic, toned in a way that was still incredibly feminine, with defined muscles under satin skin. She looked so comfortable Sheridan nearly bolted, if it was possible to bolt in a wheelchair. Sheridan figured it was. Finally, Lark's words registered.

"Mr. Johnson? Why?"

"I can't help you into the water on my own. It's not safe. After we practice getting you out of the wheelchair and onto the floor or ground, and back up again on your own, then we can do this by ourselves. You have a way to go there yet. Also, your fear of water could be a problem before you become used to this particular exercise." Lark opened a large plastic bag that Sheridan had just noticed. "Here's what we'll need. I found these stored in the pool house." She pulled out several different floating devices, and Sheridan felt a bit less stressed.

"I'm going to wear arm-floaters?" she asked sardonically. "They're for kids!"

"Brilliant, huh? They'll keep you afloat no matter what, but I won't leave you for a second. I'll hold onto you the entire time."

Always something. "All right. How do we do this?"

"Since we don't have a ramp or lift here, at least not yet, I had to be a bit clever." Lark looked adorable when she wrinkled her nose and pursed her lips. "I'll grab one of the recliners."

She removed the cushions from one of the chairs that lined the fence and pulled it to where Sheridan sat. "Look, the bottom third of the recliner can be folded as a ramp, almost." She flipped the end of the chair down so it met the ground. "Here's what we'll do. Mr. Johnson and I'll help you onto the recliner, and then I'll go into the water as he helps you slide down into my arms." Lark blushed unexpectedly. "Eh, well. You'll be wearing the arm-floaters, so you'll be fine. The water is at least eighty degrees."

"It's not the cold that's bothering me."

"I know. But it'd add more negativity, I think, if the water was cold. Ah, here's Mr. Johnson. Great that you could join us."

"There's nothing I wouldn't do to help Ms. Ward." Mr. Johnson stood next to Lark, smiling down at her as if he had practically adopted her. Lark in turn patted his arm and smiled that open, immediate smile that made a person want to make it reappear. Mr. Johnson was no exception; he straightened his back and regarded them both with equal parts protectiveness and enthusiasm. "What do you want me to do, Ms. Mitchell?"

"Call me Lark, please."

Mr. Johnson looked nonplussed. "Eh, thank you, Ms. Mitch— Lark. I'm Burt."

Sheridan blinked. As with Erica, her attempts to get on a first-name basis with Mr. or Mrs. Johnson had been fruitless. Her expression didn't pass Mr. Johnson by, and he shrugged helplessly. "She ambushed me, ma'am."

"Since she did, you can hardly keep calling me Ms. Ward, can you?" Sheridan asked sweetly. "I think I win."

"Hmm." Lark looked back and forth between them. "I think I win, actually. So, Burt, meet Sheridan—Sheridan, this is Burt, your new PT assistant. You may have to give him a raise, for doing double duty."

Sheridan had to laugh at the expression of shock on Burt's face. "No problem," she said, feigning sincerity but meaning every word.

"Good." Lark grinned, then told Burt how to help Sheridan onto the low recliner. Lark gave her the arm-floaters, then slipped into the water. She smiled broadly before she went under completely, and Sheridan felt a tinge of concern that she might be expected to do the same. *God, I'm going to seem like such a wimp.*

"All right, Burt, move Sheridan forward, slowly, but let her be in control. No sudden movements."

Burt was gentle as Sheridan glided toward the water. She wore boxers and a sports bra, and it was easier than she thought to push herself forward. Her feet made contact with the water, which was as warm as Lark had promised. Sheridan dug deep for courage and pushed forward, but she used a bit too much force and landed in the water with a splash. Her useless legs did nothing to support her, and she clung to Lark.

"There, there," Lark hummed in her ear. "You're fine. Let go and you'll see that you can float. Like that. One arm at a time."

Sheridan refused to be such a coward and slowly let go of Lark. To her relief, the arm-floaters easily held her body up. She extended her arms, which elevated her even more.

"Great. I'll take it from here. Unless you hear me call, you can come back in fifteen or twenty minutes, Burt."

"Y'all sure you're fine here alone?" Burt didn't look convinced.

"Yes. I've done this many times, both with adults and children. Sheridan is perfectly safe."

"All right. I'll be near the bungalow weeding, and I have my cell if you can't yell that loud."

"Good. I have the phone nearby. We'll be fine."

Sheridan wished she could believe that statement wholeheartedly. Instead, she looked at Lark and tried to focus on her attractive exterior. Anything to keep from panicking.

"All right. We're going to start with some floating exercises that you'll find useful. I take it you can swim but just don't like it."

"Correct."

"Then lay back here, with your head in my hands, and I'll pull you backward. You'll feel your legs come to the surface—"

"I don't want my head wet."

"You won't. I promise. I'll keep you high and dry."

"All right." Sheridan drew a trembling breath and leaned back. Lark's hands were in her hair and steadied her head and neck, keeping the top of her neck pressed against Lark's soft breasts. The contact was unexpectedly intimate and Sheridan felt herself grow heavy. Fortunately, she floated just as before.

"Now I'm going to swim backward using only my legs, and you can help by moving your arms as if you're doing the backstroke, but with smaller movements. Let's go."

The water moved like an entity around Sheridan, and her blood seemed to flow in the same kind of waves through her veins.

"Relax. You're really stiff. Don't try to do anything. Just float with me." Lark's voice was hypnotic, and she kept reassuring Sheridan. Even if her words were impersonal, her tone suggested intimate endearments. Eventually, when nothing unpleasant had occurred, Sheridan managed to relax in Lark's hands.

"That's it. Great! Now begin to move your arms. Never mind your legs. They're floating. Move your arms in a slow circle. It doesn't matter how."

Sheridan did as Lark said and felt that she actually helped propel them a little faster. "How am I doing?" she asked breathlessly.

"Wonderfully. I'm proud that you're doing this. Just look at you." Lark spoke close to Sheridan's ear. She felt Lark's breath against her cheek, and the intimacy made her skin tingle.

Sheridan kept moving her arms in increasingly bigger circles and found she took pleasure in the resistance that the water provided. Stronger these days from wheeling herself around, she managed almost another lap. Sheridan stopped, gasping, and turned within Lark's arms. Without thinking, she wrapped her own around Lark and hugged her. "That was fantastic. Thank you."

Lark returned the hug, and Sheridan couldn't help but moan when their bodies pressed together. She wanted to keep holding onto Lark, but knew this wouldn't happen. Reluctantly she let go, smiling at Lark's pink cheeks.

"You did so well. Much better than I could have hoped. I know how you feel about water, so the fact that you swam around the pool almost two laps is pretty awesome." Lark beamed, and her blush emphasized the glitter in her eyes.

"You did most of the work," Sheridan objected.

"Not true. Most of the time, my feet were off the bottom. You pushed us both with just your arms. Now, do you believe me when I say that you'll swim on your own soon?"

Startled, Sheridan gazed around the pool area.

"Hold on there. Not today!" Lark shook her head. "We're going to do some stretching while we're in the warm water, which you will find much less of a pain in the a—" Lark blushed even deeper. "Less of a discomfort."

"Pain in the ass is a good description." Sheridan winked. "Don't edit yourself. I like it when you're casual around me."

Lark's eyes grew into two dark pools full of undecipherable emotions. "All right. You sure, though? I can sometimes plant my foot pretty firmly in my mouth. Shoe and all."

Sheridan laughed. "You could chew on alligator boots, for all I care. I'd still like the unembellished truth."

Something passed over Lark's face, perhaps a sense of doubt? Granted, Sheridan hadn't allowed much leeway or forgiven very readily so far, but surely Lark knew that things had changed between them? Realizing that they were still holding onto each other, Sheridan let go of Lark. She searched Lark's expression for signs of anger or displeasure, and was totally taken aback when Lark suddenly tossed her head back and laughed.

"What?"

"You. You can be so funny." Lark held on to the ledge while she unleashed another fit of laughter. "And what's more, look. Isn't it great? You're floating all by yourself and you're laughing!"

The laughter nearly closed Sheridan's airways, but she grinned broadly when she noticed that Lark was telling the truth. She was floating, with the help of her arm-floaters, relaxed and carrying on a flirtatious conversation in the pool. *Flirtatious?* Yes, that was it. It was there in Lark's eyes, their glitter and the way she squinted with her head tilted to the side. Her hair laid slicked back against her head, revealing a tall, rounded forehead.

"Imagine that." Sheridan moved in close to Lark and placed her hands on her shoulder. "I just think it's safer like this."

"Oh, yeah?"

Lark didn't push her away so Sheridan slid closer. "Yes. I do. I feel much…safer, this way."

"You're trying to change the subject so I'll forget the rest of our exercises."

"No, no. Not at all. This is just while we're on a break." Sheridan cupped Lark's chin. "Keep still. You have something on your lips." She stroked her thumb along Lark's bottom lip once, then again, wiping away a tiny blade of grass that had glued itself there. "Better."

"Thank you," Lark whispered, sounding as if her breath was out of sync. "Sheridan—"

"You're welcome. Lark. By the way. How did your parents come up with a name like Lark?"

"I was born ruffled, my mom says." Lark touched Sheridan's lingering hand. "Lots of dark hair standing on end."

"No doubt just as cute." Sheridan knew as the words had just left her lips that she'd said something she didn't mean to.

"I'm cute?" Lark wrinkled her nose. "I'm nearly thirty! Cuteness, if any, is long gone."

Sheridan laughed, nervous, but also feeling happier than she had in a while. She couldn't remember laughing at all, after the illness. "You make it sound like you're an old woman. Cuteness, babe, is in the eyes of the beholder."

"Babe?" Lark's eyes grew wide. She blinked several times and then the now-familiar blush crept up her cheeks.

"Geez, I managed to call you cute and babe within one minute, didn't I?" Sheridan groaned, but couldn't keep the wide grin from her face.

"A record?" Lark splashed some water on Sheridan.

"It must be. I don't remember calling anyone cute before."

"I suppose it's good to be original." Lark inched away, and now her smile faded to polite. "Have to remember that for future reference when I need leverage."

"Hey, there's nothing wrong with being cute."

"Children are cute, Sheridan. Dogs, cats, or other pets are cute. The word implies belittling. And if you add babe to that…it finishes the imagery off, doesn't it?"

Sheridan simply didn't know what to say.

"Would you like it if anyone called you cute?"

About to argue the preposterousness of the whole idea, Sheridan slammed her jaw shut. Lark had a point, a very valid point. There was nothing wrong with being cute. *Sure.* "I'm sorry. I've honestly never thought of it that way. I don't like condescending people and certainly don't want to be one myself." Sheridan grasped Lark's shoulders and pulled her closer. "If I ever blurt out something along the lines of 'cute' or 'babe' again, please hit me over the head."

Lark studied her for a moment, her eyes piercing and sharp, belying their soft color. Slowly, her expression softened and her eyes sparkled again. "Over the head? Nah, I have better ways of getting someone's undivided attention."

Relief washed through Sheridan, and she knew they were back on track. What exact track or toward what, she had no idea. She only knew that she felt as if she'd stopped a train wreck from happening.

"Y'all ought to be growin' gills by now."

Burt's dark voice sent them flying apart.

Sheridan lifted her arms and, when she did that, the floaters moved upward and she sank a few inches. Water on her face made her splutter and cough for a few seconds before Lark grabbed her.

"I've got you! Sheridan, you're okay." Lark pressed her close. "Take a couple of slow, deep breaths."

Sheridan wrapped her arms around Lark's shoulders, unafraid, which was beyond amazing, really, but all she could think about was how well their bodies fit together. "I'm okay."

"Yes. Yes. Okay. That's it. You're okay." Lark obviously thought Sheridan's faint voice was due to her fear in the water. "I won't let go."

"I'm fine. Really. And weirdly enough." Sheridan let go of Lark with one hand and pushed drenched hair out of her face. "Just a bit taken off guard. No thanks to you." She glared mockingly at Burt, who merely shrugged and grinned. Sheridan had never seen him look this mischievous, for lack of a better word to describe the sparkle in the man's eyes.

"We might as well call it quits and do more of our bar exercises after lunch," Lark said. "Burt, it's time to help Sheridan out of the water. We're beginning to look like prunes."

With Lark's help, Burt lifted Sheridan out, and soon she sat on the recliner with a towel around her shoulders. "This did wonders for my confidence, when it comes to the pool, anyway. I'm not so sure I'd be as daring in the lake, so I hope you won't come up with any ideas like that."

"I'm only interested in having you with me in the water for PT reasons. I promise not to plot to send you swimming across Lake Travis."

"How kind." Sheridan wrapped a towel around her hair. "Time for a shower."

Her bathroom had undergone a makeshift accessibility overhaul, and she was confident that she'd manage on her own. Three weeks ago, she'd never have believed she'd gain so much independence in such a short time.

Is it because Lark is even more stubborn than I am? Lark took advantage of every situation to train her body, and Sheridan's newfound confidence was undeniably why she was overcoming some of her fears. Though she deliberately shied away from thinking about how Lark's proximity affected her, an inner voice insisted that part of her recent success was because she wanted to impress Lark.

Back in her wheelchair, Sheridan rolled into her bathroom. As she gazed into the mirror, she thought she could detect the remnants of her bout with desire, a faint glow deep in her eyes. Her sex felt more alive than it had in a long time, and her aching nipples weren't hard only because of the cooling swimwear. Sheridan remembered the feel of her thumb caressing Lark's lips, and she wondered how it would have felt to cover them with her own and taste all that softness.

Startled, Sheridan put a stop to her train of thought. She couldn't afford to do anything to repel Lark, in case she made good on her threat to quit her job if Sheridan didn't stick to their therapy plan. *Should be easy. I never mix business with pleasure.* Sheridan tried to be pragmatic, but her reaction in the pool had shifted from laughter to desire and back again so fast, she wasn't sure it wouldn't happen again.

Sheridan got ready for the shower and slid over to the plastic garden stool that doubled as a shower chair. The hot water rinsed off the smell of chlorine, but she could still feel Lark's arms around her. It was amazing how safe she'd felt.

CHAPTER SIXTEEN

Lark had been to Austin many times, but was unfamiliar with the neighborhood around The University of Texas. She had spent most of her time visiting relatives northwest of the city. Lark hoped going shopping with Sheridan would turn out to be a great learning experience. They were bound to encounter logistic challenges with curbs, steps, and other hurdles in this busy part of town.

"I want to take you out to lunch," Sheridan said, breaking into Lark's musings. "I have some favorite restaurants, so pick your poison, and I'll know just where to go."

"All right." Lark grinned. "That's courageous. You never know what I'm in the mood for."

Sheridan raised an eyebrow and looked sardonically at Lark. "Oh, I have my suspicions what your taste might be. It's quite clear actually."

Lark hiccupped, then laughed. "Are we still talking about food?"

"Sure."

"And what's my taste then? Since it's so obvious."

"You're a fish kind of girl."

"Fish?" Lark was stunned.

"Fish in general, salmon in particular. Preferably with pasta. Angel hair pasta."

Lark was speechless until she saw little quivers at the corners of Sheridan's mouth. "You've talked to Mrs. D!"

"I did better than that. I happened to pick up the phone when your mother called yesterday, and we had a little talk."

"Oh, I didn't know that. Mom didn't mention it."

"I asked her not to. She also told me that you like Haagen-Dazs vanilla ice cream, with raspberry sauce, and your favorite candy is salty licorice. Where in the world did you learn to like *salty* licorice? Never heard of such a thing."

"Sweden. And my mom is such a blabbermouth."

"So, you see. That's how you make someone easy to read. You interview their parents." Sheridan looked smug.

Lark patted Sheridan's laced hands. "Then you won't mind if I confess that I *interviewed* Mrs. D. I needed some inside help too."

"What? You did? About what?"

"That's for me to know and you to find out, possibly."

"Possibly?"

Lark laughed. It was delicious to tease Sheridan like this and watch her lose her advantage just a tad. "Possibly."

Sheridan joined in the laughter, shaking her head. "I can't imagine what Mrs. D had to share about me that could be remotely interesting. As you know, I don't do anything but work. Well, I did."

"She filled in the gaps. Told me about stuff unrelated to work." Lark pursed her lips, mimicking having deep thoughts. "For instance, she let me know how stubborn you can be, so it's up to me to be even more pigheaded."

"God. She really said that?"

"Pretty much." It was funny to watch the disgust on Sheridan's face, especially as a smile obviously threatened to break through. "And since you used the same approach with my mother, my flesh and blood, for heaven's sake, I'd say we're even."

"Hmm." Sheridan smiled. "If you say so."

"I do."

The chauffeur pulled the minivan out of the busy downtown traffic and stopped close to the curb. "When would you like me to return, ma'am?"

"I think in two and a half hours. Four o'clock. Sound good to you, Lark?"

Lark nodded and helped Sheridan out of the minivan. Once her charge was successfully on the sidewalk, she stepped to the side and let Sheridan take over.

They rolled and walked, respectively, in and out of a few stores and didn't have any problems in the first two. In the third store, a nervous clerk kept talking above Sheridan's head, directing herself to

Lark although Sheridan was the one shopping.

"Miss? I believe I'm your customer. Not Ms. Mitchell." Sheridan's voice was polite, but Lark had no problem imagining icicles dangling from every word.

"Of course, ma'am." The woman turned to Lark again. "Does she want this gift wrapped?"

"Why don't you ask her? There's nothing wrong with her mind." Lark also became annoyed, even if she'd seen or heard worse than this while she was out and about with patients.

"Oh. I see. I apologize. Would you like it gift wrapped, ma'am?"

"Yes, please." Sheridan's expression was still cool.

The clerk hurried through the wrapping and charged the set of twelve silver teaspoons to Sheridan's credit card. "There you go, ma'am. I apologize again for the misconception."

Sheridan's eyes finally grew warmer. "Live and learn, miss." Sheridan shrugged. "We all forget that we should never assume. Just remember that the next time."

"Point taken." The girl blushed deeply, and Lark watched with fascination how quickly she fluctuated between nervous condescension and fluster.

Outside, Lark searched Sheridan's face for signs of how she felt and knew she had to say something. "You handled that well."

"Even I'm amazed, actually. I'm more known for biting people's heads off. I usually don't have any patience for fools."

Sheridan's pensive expression tugged at something buried deeply inside Lark. "Maybe you've realized that people are often ignorant, but seldom deliberately malicious."

Sheridan blinked. "Yeah, you're probably right. I've always thought that people just don't focus, that they're usually pretty oblivious to what life can bring. I believed they could get so much more if they only had the energy, or stamina, to reach for it."

"And now?"

"I never quite understood before that people are different, I mean, in what they find important or desirable." Sheridan began to roll along the sidewalk. "There's a restaurant just around the corner that I think you'll like. They have great seafood. All right with you?"

"Sure." Lark didn't want Sheridan to stop talking, but knew they couldn't very well discuss this topic on the street with hundreds of people brushing by them. "I've worked up an appetite."

A waiter guided them to a corner table and pulled out a chair without a word, to make room for Sheridan's wheelchair. The menu included almost all of Lark's favorite seafood, and it took her a while to choose. "I'll have the salmon pasta, please," she finally decided and handed the menu back to the waiter. Sheridan ordered her food, a similar dish but with shrimp, then leaned back, rolling her shoulders discreetly.

"You in pain?" Lark said, frowning.

"No. Just a bit stiff."

"I'll give you a massage when we're home. You've worked hard the last week, and maybe we've been over-eager."

"I don't think so. I feel fine. We'd better take advantage of these weeks."

"True. But overdoing it won't make you stronger or give you results quicker. Just the opposite, in fact."

"You're the expert." Sheridan raised her glass of iced tea. "To mutual success."

"To success." After sipping her water, Lark said, "So, tell me, what do you think about your new ideas regarding people's imperfections?"

"Oh, that." Sheridan's laugh was brief and tinged with surprise. "I honestly can't say. If I had to guess, though, I'd say my illness, coming completely out of the blue like it did, was life-altering."

"I know it was. It would've been strange if it wasn't."

"Before then, I had my own idea about people who 'succumbed' to illness. Shows what a hypocrite I am."

"What made you draw such conclusions in the first place?" Lark let her fingers trace the rim of her glass and wipe off the condensation on its sides.

"Many things. Being a Ward, for one. Wards bear it. They're never sick. And if they are sick, they clench their teeth, say 'screw you' to any docs that suggest any treatment, and just push through." Bitterness snuck into Sheridan's voice. "Wards are inhuman, if you want the truth. We don't need any help, and we certainly don't show any discomfort or pain."

"But that's completely unreasonable!" Lark was shocked. She'd suspected that Ward traditions were behind Sheridan's attitude, but to hear them put in such uncertain terms was something entirely different. "To teach a child that a person is to blame for his own illness or disability is beyond inhuman. I don't mean to criticize your parents—"

"My daddy. My mother was a saint. She stood by his side, always defending him, and I don't mean to make her sound weak. In fact, my mother was the strongest woman I've ever met." Sheridan's eyes darkened. "She lived two years longer than the doctors estimated, on sheer willpower. She showed true Ward grit, but my father couldn't even admit that. He kept saying that if she stopped seeing those 'quacks' she'd be a lot better off. Fortunately she didn't do as he said, but he made it so difficult for her with all his disapproval and nagging."

The waiter showed up with their food and they ate in silence for a few minutes. "Did your mother let you in? I mean, did she level with you?"

"Yes, she did. This of course only annoyed my father more, and he tried to make my mother stop. Once in a while he'd tell me her illness was mostly in her head."

"Oh, God." Lark shook her head. "How did *he* handle being ill? I mean, after all he'd said before?"

Sheridan looked genuinely cynical. "He claimed that he was experiencing a temporary lapse and denied his condition completely. Business as usual, you could say."

"But you stayed."

"I honestly didn't know what to do at first." Sheridan speared a steamed shrimp and chewed it carefully. "I had my life and my friends in Boston. I had job offers constantly, head hunters who offered me the moon and then some. But when I saw Daddy, pale, thin, and so determined to work himself to death, my choice wasn't difficult at all. I'd already lost one parent. I didn't want to lose him. Not without us being on speaking terms at least."

"So what happened?"

Sheridan laughed, and now her smile was soft and kind. "During the following few years he made me work in every executive position. When he finally gave me the office next to his, I knew I'd gained his approval, perhaps even his pride. He...he actually kissed my cheek. Just that time, and only once, but I'll never forget it."

"And hearing this, hearing you be so clear-sighted, it still bothers me that you can be so Ward-like, so like your father, when it comes to the aftermath of your illness." Completely absorbed with the topic, Lark put down her utensils and leaned across the table. "Why can't, or couldn't, you see this trend in your own reactions?"

"Oh, don't think for a minute I acted only like my father would have expected. There's a difference. The Ward industry, its future, its success, lies on my shoulders. My responsibility. I have no close relatives, no heirs. I have nobody that I can turn the company over to, in whole or in part. Ward Industries employs approximately 210,000 people worldwide that I—me, nobody else—am ultimately responsible for. No matter what happens or who screws up, the buck stops at my desk. So..." Sheridan extended the last word and placed her hand over Lark's, squeezing it for emphasis, "perhaps you can understand that I can't show weakness, perceived or real, and I have to get back on my feet, metaphorically and physically speaking. I have to."

"I see." Lark's heart plummeted as she realized, for the first time, Sheridan's point of view. *This explains why she doesn't even relate to what her neurologists have predicted.* Lark wondered how Sheridan would react when reality hit, which it would, sooner or later. One day, and this would happen within the upcoming weeks, or months, she would realize that her legs would never obey her again. Granted, she had undamaged neural paths that could take over lost functions to a degree, but any hope of a full recovery was a sad delusion. There was no way Lark would discuss that topic over lunch in a crowded room. She thought quickly of what more to say and had opened her mouth when a female voice cut in.

"Sheri, honey, you're back!" A whirlwind, consisting of a thin, blond woman, leaned down and kissed Sheridan on the cheek. "What have you been up to, gorgeous?"

"Hi, Fergie." Sheridan had paled considerably, but still managed to smile politely. "Didn't think you frequented this type of place. Isn't it too bourgeois for you?"

Her words were abrupt, and Lark expected the other woman to be offended, but to her surprise, Fergie just laughed.

"You know me well. Gaby and Mo's is more my thing, but I was shopping for a present for my mom, and...Oh, I'm being ruder than usual. Please introduce me. Who is this doe-eyed creature?"

Lark felt her eyes grow wide as she stared at Fergie with her black leather slacks, black T-shirt, and black leather vest, along with black tribal tattoos on her wrists. Fergie in turn looked appreciatively at Lark, raking her eyes up and down her body.

"Lark, this is Fergie, a friend of mine. Fergie, this is Lark, my… associate." Sheridan tripped over the last word, and Lark tried to figure out why she'd become "promoted."

"Nice to meet you, Fergie," Lark said and extended her hand.

Fergie took it, and before Lark realized her intentions, she had placed a feather-light kiss on her knuckles. "My pleasure," she murmured, nailing Lark with intense green eyes.

Sheridan had clearly not missed Fergie's overly polite gesture. "Behave now, Fergie."

"I am. This is me on my best behavior." Fergie winked at Lark. "You should know that."

"Guess so."

Fergie's eyes dropped to the floor, and her quick intake of breath made Lark realize that until now the exuberant woman hadn't realized that anything was wrong with her friend.

"Sheri? What's happened to you?" Without asking, she pulled up a free chair and sat down, her face devoid of all flirtation or teasing. "Honey?"

"I've been ill. But I'm feeling better." Sheridan looked uncomfortable, but her smile was indulgent, if a bit forced.

"When did this happen? Babe, you should've told us. We're your friends, even if you don't come around as much as you used to. We would've helped."

"Thanks, Fergie, but I don't think so. I know you're my friend, as are the other girls, but I had so much on my plate, too much to handle, to spread myself too thin. I've just begun to move about this effortlessly." Sheridan glanced at Lark, and the look didn't pass Fergie by.

"So I take it Lark here is more than an associate. She's the one who stands in for your friends?"

Sheridan looked flabbergasted by the sudden tone of jealousy and hostility Fergie showed toward her. This after having flirted insistently only a minute ago.

"Fergie. You know I'm a private person who doesn't move in the fast lane like some of the crowd we hang with. I enjoy it when we're together, but I always withdraw when it becomes too wild. That's simply not my thing. I was trying to…well, fly under the radar a bit.

Lark is my physical therapist."

"Your…oh!" Warmth returned to Fergie's features. "Sorry 'bout the lousy attitude, Lark. I can be such a bitch."

"Apology accepted." Lark had to smile. Fergie's immediate reactions were fascinating. She seemed to be one of those people who didn't hold anything back. An unruly, confrontational, and no doubt eccentric woman. *And she's Sheridan's friend?* It was hard to judge Fergie's age, but Lark thought she had to be a couple of years younger than herself. "We all have days like that."

"Days?" Fergie huffed with a sparkling smile. "Try weeks, months even. I'm surprised that Sheri wants to be friends with someone like me. But I suppose the girls and I have shown you a good time or two." She winked at Sheridan, who suddenly blushed faintly.

Fergie laughed loudly. "Damn, never seen you blush so sweetly! Could it be because we're in the presence of the lovely Ms. Lark? Perhaps you're worried that I'll share all our hot and steamy memories."

Sheridan, looking flustered and with her lips pressed tightly together, glowered at her. "Fergie."

"I know. I know. Behave. I'll start now." Fergie sighed. "But let me know when you want to hang out with the gang. Drew especially misses you. She says the rest of us are ignorant babies without any culture or manners."

"She has a point." Sheridan shook her head.

"So, don't be a stranger. And feel better, gorgeous." Fergie leaned forward and kissed Sheridan lightly on the lips.

Lark clenched her fists under the table as jealousy stabbed her in the chest. If she hadn't known better, she would've sworn it made a resounding thud when it buried itself to the hilt.

"See you around, ladies." Fergie rose and left with a casual wave. "Ciao!"

Silence hung between Sheridan and Lark like morning mist over Lake Travis. Lark studied the half-melted ice cubes in her glass and drew patterns in the condensation, as she had before.

"That was Fergie," Sheridan said superfluously. "A friend from here."

"I guessed as much." The green monster still clawed at Lark's midsection, the sensation surpassed only by the strong conviction that she was being ridiculous.

"We used to hang out, with some mutual friends. You know. The bar scene." Sheridan shrugged.

"Actually, I don't. Not much for bars." Why was her tongue so stiff all of a sudden?

"No? What do you do for fun then?" Sheridan finished her iced tea only to have it refilled as soon as she put her glass down.

"Dinner. A movie. Walks. Sometimes dancing. Guess that sounds boring."

Sheridan regarded her for several seconds. "Actually it sounds nice, when done with the right person. Laid back and relaxing."

"Really?"

"Yeah."

"You'll do fun things again, even bars." Lark wanted to reassure Sheridan, despite her mixed emotions. It wasn't Sheridan's fault that she attracted interest from several women. Lark guessed that Austin had been a safe haven of sorts, away from her strict business circles in San Antonio.

"Somehow I doubt it," Sheridan sighed. "I haven't even missed it."

"You'll get that feeling back."

"I may not want to." Sheridan looked intently at Lark, then waved the waiter over. She paid the bill without listening to any of Lark's objections and began to wheel out of the restaurant.

Lark caught up with her on the sidewalk. "Hey. Wait up."

"I had to go outside. The walls were suddenly falling in." Sheridan seemed out of breath. "Weird."

Lark's jealousy, seeming very petty now, evaporated. "Let's go home. I'll call for the car."

"Good." Sweat formed beads on Sheridan's forehead and she began to lean in her wheelchair. "I don't feel very well."

"I've got you." Lark stood next to Sheridan with an arm around her shoulders and squeezed gently. "Just breathe, sweetie. Just breathe."

Sheridan leaned her head against Lark's hip as Lark pulled out her cell phone, dialed the driver, and asked him to bring the car to their location. *Sweetie? God Almighty, what was I thinking?*

CHAPTER SEVENTEEN

"Fetch, Frank, come on! Get the ball!"

Sheridan pulled her baseball cap down a bit to shade her eyes. She didn't want to miss a thing as the game unfolded on the lawn. Her Irish setter, still so hesitant around her, had fallen madly in love with Lark. He followed her everywhere, often after a suspicious glance in Sheridan's direction. Lark wasn't overly affectionate with him. Instead she seemed set on exercising him and making sure he was walked. The Johnsons mostly let him run loose on the grounds, which according to Lark wasn't enough.

They had discussed the situation a few days earlier. "My youngest sister has two German shepherds that she's taken to several obedience classes. She's a strong believer in positive reinforcement. Also, if you want to catch a dog's attention, you have to exercise him properly. Several walks a day, at least one long one."

"Well, that kind of excludes me," Sheridan had said with a smirk to hide the sting in her heart. "I'll ask Burt if I can add this to his duties."

"Burt's a strong man. He can lift things and does a great job around the house. He has rheumatism though, in his knees, which limits his ability to walk a dog properly. Mrs. Johnson has high blood pressure, so that's not a good solution either."

"Damn, I'll have to think of something else, then. I've heard of professional dog walkers, but I don't know if they operate out here by the lake."

"In the meantime, let me take care of him. At least while you work."

"You wouldn't mind?"

"I'd be happy to."

Lark's expression had lit up, and now she worked and exercised Frank on a daily basis. Sheridan tried to convince herself that being jealous was completely ridiculous. She knew that dogs related to people around them in a very basic way. Frank wasn't betraying anyone. He'd simply found a new friend in Lark, one who could run with him.

Sheridan's throat ached, and she had begun to wheel back toward the house when Lark's voice stopped her.

"Sheridan! Wait! Check this out."

"All right." Sheridan turned around, a polite smile firmly in place.

"I want to show you something." Lark sat Frank down and walked toward Sheridan. Halfway there, she dropped something white on the grass. She stopped, looked down at the item, then over at Frank. "Frank, I *dropped* it. Pick it up. Pick it up!"

Sheridan frowned as her free-spirited dog looked inquisitively at Lark. He wagged his tail, clearly eager to do something.

"Come on, pick it up, Frank."

Frank bounced across the lawn and stopped in front of Lark so fast he tore up part of the grass. He dove onto the object and sat down, wagging his tail vigorously.

"Thank you, Frank. Good boy, good boy." Lark held up the object to Sheridan. "See? He fetched my pack of tissues!"

"You taught him that?" Sheridan was amazed. Frank was the type of dog who was naturally nice and fairly well behaved. He ran loose around the property and never bothered anybody, and he had received very little training apart from the normal cues for sit, down, come, and stay. To watch him pick something up on cue and hand it over was practically a miracle.

"Yeah, he learns really easily. Let's try something a little harder. Do you have anything you can drop?"

"Me?" Sheridan flinched, unprepared. "Eh, I don't know. Will my baseball cap do?"

"Unless you're scared of teeth marks on it. Frank could chew it halfway up, you know."

"No problem. What do I do?"

"Drop it when you wheel back toward the house, like you were doing before. Notice it, stop, point, and ask Frank to pick it up like I did."

"I don't think he'll obey me. He doesn't come near me these days."

"Let's try anyway. If nothing else, it'll give me an idea of how to proceed with his training."

"Okay." Sheridan began to wheel, and after a few yards she let her baseball cap fall to the ground. She stopped the wheelchair and turned around, trying her best to look dismayed. "Oh, I dropped my cap. Pick it up, Frank." When nothing happened, she repeated the cue. Still nothing. "You see?" Sheridan spread her hands, palms up, in a defeated gesture.

"Try calling him again." Lark didn't seem the least deterred.

Sheridan called Frank's name again, pointing at the baseball cap. "Come on, boy. Fetch it for Mommy." She knew she sounded terribly mushy, but it was all she could think of to say.

Suddenly Frank barked and ran toward Sheridan. He skidded across the limestone tiles and stopped in front of her, then gave another low bark.

"Pick up the hat, boy," Sheridan said, her voice trembling. This was the first time the dog had shown any interest in her since they had arrived at Lake Travis. "Come on."

Frank grabbed the cap between his teeth, then sat down with a thud. Wagging his tail, he looked at her with big eyes. He wagged only the very tip of his tail, as if he was uncertain how she'd react. Sheridan felt something inside loosen, as if an icicle dislodged from a fine piece of crystal. "Good boy," she said, tears rising to cloud her sight. "Give it to Mommy. Come on."

Frank hesitated for a moment, then placed his head on her lap, the cap still in his mouth. Sheridan cupped his cheeks, the way she used to, and scratched along his nose. Frank whimpered and, letting go of the cap, licked her wrists, his tail now wagging madly, sweeping the tiles.

"Oh, Frankie. I've missed you." Sheridan buried her face into his fur and inhaled the typical smell of dog, which was the sweetest scent she'd come across in a long time. Frank scooted closer to her, pressing his nose up under her chin. The familiar movement felt so good; Sheridan sobbed as she hugged her dog. "Frank."

Frank broke free after a while and looked expectantly at her. He wiggled his eyebrows and placed his paw on her knee. Sheridan knew what he was asking for. She locked the brakes on her wheelchair and patted her lap. "Come on, Frank. Lap."

Frank launched the front part of his body up on her lap. He whimpered to express his joy, and Sheridan laughed while tears streamed down her face.

"Look at the two of you," Lark said, beaming next to them. She wiped at the corners of her eyes. "You see now? He just needed some time and persuasion."

"Thank you." Sheridan hugged Frank and ruffled the wavy fur on the sides of his neck. "Honestly, it feels like I've just come home. Isn't that weird?"

"It's not weird at all. An important part of your home was missing, and now that Frank is back in the picture the way he should be, we should be able to work him into our plan and schedule."

"How do you mean?"

"I know Frank is used to being here with the Johnsons, but the truth is, you need him. He also needs to remain connected to you and your changed circumstances. He should go back to San Antonio with you."

"But that'd be so hard on him. He's used to having this." She gestured with her arm to indicate the 200-acre property.

"He'll be fine. Dogs are very good at adjusting, as long as they're loved and cared for. Besides, he's got a job to do."

"What do you mean, a job?"

"Training to be your service dog."

Sheridan recoiled. "But I won't need a working dog once I've recovered. And that breaks up Frank's routine for nothing."

Lark's gaze was firm. "You know you have a long way to go, Sheridan. We can't be sure how quickly and how much you'll heal. Frank will be a tremendous help for you. Fully trained, he'll be able to accompany you everywhere."

"You talk as if there's no hope for me." Sheridan's tongue felt stiff and threatened to make her slur her words.

"There's always hope! Just look at Fiona. She was in a coma for two months, and the doctors were very pessimistic about her future. They couldn't even say if she would live or not. And look at her now."

"I don't mean to imply that you don't understand," Sheridan managed. "It's just that I'm in this body, and you aren't. I'm the one who has to believe in a full recovery. I can't give that hope up. It would be as if I stopped breathing."

Lark looked up into the sky, and at first Sheridan thought she was looking for divine inspiration.

"Sheridan, I know this. I've seen it in other patients, and I know you better with each passing day. I understand. I really do. That said, you have to face the fact that no matter the degree of your recovery, it—will—take—time." Lark knelt next to her and Frank, looking as if he wanted to bring her into the cozy embrace with his beloved mom, licked her nose.

"I don't have time."

"You have no choice. You're Sheridan Ward, business tycoon and one of the most admired, respected, and no doubt feared women in Texas. You're richer than most, and if it came down to sheer determination and courage, you'd make a full recovery in no time. But, Sheridan, the thing is, our bodies can break and be damaged, no matter our circumstances. I know you'll do your best to regain as much of what you've lost as possible, and I know you have a lot more to gain. But in the meantime, while you still struggle, you need to *live* as well." Lark cupped Sheridan's cheek. "You need to exist here and now, and not think this journey you're on is wasted time. Trust me, I know for a fact that you'll benefit from living in the moment. You will see it too, in retrospect."

Sheridan placed her hand on top of Lark's and held it to her face. "For me, acceptance is admitting that I'm screwed, that this is as good as I'll ever become. I can't hang up my hat and just call it quits."

"I know! And that's where Frank comes in, with a little help from me. Frank can be trained to make your life easier. He's shown us how clever he is. You can put all the strength that he conserves for you into your training, if you want."

"You have a point," Sheridan admitted reluctantly.

"Yes. I know." Lark wrinkled her nose and pursed her lips. "Clever, aren't I?"

Sheridan had to laugh, despite the fact that she was still twirling inside some eternal emotional spiral. A few heavy drops of rain landed on them, creating big damp spots on Lark's light chinos. "We better go inside. It's going to start pouring any minute."

They moved toward the patio and almost made it ahead of the rain. The sky darkened with each step they took. Streaming down, the rain drenched their hair and soaked their clothes. They were barely inside and slamming the door shut behind them when lightning and thunder struck simultaneously.

Lark whimpered and clasped a hand over her mouth.

"Don't worry. We have a lightning conductor installed." Sheridan tried to sound reassuring.

"It's not so much the lightning, believe it or not. I just hate the thunder."

"I see. Well, what if we dry off poor Frank, he looks miserable, and then ourselves. I'll try to call the Johnsons and let them know that we're indoors and can take care of ourselves. I don't want them outside unnecessarily. Being this close to the lake tends to make lightning a bit antsy." Sheridan's joke fell flat to the ground. "Towels, first of all." She pulled out her cell phone and called Burt. He picked up right away and assured her that he and his wife were fine and would sit out the storm in the bungalow.

Lark returned with towels for all of them and began to rub Frank, who appeared to enjoy the procedure.

"Something about handling Frank is reassuring. Funny that," Lark murmured as she toweled the delighted dog. "You think this is all about you, don't you, Frankie boy? Trust a dog to be conceited like that. You brat." Despite her choice of words, Lark sounded like she was talking tenderly to a child. "There you go," she said and swatted Frank softly with the wet towel. "You're done."

Sheridan sat motionless, mesmerized with the sight of Lark and Frank.

Lark turned around and frowned. "Sheridan! You haven't even started. Here, let me." Lark took the towel and began to rub Sheridan's hair. "You're still vulnerable, and being cold like this stiffens your muscles. We have to get you out of these clothes."

"You too," Sheridan said and immediately wanted to kick herself.

"I know. But you first. Let's go to your room."

As Lark helped Sheridan out of the clinging wet clothes, another lightning bolt seared the sky. The thunder followed almost instantly and Sheridan felt Lark tremble. "It's okay to be uncomfortable," Sheridan tried to reassure her. "We both know that until you've been through a Texas thunderstorm, you ain't seen nuthin'."

Lark smiled, which Sheridan found encouraging. She raised her arms for Lark to peel her long-sleeve T-shirt off and only then realized that she hadn't worn a bra. Sheridan's breasts bounced free of the wet fabric and drew Lark's attention. Instead of offering Sheridan the towel, Lark rubbed it along her back and dried her off. When she reached Sheridan's front, she hesitated for a fraction of a second before she handed her the towel. "Here. I'll find a shirt for you. Want some sweatpants?"

"Yeah, that'd be great, thanks. And dry underwear. Even my briefs are soaked." Sheridan couldn't believe how she managed to spout double entendres, one after another. Groaning inwardly, she dried off her chest. Her nipples were diamond hard, from being cold, Sheridan insisted to herself, and the soft terry-cloth fabric didn't do anything to soften them.

Lark returned with some clothes, and that's when Sheridan noticed that Lark didn't wear a bra either. Her smaller breasts quivered beneath the white, semitransparent T-shirt. Her nipples looked small too, but just as hard as Sheridan's. Unable to look away, Sheridan forgot that she was half naked, and only when Lark pulled a golf shirt over her head did she become aware that Lark was touching her skin. The sensation was very different from their massage sessions when Lark worked through Sheridan's muscle groups. Now the soft hands smoothed down the shirt over her shoulders, and the touch made her skin tingle all over.

Another flash of lightning and subsequent crash of thunder made Lark step closer and press her hands firmer against Sheridan.

"Shh. We're fine." Sheridan loosened the left armrest and moved over onto the bed. Wiggling from side to side, she managed to push her jeans down, but then they became stuck. "Damn it. Guess I need more help."

"No worries." Lark knelt before her and tugged.

Sheridan saw her jeans glide down her legs and knew she would always remember this moment because Lark was privy to everything. She didn't know if Lark found her remotely attractive, but she thought she could see her temple artery throb.

"Can you wiggle some more?" Lark looked up at Sheridan, her eyes like dark honey.

"Sure." Sheridan moved her hips as Lark had taught her, and only when Lark pulled her briefs off did she realize that she was now fully naked. Sheridan drew a deep breath when she sensed Lark touch and move her legs.

Lark pulled the clean pair of briefs up her legs until she reached Sheridan's upper thighs. Sheridan's skin tingled and she wanted to spread her legs, wanted to be touched so badly she almost choked. Instead, she held on to Lark and rolled back and forth until her panties were in place. Out of breath and trembling, Sheridan hardly paid attention as Lark pulled the sweatpants up her legs. As she warmed up, Sheridan stopped shivering, but still felt a persistent tremor deep within her.

"Lark," Sheridan said, "you're even wetter than I was. Go take care of yourself. Frank and I'll go warm some canned soup."

"All right. Be there in a sec." Lark smoothed Sheridan's hair with quick hands and left the room.

Sheridan moved back into her chair, rolled toward the kitchen, and was just about to reach for a can of tomato soup in the pantry when several bolts of lightning struck around the house. The deafening thunder made Sheridan drop the can, which rolled out of sight. A second later, Sheridan couldn't see anything. The storm clouds grew denser, darkening the sky, and the lights began to flicker. Then, when they all went out, she heard a scream, which echoed through the house.

"Sherida-a-an!"

CHAPTER EIGHTEEN

Sheridan!" Lark screamed for help, but she knew instantly that the thunder had drowned out her voice. As she stumbled through the corridor toward the kitchen, a low dark shadow appeared and nearly made her topple over. She grabbed for a chair that fell to the floor with a loud clatter.

"Lark? Are you okay?" Sheridan's voice came from the kitchen.

"Yeah…" Lark knew she didn't sound convincing. "Think I tripped over Frank."

Another lightning bolt, followed by roaring thunder, tore across the sky. Lark's heart nearly stopped as she hurried toward Sheridan. She stubbed her toe against the door frame and entered the kitchen with a loud moan.

"God, what did you do?" Sheridan rolled up to Lark and took both her hands.

"Tried to wreck your house, it looks like." An army of ants wearing combat boots threatened to march under her skin when she thought of the next eruption outside.

"We've lost power and I suspect the Johnsons have too." Sheridan stroked the back of Lark's hand with her thumbs. "But we have supplies and everything we need, so we'll be all right. Hopefully the storm won't last long."

Lark clung to Sheridan's hands. One roll of thunder after another made her flash back to the terrible night when Fiona was shot. She could still hear the thunder of that humid evening, the booming sound that had masked the sound of the gun fired at a gang member, which instead hit her little sister. Nobody had heard the screeching tires or Fiona's screams as the carload of men drove away.

"I hope it won't," Lark managed, trying to shake off the haunting images.

"Your hands are ice cold. We really do need to warm this soup up. That means firing up the old wood stove." Sheridan let go of Lark and wheeled over to the opposite end of the kitchen. She grabbed a few logs and some kindling, and quickly had a fire roaring. "Grab a pan and open the can, please? I think it rolled toward the stove when I dropped it." Sheridan said over her shoulder.

Lark knelt and spotted the can over by the sink. With trembling fingers, she poured the soup into a pan and handed it to Sheridan, who put it on the stove, and within minutes, they were sipping the soup from large mugs. Lark clung to hers, willing her hands to warm up.

"Why don't we eat in my room? We can light another fire there." Sheridan handed her mug to Lark and wheeled into the hallway. "It'll warm up faster, since it's smaller than the living room."

"Sounds like a plan." Lark did her best to sound casual. She didn't want to act like a complete idiot. How could her normal calm, collected persona crumble this easily?

Under Sheridan's supervision, Lark soon had the fire going, feeling quite proud of her accomplishment. She'd never been a Girl Scout, or even very outdoorsy. Stacking the firewood and learning how to ignite kindling took her mind off the volatile weather for a while.

"You comfortable with sitting on the bed?" Sheridan asked, studying Lark intently.

"Sure. Why not? Most comfortable place in the room." Lark heard the forced casualness sneak back into her voice as she climbed onto the bed. She was shivering again.

"All right." Sheridan moved effortlessly over onto the bed, pulling at her legs with her hands. "Can you reach the blanket?"

"Sure." Lark tugged the cashmere blanket over their legs, then handed Sheridan her mug of soup, sipped her own, and tried to relax. Acutely aware of Sheridan's proximity, Lark found it nearly impossible not to turn to her, snuggle up, and hide. She couldn't think of anything more tempting.

A new onslaught of thunder made Lark tremble so hard, she had to put down the mug. She was taken aback by the intensity of her reaction. Normally, she suffered through thunderstorms on her own, shutting out bad memories through sheer willpower. Now, here with Sheridan, she felt raw, her heart and soul bared for the elements to tear apart.

"You want to talk about why, exactly, you hate the thunder?" Sheridan's voice was closer than Lark expected, and when she turned her head, she found Sheridan tucked in on her side, her empty mug dangling from her fingers. After Lark put it on the nightstand next to her own, she found it hard to look Sheridan in the eyes, but forced herself to do so. It would have been cowardly not to, she thought, and she wasn't prepared to add that weakness to her persona.

"The night Fiona was shot was just like this."

Sheridan didn't speak.

"She was shot by gang members who missed their target and ended up nearly killing her instead." Lark plucked at the blanket and used it as a valid reason to avert her eyes. "Nobody heard the shots fired in the street, because of the thunder. Nobody heard her cries for help or her cries of pain, initially, either. "

"Oh, God."

"She lay in the street until a neighbor pulled out of her driveway and nearly backed over her. If she hadn't been so observant…well, you know." Lark shrugged.

"I understand. And I bet you were the first one out the door when your family learned that she was injured."

"She was my little sister. My responsibility." Lark's jaws felt stiff. "I know my mother was the head of our household, but I was always left in charge when we kids were home alone, even if I wasn't the oldest."

"Always the mediator."

Lark looked up, surprised. "Yes. You remember that?"

"I remember everything you've said. And what your family said when I came by." She colored faintly in the light from the fireplace. "You're not like any person I've ever met, so that might be why."

"But…I'm just me. I mean, ordinary." Lark was puzzled. "You meet the most amazing people—industrial magnates, political leaders. You've traveled far more than I, and I've worked on all five continents."

"And still, I haven't met anyone who gets under my skin and makes me focus like you do." Sheridan cupped Lark's cheek for a moment. "You're complex, kind, committed to your job, and more patient than I could ever hope to be."

"You're being patient with my childish fears right now."

"I disagree. They aren't childish fears. You went through hell during a thunderstorm when you were young. They're completely understandable."

"You've been through hell too," Lark said. "Your mother's illness and the way it was handled. Your father's death. Your own illness."

"Yeah. Probably the same thing. Hadn't thought of it quite like that."

Thunder rolled again, this time louder than before, and Lark knew the storm had come back full circle. "Damn it. Why can't it just stop?" she muttered.

"It's the lake. A lot of times, it circles the lake several times before it runs out of juice."

"Oh, great." Lark sighed and squeezed her eyes shut. "This is going to be a rough evening."

"Yeah. But I'm here, if that's any consolation. And what's more, Fiona's safe back in Boerne."

"Yes, thank God." Lark couldn't resist the low purr in Sheridan's voice any longer. She turned on her side, pressing her forehead against Sheridan's shoulder. "I worked hard for years to get the picture of her, bleeding and broken, out of my mind. She was unconscious when I reached her. I knew we shouldn't move her, and Mom and I had to fight off my other sisters. They wanted to pull her into the house."

"That probably also helped save her life," Sheridan said softly. She brushed back Lark's hair with gentle fingers.

"Yes. The doctors said so." Lark moved into Sheridan's touch. "It just took so long before we knew if she would make it, and when she finally woke up…she couldn't move at all. It took her a long time to regain what she has now. *Fiona* was the brave one. She was the fighter who inspired me to become a physical therapist. I wanted to help others the same way Fiona's PTs helped her."

"Makes sense, given your sweet nature."

The words, uttered with such sincerity, made Lark look up at Sheridan. "Sweet?"

"Yes. I don't mean it in a meek way, far from it. You're as tough as they come. At least you are with me." Sheridan winked. Her dark gray eyes, even darker in the light of the fire, swept up and down Lark's body.

Heat spread throughout Lark's system, creating beads of sweat on her forehead and upper lip. She wiped them, self-conscious and aroused at the same time. Sheridan radiated a mix of concern and attraction, unless Lark misread her completely. She wanted to press close to Sheridan, feel her arms around her, and hide from the thunder. More than that, she wanted to finally feel Sheridan's lips against hers, to find out if all these rampant feelings she harbored were real.

Sheridan kept smoothing Lark's hair back. Leaning into the touch, Lark trembled at the way Sheridan looked at her. She could almost feel the glances against her skin, and the tension between them grew with every quick breath. Sitting so close, their bodies touching, Lark knew she'd never been so exhilarated or nervous before. Sheridan kept touching her and soon Lark would want more. Her breasts ached, and she felt as if only Sheridan's hands could quench the fire under her skin.

"You not only look sweet, I bet you taste just as sweet." Sheridan's voice was tense, lower than usual.

"You might just have to wait your turn." Lark grabbed the hand that stroked her hair and held it a fraction of an inch from her lips. She kissed Sheridan's palm languidly. "Mmm. You taste very good."

"I do?" Sheridan was considerably more breathless, and the hand Lark held was definitely shaking. "You vixen." She turned somewhat and, by doing so, towered over Lark in the bed. "You a closeted flirt, Ms. Mitchell?"

"Never flirt. Well. Not really." Lark nibbled the knuckle of Sheridan's index finger. "I'm just interested in people. Some might call that being…" she nibbled some more "…flirtatious."

Sheridan growled in the back of her throat, pressed Lark's hand into the bed, and brushed her lips along the right side of Lark's face. Overwhelmed by her arousal and needing Sheridan's touch more than she had needed anything in a long time, Lark captured Sheridan's mouth with hers and slid her tongue along Sheridan's lower lip.

A sharp breath proved that she'd managed to take Sheridan by surprise. Lark inhaled the scent of the men's soap Sheridan used, with a musk tinge, so unlike her own fruity gel variety. As Lark buried her face against Sheridan's neck, she found her scent alluring.

"Lark…" Sheridan framed Lark's face with both hands and kissed her forehead. She kissed softly down Lark's nose and captured her lips. The thunder boomed again and Sheridan trapped Lark's whimper in her mouth.

"Sheridan, hold me," Lark whispered.

"I won't let go."

"Hold me."

"Feel me." Sheridan moved closer, pressing her chest to Lark's. "Open your mouth for me."

"I shouldn't. I really shouldn't, but I can't seem to help myself…" Lark whimpered again, but this time from sheer desire, as she complied.

❖

Sheridan couldn't move her legs sufficiently to slide fully on top of Lark, but she was happy where she was. Lark's half-open mouth met hers with trust and desire, and Sheridan explored it gratefully. Responsive, and with a taste that was entirely her own, Lark's mouth enticed Sheridan to take the kiss further. Sheridan devoured her, and her heart thundered louder and louder as Lark returned the kiss.

"God, Lark, you feel so good," Sheridan murmured as she kissed her way down Lark's neck. She pushed the shirt open more fully, wanting to reach the indentation above Lark's collarbone.

"Ah…" Lark arched against Sheridan. "Please. Please."

"You don't have to beg, Lark. Don't you know what you do to me?" Sheridan licked a trail over to the other collarbone. "I want to taste all of you. I've wanted that for a long time."

"I thought it was only me. I thought I'd go out of my mind when I gave you that first massage…and—"

"Really, then?" Sheridan raised her head, gazing into Lark's eyes, which burned with an amber glow.

"Yes." Lark wrapped her free arm around Sheridan and pulled her close. "You're extraordinary, and I've ached to touch you—like this. I know it's wrong. Unprofessional. Unethical. And I've never felt, or done, anything like this before." Lark pressed her cheek against Sheridan's shoulder. "Oh, God, the way you make me feel—"

"Show me." Sheridan's throat was dry from her being so hot and aroused.

"You sure?"

"Show me," Sheridan repeated, trembling all over.

"Mmm…yes." Lark rolled Sheridan over onto her back, stared down at her, and smiled, her cheeks a deep red. Slowly, Lark ran the tip of her tongue along her upper lip in an obvious challenge. "Like this." She lowered her head and took Sheridan's mouth in a simple, but powerful kiss that sent new floods of moisture between her legs. Sheridan wanted to rub her legs together, to harness her arousal before she ignited and went into orbit, but focused on Lark instead.

Sheridan found she only had to focus on Lark's incredible softness as their hands roamed up and down each other. Sheridan wanted to cup Lark's breasts, but something, shyness or a feeling that it was too much too soon, kept her from taking their mutual exploration further.

Lark seemed more trusting, more open, and she nuzzled the curve of Sheridan's breasts with her nose, pushing the fabric out of the way.

"Lark. You drive me crazy," Sheridan gasped. "You're like fire."

"I am?" Lark didn't raise her head, but slowed her caresses. "Yes, I think so. Your fault. All your fault."

She spoke so tenderly that Sheridan hugged her firmly and kissed her with the same determination as she answered, "Let me hold you. I just need this, to hold you and feel you against me—"

"Hello? You gals all right?" A male voice tore through the silent house. "Hello?"

"Damn it," Sheridan muttered under her breath. "Yes. We're fine. We're here. Staying warm." Sheridan didn't have to push Lark off her. She had withdrawn the second Burt's voice echoed through the room.

He showed up in the doorway with a flashlight in his hand. "The missus was worried that y'all couldn't cope on your own. You seem fine though." He looked at them under his dripping baseball cap. "Something I can do for you?"

To Sheridan's dismay, Lark snuck out of the bed, her voice not quite steady as she replied. "No, that's all right. Sweet of you to ask, but you shouldn't have ventured out in this weather."

"I can take the dog off your hands, at least."

"No," Sheridan said from the bed, hoisting herself up against the pillows. "We've just started to make progress. I don't want to lose the connection."

Burt looked as if he didn't quite follow but nodded amicably. "All right. Well, Cora will be glad when I tell her you're okay."

"Thanks. The storm can't last forever."

"Bye, then." Burt touched his cap in a cordial gesture and walked toward the front door.

Lark looked at Sheridan, her hands restless as she tugged at her fingers. "I should make sure all the windows are closed. The worst of the thunder seems to have passed."

"Lark…" Sheridan raised her hand, not sure what to say.

"I'll be back in a few minutes. All right?" Lark's pleading expression pierced through Sheridan's residual arousal.

"All right. Hurry back." Adding those last two words made Sheridan feel vulnerable, and she tried to hide her openness by straightening the blanket and pushing at the pillows behind her.

Lark's features softened, and she leaned forward and placed one knee on the bed. As she ran her hand along Sheridan's arm, she smiled faintly. "I'll hurry back."

As Lark left, with Frank right behind her, Sheridan tried to understand what had happened between them. Clearly the attraction was mutual, but there was more. Sheridan knew what great integrity Lark possessed, and the fact that Lark was attracted to a patient and acted on her feelings had to be huge. Sheridan wondered how she herself had gone from being sensitive and listening, to horny and ready to tear Lark's clothes off in a matter of—minutes? If Burt hadn't interrupted them, Sheridan knew they would have been undressed by now and making love.

At least that's what she thought, but Lark's reaction to the interruption suggested more complicated emotions. Perhaps Lark's sense of duty and responsibility had surfaced once she had time to think. Or was she just looking for understanding and empathy, never meaning for their physical intimacy to escalate like it had? Sheridan sighed and wanted to hide under the blanket and not have to decipher Lark's expression when she returned. This uncharacteristic reaction startled her. Sheridan Ward never hid from anything life threw at her! *Or does she?* Wasn't that what she was doing here, at the lake? Or in the old days, before the illness, when she had used her bachelor den in the center of Austin as a refuge, wasn't that hiding?

Sheridan tossed a pillow across the room, groaning at her futile reasoning. All she really wanted was for Lark to come back so they could either continue what they had started or talk so she knew they were okay. She felt lonelier and colder than ever, and only Lark's presence could remedy her ache.

CHAPTER NINETEEN

They here yet?" Sheridan asked and looked up from her laptop.

Lark couldn't speak at first. Sheridan sat by the window in the rustic living room, and the sun shone in on her from the side, highlighting her chocolate brown hair and adding a golden streak to her silver-gray eyes. Her skin seemed transparent and her pale pink lips so tempting, Lark had to close her hands into tight fists so she wouldn't rush over and kiss her. They hadn't gone as far as they had the evening of the big electrical storm, but they had shared lingering touches and snuggled on the couch by the fireplace more often than Lark could count. *Cozy.* That was the only word to describe it. And the underlying, hot feeling that something could ignite at any given time persisted. Lark couldn't look at Sheridan's long neck without wanting to shower it with kisses and love bites.

"Fiona called from the car. They'll be here in ten minutes."

"Good. That gives me the perfect excuse to chuck the laptop for a while. I'm stiff from typing all day." Sheridan rolled her shoulder and grinned.

"You stiff, huh. Let me help you." Lark circled Sheridan and put the laptop on the desk. Feeling her hands under Sheridan's collar, she examined the muscles that led up to her neck and frowned. "You're beyond stiff. You need a massage."

"I know, but it'll have to wait until your family's gone. It'll take longer than ten minutes."

"Ah, but you don't know how fast I can be." Lark leaned forward and to the side so Sheridan could see her.

"You can be quick, eh?" Sheridan blinked. "Well, I suppose that's a good trait—sometimes."

Lark laughed, a tad breathlessly, and began to massage the taut muscles under Sheridan's silken skin. "Yeah, sometimes," she agreed. "I don't want any of your migraines to be for lack of care on my part, you know."

"Lack of care. Would never happen."

Sheridan spoke with a certainty that warmed Lark. "Thanks for the vote of confidence," she managed. "That kind of makes me glad to hear."

"Kind of?"

"No. Wrong words. Very much so."

"You're by far the most caring person I've met, so that's a no-brainer rather than a compliment." Sheridan glanced back at Lark over her shoulder. "Oh, boy, are you blushing?" She smiled broadly.

"Unexpected compliments, or no-brainers, as you put it, do that to me."

"Looks adorable." Sheridan winked.

"Hmm. Another cute kind of word." Lark tried to frown, but it was impossible not to laugh.

"*Mea culpa.* Just speaking the truth though."

"Ms. Ward, your guests are pulling into the driveway." Mrs. Johnson poked her head through the doorway. "I'll have welcome drinks, hot and cold, ready on the porch in a minute."

"Perfect," Sheridan said and turned to Lark. "We better greet them." She sounded genuinely enthusiastic, and Lark thought she looked as close as she would ever come to resembling a giddy child.

"Yes, come on." Lark walked next to Sheridan to the doors that led directly out from the living room to the wraparound porch. She saw her parents' minivan pull up in front of the building.

"Lark! Sheridan! So great to be here." Arthur grinned as he opened the side door and extended the ramp, making it possible for Fiona to guide her wheelchair out of the vehicle. "Here's someone who's eager to leave Boerne for a while."

"You got that right, Dad." Fiona laughed. "I love Boerne, but it can become a bit monotonous."

"Welcome, all of you. Any of the kids with you?" Sheridan asked, sounding quite hopeful.

"Yup," Doris said and emerged from the car. "We brought Sean and

Michael. When they heard you have a pool, we couldn't stop them."

"Good. I was hoping y'all would be interested in a dip, either in the pool or the lake."

"Hmm, the pool's good enough for me," Arthur said. "Not so much for open water, you see."

"You and me both," Sheridan muttered. "Fiona, it's great to see you. This house isn't as outfitted as yours, but it's fully accessible."

"I'll be fine," Fiona said. "I'm used to winging it. You should see me when I fly to any of my exhibitions. The gate attendants sometimes look like they're going to have a cow right then and there when I drive up to the gate. Probably wondering if they'll have to carry me."

"I bet. I haven't tried that yet. I've had to fly a couple of times, but I've gone in the company jet."

"Oh, I do want to get me one of those," Fiona pouted, then burst out laughing.

"Who else is coming?" Lark asked as she spotted a dust cloud at the far end of the road leading to the estate.

"No clue. Wait." Sheridan squinted and shaded her eyes. "I think that's Erica's car. She drives a Crossfire."

Oh, no. Lark's good mood plummeted. "Any special reason, you think?" *As in, is she coming to hog you for the rest of the day, to make you work?*

"I have no idea. I didn't hear anything beforehand. Here she is now."

Erica stepped out of the car, carrying a briefcase. Perhaps she read the expression on Lark's face very clearly because her first words to Sheridan seemed designed to reassure her. "I'm not here to create a problem. I just brought some urgent documents for you to sign. I see I came at a bad time. That'll teach me to do things on the spur of the moment."

"No, no," Sheridan said and held out her hand. "Let me introduce you."

As Sheridan did so, Lark exhaled, glad Sheridan didn't have to go back to San Antonio just yet.

"I can't believe it." Erica stared at Sheridan, her mouth half open.

"What?" Sheridan frowned.

"You—you remembered all their names. Just like that."

Lark had to cough to disguise the laughter that threatened to explode. Sheridan gave her a penetrating glance before she turned back to Erica. "I know. Weird, huh?"

"Maybe not." Erica shook hands with Lark's parents, then stopped at Fiona's electric wheelchair. "Nice to meet you, Fiona. What a lovely name."

Fiona looked up at Erica, and her smile faded for a moment, only to reignite in full force within seconds. "A little too old-fashioned for me," Fiona said with a faint blush. "But what can you do?"

"It suits you so well. "

"Oh." Fiona's smile widened and she laughed, the small, breathless laughter that told Lark that she was entranced and feeling shy at the same time.

"We have drinks ready on the patio." Sheridan motioned for everyone to move out there. "Mr. Johnson will fire up the grill soon, and Mrs. Johnson's the best cook you could imagine."

Once they were outside, Michael's face lit up. "Check out the pool over there, Sean. Grandma, can we change? Please?"

"Sure, why not. You won't let me off the hook until I say yes," Doris grumbled good-naturedly. "Let's go inside, guys." She disappeared back into the house with the two boys, guided by Mrs. Johnson.

"You have a fantastic place here." Fiona sighed and parked her wheelchair in the shade on the patio. "I could imagine living like this one day."

"Me too," Lark said, without thinking how her remark might sound. "I mean, I love the view and the solitude here. The grounds are so big that the nearest neighbor's more than a mile away."

"Quite a difference from where we grew up in Houston," Fiona said. "We had the cutest little house, but it was almost a townhouse, built so close to the neighbors' that they nearly leaned against each other."

"Well, you should know." Lark grinned. "You got stuck between our house and the neighbor's when you were four. I had to crawl in and coax you out."

"I was a chubby baby. You were a skinny, energetic little thing." Fiona stuck her tongue out and laughed.

Lark noticed that Erica, who had taken the seat closest to Fiona, followed her sister's every move.

"I was skinny because I chased you and the others around, trying to keep you in line." Lark grinned. "You were a handful, sis."

"I know."

"Your mom's always said that you were the most responsible, serious little girl in Texas," Arthur said. "A real mini-mom to all your sisters."

Lark shrugged, feeling a little self-conscious. "Don't make me sound like a total bore."

"Oh, nothing could be further from the truth. You're anything but," Sheridan said.

Lark hadn't realized that Sheridan had parked her wheelchair a little behind her.

"You're no bore. Trust me," Sheridan said as she wheeled forward and touched Lark's shoulder gently.

"I never meant that!" Arthur looked dismayed.

"I know, Dad," Lark reassured him.

"We've been grateful so many times that Lark's so calm and levelheaded," Fiona said. "I wouldn't be here if she wasn't. I...I..." She paled. "Oh, damn it."

Fiona's only mobile hand began to tremble. She clung to her armrest, and Lark knew she was counting backwards from a hundred, like she'd learned to do when flashbacks hit out of nowhere like this. Lark didn't want to add to the panic by rushing over to her, and Arthur didn't move either. Praying that Fiona would make herself snap out of it, Lark looked over her shoulder for their mother, but saw no sign of Doris yet.

"I can't...I can't seem to..." Fiona's eyes now filled with tears and her back arched in the chair.

"Hey. It's okay, Fiona. Just relax." Erica took Fiona's shaking hand in her left and placed the other on her knee. "Look at me. You're okay."

Lark was about to tell Erica that Fiona didn't like anyone to interfere, but her sister raised Erica's hand to her cheek and wiped at her tears with it. The movement was beautiful and endearing, and Erica kissed Fiona's temple.

"There you go. You're all right now. Just breathe and it'll go away." Erica cupped Fiona's neck under her long hair. "I used to get panic attacks when I was a teenager. You'll be fine. Trust me."

"I'll be damned," Sheridan breathed behind Lark. "Who would've guessed? Look at Fiona. Whatever Erica's doing, it seems to be helping."

"Never seen an attack avoided so quickly." Lark glanced at Sheridan. "You're right. Who would've guessed?"

The sound of the two boys running out of the house and crossing the patio to reach the pool area, followed by their slightly ruffled grandmother, broke the magical mood.

"Arthur, will you volunteer to watch them while they swim?" Doris asked and plopped down in a deck chair. "Just helping them change took most of my strength."

"Sure. I always volunteer, don't I?" Arthur chuckled and walked toward the pool.

Doris reached for a glass of orange juice, then looked searchingly at Fiona as she sipped it. "You all right, darling?" she asked as she placed the glass on the armrest.

"Yes. I'm fine," Fiona replied. That Fiona was still clutching Erica's hand didn't escape Doris's attention.

"So I see," Doris said slowly, but not unkindly. "Excellent."

A wonderful scent of grilling meat and vegetables spread over the patio. Lark relaxed back in the deck chair and watched her family, all the time conscious of Sheridan's presence next to her.

Sheridan ran her fingers up and down Lark's arm, twice, as if she sensed Lark's thoughts. "I like your family. A lot."

"I'm glad. So do I."

"Fiona's smiling again."

"I see that. I got nervous."

Sheridan squeezed Lark's hand out of sight of the others. "I know. But she's doing great now. Look at her. She has Erica eating out of her hand."

Lark giggled quietly at the last comment. It was true. Erica looked transfixed.

"Shows how much I notice about my employees," Sheridan huffed.

"What do you mean?"

"Surely you see why Erica's so interested. She's smitten."

Lark scrutinized the two women across the table. "You're right!"

she whispered. "But Fiona, she's not—"

Lark stopped talking when she looked over at her sister, who now boasted pink, glowing cheeks and sparkling blue eyes. Her dark hair flowed around her shoulders in a soft cloud, and she gestured emphatically as she spoke with Erica. "Actually, I don't know if she could find a woman attractive. She's never had either a boyfriend or a girlfriend, as far as I know."

"Then let's just see what happens. I may not have picked up on Erica's vibes," Sheridan whispered, "but I know she's a good person. Very patient."

"She would have to be, to work for you." Lark's grin turned into a giggle at the sight of Sheridan's surprise. "I speak from experience, you see." Lark wiggled her eyebrows. "I know what I'm talking about, and speaking of that, Erica and I would probably have a *lot* to talk about."

Sheridan leaned closer, a devilish gleam in her eyes. "There's just one thing you can't compare. I've never kissed Erica."

Lark couldn't help but blush, and as she did, she looked up and noticed Fiona watching her with something between helplessness and exhilaration in her eyes. *Oh, sis, I know so well how that feels. I do.*

❖

Sheri_star: Hey, long time no see.
Grey_bird: Been working, actually.
Sheri_star: Good for you. Happy with your new job?
Grey_bird: Yes, this new boss is much better.
Sheri_star: Guy or gal?
Grey_bird: Gal. Classy and very nice, once you get to know her. How about you?
Sheri_star: I'm in a bit of a bind.
Grey_bird: Oh?
Sheri_star: You remember the woman I fired. My PT?
Grey_bird: Sure.
Sheri_star: Well, believe it or not, we made out.
Grey_bird: What? You did? Oh, my.
Sheri_star: Exactly. It only happened once, really. But there's been lots of discreet touching, you know. In passing. And, God, the way she

looks at me.

Grey_bird: How does she look at you?

Sheri_star: Like she really cares.

Grey_bird: You mean, on a personal level?

Sheri_star: I think so. I hope so.

Grey_bird: Tricky situation. What do you want from this?

Sheri_star: I want to say that I don't know. But that's not true.

Grey_bird: Then tell me the truth.

Sheri_star: I want her. In the worst way. In my arms. In my bed.

Grey_bird: To keep or to get her out of your system?

Sheri_star: I'm not a predator, you know.

Grey_bird: Didn't say you were. From her POV, I'd imagine this is harder, though.

Sheri_star: How so?

Grey_bird: There are pretty strict ethical rules about what goes on between caregiver and patient. If anybody found out, it would hurt her professionally.

Sheri_star: Damn, I'm such an ass. I never even thought of that!

Grey_bird: That's why I asked. What's your intention?

Sheri_star: She should be the one who hears that from me first, don't you agree?

Grey_bird: Absolutely. Only meant to raise the question like a good chat-buddy.

Sheri_star: You really are. Thanks for listening to me.

Grey_bird: No problem. I'm all for happy endings.

Sheri_star: And your new lady boss, is she hot?

Grey_bird: *grin* Sizzling!

Sheri_star: Plan to make any moves?

Grey_bird: I don't think so. I might lose my job.

Sheri_star: Anybody would be lucky to have a girl like you.

Grey_bird: How can you be so sure of that?

Sheri_star: Because you remind me of her.

Sheri_star: Bird? You there?
Sheri_star: Bird?
Grey_bird: Yeah. I'm here. Something came up. Can we
          chat more another evening?
Sheri_star: Sure. Time to go to sleep anyway.
Grey_bird: Sleep well.
Sheri_star: You too.

Lark logged off, staring at the screen. "Because you remind me of her," she read out loud, her chest constricting. It would only be a matter of time before she slipped up, or Sheridan figured out what was going on. Lark covered her face with both hands and groaned. *I have to tell her.* But how?

CHAPTER TWENTY

Lark stretched and tried to work out the kink in her neck. She sat on the couch next to Sheridan, browsing through old family albums where Sheridan had pointed out pictures of a much younger Mrs. D and the Johnsons. Lark had felt the closeness and seen the now-familiar affection in Sheridan's eyes, which made her feel even worse for continuing her charade.

"Here are my mother and me, only weeks before she passed away." Sheridan pointed at a photo showing an emaciated, black-haired woman sitting on one of the deck chairs. A very young Sheridan knelt next to her with an arm around her shoulder.

"You resemble her a lot." Lark couldn't stop looking. She noticed something of the "angry young woman" about Sheridan, contradicted by the ocean of tenderness directed toward her mother.

"Her name was Amanda. Amanda Louise." Sheridan's voice was low, warm, and tinged with remorse. "I hope I helped make her last days somewhat decent. I ditched so many classes to be with her. I sat by her side at the hospital, slept in a chair by the bed, or simply held her. Toward the end, I couldn't do anything but hold her hand, she was in so much pain, but it was enough for her, she said. My father only came the last night of her life because I gave him an ultimatum."

"What did you say to him?" Lark leaned her head against Sheridan's shoulder and stroked her arm.

"I simply told him that if he didn't come to show his wife his love and affection for her on the last day of her life, he'd lose me too. He showed up and stood by the window most of the night, staring at her or the sky, but he was there, and I think she knew it."

"Poor man."

"What do you mean?" Sheridan stiffened.

"To be so afraid, so locked into his own fear. Your strength was obvious, your compassion too. His was trapped inside, and if you hadn't insisted, he'd have stayed in his ivory tower, unable to even try to reach out." Lark smiled sorrowfully. "Do I sound like some cheesy greeting card? I don't mean to."

Sheridan blinked several times. "No, no. You don't. You have a way with words, Lark. You make sense of things and seem to understand even the most unfathomable reactions."

"Perhaps because I went through so many contradictory feelings after Fiona's injury."

"How do you mean, contradictory?"

"I was angry, scared, and sometimes depressed, not to mention frustrated. Overwhelmed, also, by the protectiveness that welled up in me at the oddest times, regarding all of my sisters. I joined a karate dojo and managed to earn a blue belt. I knew my self-defense and karate skills wouldn't stop a bullet, but they made me feel less vulnerable and more in control."

"Ever had to use them?"

Lark shrugged. "One reason I didn't want to work in a private home any more was that I longed to have real workmates. You know. A lunchroom to eat in and the chance to focus on more than one patient, spread my care around a bit so it wouldn't all be so personal. And more than once, male members of the family I worked with thought I should include extracurricular duties on my schedule."

Sheridan gasped and stared at Lark. "You're kidding!"

"No."

"And...oh..." Sheridan suddenly looked flustered. "I haven't been much better, have I?" She pulled back while lowering her darkening eyes.

"Sheridan. No. Don't think that. Please!" Appalled at how the conversation had derailed, she pulled Sheridan's stiff body to her. "You're nothing like those guys. Not even by a long shot. Anything that happened between us, especially here by the lake, was completely mutual. I...I really care about you." It wasn't a declaration of love, but it was as close as Lark had ever come. She explored Sheridan's features for any signs that she understood.

"Mutual." It wasn't a question.

"Yes. Mutual." Lark pushed her jumbled thoughts away. All that mattered right now was to reassure Sheridan. She leaned forward, slowly, and brushed her lips against Sheridan's, feather light. "Mmm, mutual," Lark murmured against Sheridan's mouth. Parting Sheridan's lips, she slid her tongue just inside and explored the softness there.

Sheridan whimpered, a thoroughly sexy sound, stemming from the same helpless desire that permeated Lark. Not knowing if this was the last time she'd have the pleasure of feeling Sheridan pressed against her, Lark angled her head and deepened the kiss. Sheridan returned the feverish caresses and sucked Lark's tongue deeper into her mouth. Lark knew she'd never wanted another woman like she wanted Sheridan right then. They were both trembling, and Lark felt small drops of sweat run down her throat and between her breasts.

"I need to…touch you," Sheridan moaned. "You feel so amazing, so soft and sexy. I never meant for this to be wrong—"

"It isn't!" Lark said and moved up on Sheridan's lap, careful to not put all her weight on her legs. "It's fine. Better than fine."

"Better?"

Lark could sense Sheridan smiling against her skin. "Yes. Much better."

Sheridan bit gently on Lark's neck, painting wet, scorching traces along her skin with her tongue. "I'm glad. Very glad."

"How glad, would you say?" Lark smiled and tipped her head back. "Glad enough to take this up a notch?" She looked at Sheridan between her eyelashes. *If she locks those amazing eyes on me, I'll self-combust.*

"I'll take it anywhere you want." Sheridan played with a button on Lark's denim shirt. "I can't remember ever wanting anything this much. I have to look at you. I have to."

Lark raised her hands and unfastened the three top buttons. "Like this?" She glanced down and saw that Sheridan had an unobstructed view of the top curve of her breasts. She wore only a small sports bra, which pushed her breasts up and together.

"God, yes. But it won't be enough for long." Sheridan was breathing harder now. She ran her hand along the exposed skin, then slipped two fingers under the sports bra and barely grazed a nipple.

Lark couldn't look away from the expression of desire on Sheridan's face. Her cheeks were flushed and her white teeth glistened between her half-open lips.

"Then I may just have to do this," Lark breathed and undid one more button. "I don't want to disappoint you. If you want to see more, feel more...here." Lark tugged the shirt off her own shoulder and saw an immediate response in Sheridan's eyes.

"You're like gold. Your hair, your eyes, your skin." Sheridan ran her tongue along Lark's shoulders. "You're beautiful."

"So are you." Lark thought Sheridan looked like a goddess fashioned of silver and ebony. Her skin glittered as perspiration made it shiny. She tugged gently on the zipper of Sheridan's black hooded jacket, and Sheridan ran her fingers through Lark's hair as she tugged the zipper down, revealing a black top. Hard nipples poked the satin enticingly as Sheridan moved her arms.

Lark nuzzled the soft mounds through the fabric, teasing the nipples with her lips. "Mmm, you smell so good," she moaned. "I love how you feel."

"You too. You feel amazing. And it's been so long."

Lark looked up. "For me too. Too long, really, but I'm glad you're here, and I'm here. This—" She cupped Sheridan's breast through the fabric and kissed it gently. "This, you, are worth waiting for."

Sheridan sobbed, a nearly inaudible intake of breath that startled Lark.

"Sheridan?" She let go of her breast and sat up farther. "Hey, you all right?"

"Yes. No." Sheridan leaned her forehead against Lark's shoulder. "I'm okay. I just...I never thought there'd ever be anything like this. Again."

"You're gorgeous. That and a thousand other great things. Why wouldn't there be something like this?" Lark laced her fingers through Sheridan's disheveled hair.

"Because of that." Sheridan motioned toward the abandoned wheelchair. "Because I'm not the same person I was before."

"I think you are. The wheelchair aside, very little has changed. You're still the same Sheridan Ward."

"But I don't *feel* the same."

"That's just it. I didn't say that nothing had changed. But you know what I think?" Lark kissed Sheridan's trembling lips gently. "Your opinions and views of yourself have changed. You're still the daring, bright business tycoon, enterprising, smart...brilliant, even. But you feel different about yourself because you see other sides of yourself. I bet they were there before, unrecognized and unseen."

"You mean I've always been a weepy, mushy pushover?" Sheridan huffed, but a smile began to play on her lips.

"Probably. But you had to be strong, all the time, for your mother and, later, for your father as well."

"How do you know all these things?"

"I'm not saying that I know, but I'm good at guessing. Call it intuition. Going through all Fiona's trials with her, physically and emotionally, has made me aware of how we humans react to adversity. My education and experience fill in some of the blanks. And my heart says the rest, when it comes to you."

"Your heart?" Sheridan spoke quietly and seemed out of breath.

"Yes, I listen to my heart a lot. I follow my gut feeling. And, with you, that has been both the hardest and the easiest thing I've ever done."

"How so?" Sheridan slumped back in the couch, pulling Lark with her.

"You're pretty transparent regarding some things, but with others…you clam up."

"Not with you, do I? Not much."

"Not much, but enough to keep me guessing. And I don't want to guess. It makes me uncomfortable."

"I don't mean to." Sheridan smiled broader now. "But then again, I don't want to come across as too predictable."

"Predictable? I don't think there'd ever be a risk of that." Lark reached around Sheridan's neck with both arms and hugged her. "Sure you're all right? I don't want you to feel upset in any way."

"I am. I *am* fine." Sheridan returned the embrace. "But perhaps, as much as I dislike saying this, it isn't the time or the place…yet."

"I know you're right." Lark groaned. "But I don't like it."

"Neither do I. I just feel like we've shared so much, you know, deeply personal things, and I need time to digest them. Make sense?"

"Yes. I feel the same way." Lark willed her body to calm down. She didn't want this to be just about the overpowering lust and passion that simmered under the surface. She felt much more than that for Sheridan. And Sheridan might never forgive her for the chat sessions. If she made love with Sheridan and then was rejected, it would devastate her.

Sheridan kissed her again, lingeringly and with nearly as much passion as before. "I'll never be able to settle down tonight. I'll see you in my dreams."

"And we have an early morning tomorrow, driving back to San Antonio."

"Feels like we just got here."

Lark agreed. They'd spent six weeks at the lake, and the days had passed so quickly. They'd focused almost entirely on physiotherapy, and it was amazing how much progress Sheridan had made. She drove her wheelchair effortlessly up and down curves, even a few steps. With a little help, Sheridan could also manage to navigate an escalator. Her arms were toned and so was her abdomen, and her cardiac training had made it possible for her to actually race Frank with the wheelchair.

The dog was another budding success story. Frank had clearly found a new mission in life. He shadowed his owner most of his waking hours, circling her, probably hoping Sheridan would drop something or need his help some other way. He was affectionate toward Lark, as if he guessed he had her to thank for this new adventure, but mostly he worshipped at Sheridan's feet.

"So, back to the real world," Lark said slowly.

"You sound like you're not happy with that." Sheridan studied her. "Surely you don't think I'll bail on my training again?"

"No. Well, I hope not. Perhaps part of me fears that you'll be swept up by all the preparations for the stockholders' meeting."

"If I do, I give you the right to come and drag me away, literally."

Lark knew her smile showed some uncertainty. "I'll take your word for it. Speaking of dragging, let's call it a day."

"Good idea." Sheridan moved over to the wheelchair. "Frank probably needs to do his thing. I'll let him out the back door. You go on. I can manage on my own."

"You sure?"

"Yes. I think I'll sleep in the sweat suit. A bit cold, don't you think?"

"Actually, yes." Lark got up. "All right, see you tomorrow then. Bright and early."

"Yes." Sheridan took Lark's hand in hers. "Thanks."

Lark bent down and kissed Sheridan's forehead with a bittersweet, unsettling feeling.

CHAPTER TWENTY-ONE

The Tokyo office has faxed the...Ms. Ward, is everything all right?" Erica stopped inside the door to the office, her expression shifting from business-like to worried within a second.

"I'm fine. Thank you." It wasn't untrue, but the last week had been increasingly crazy. So many meetings, working lunches, and social gatherings, with hardly enough time for everything.

"Do you need anything more, besides the Tokyo documents?" Erica placed a stack of folders on Sheridan's desk.

"You know. I could use a latte, but, please, get something for yourself too. You've been here since seven this morning. Don't think I don't know that." Sheridan checked her watch. "Damn, it's already five-thirty. Lark's going to kill me."

"I can call her and let her know that you'll be late."

"Thanks, but I better do that myself, since I don't think I'll make PT tonight. Pity. I could have used the massage at least." Sheridan rolled her shoulders and winced when pain stung her neck muscles.

"It's the second time you're canceling since you've come back from the lake." Erica shook her head. "You're close to being in the dog house."

Sheridan had to laugh, since Erica had no idea how right she was. She'd actually had to cancel PT four times already, and even if Lark said she understood, it was clear that she was less than pleased.

Erica returned with the coffee, and Sheridan sipped it as she flipped open her private cell phone. She speed dialed Lark's phone and rapped her fingertips on the desk as she waited.

"Mitchell."

"Lark, it's me."

"Sheridan. How's your day been?" Lark's voice was noncommittal. Not a good sign.

"Busy. I told you it would be."

"I know. And I understand. I'm just afraid that you're burning the candle at both ends and that you'll undo some of your progress."

"That won't happen." Sheridan tried to sound reassuring, but her neck hurt badly.

"I hope not. I worry."

And I miss you. "If it was just about me, then I'd be home in a heartbeat. I have two more teleconferences to do, one with Tokyo and one with Cincinnati."

"It's already late. Guess I'll see you tomorrow morning then." Lark still sounded calm and friendly, which made Sheridan wonder if she was imagining her undertone of disappointment.

"I guess so." She ran a finger up and down the edge of her desktop lamp. "And Frank. How's he doing?"

"He's acclimatizing pretty well, actually. That's another thing. We need to keep up the connection between the two of you. Perhaps tomorrow morning once we've done the bar exercises."

"It's a deal." No matter what, Sheridan wasn't going to let work lure her into the office too soon. "Good night then, Lark, if I don't see you when I come home."

"'Night, Sheridan."

A click told Sheridan that Lark had hung up. She was usually happy to deal with concise people who didn't linger too long with good-byes, but she also knew that Lark wasn't normally abrupt.

Her cell phone rang and made her jump. Thinking it was Lark, she pressed the button eagerly. "Wanted to say good night one more time? Or be tucked in?"

"What? Hello? Is this Sheridan?" a vaguely familiar voice asked, sounding puzzled.

"Yes. Who is this, please?"

"This is Fiona Mitchell. I hope I haven't caught you at a bad time. I know you're busy with the stockholders' meeting coming up."

Sheridan straightened. "What a nice surprise, Fiona. No, you're not disturbing me. What can I do for you?" Sheridan assumed that Fiona hadn't called just to chat.

"I talked to Lark earlier today, and she's going to hate me for this, but I had to give you a call because I'm worried."

A sliver of something icy slipped down Sheridan's back. "Why? What's the matter?"

"Lark doesn't know that I'm calling, and I know she'll be mad at me, but I couldn't just sit idly by. So much is at stake for her, and she's my sister, you know."

"Sure."

"Here's the deal. I talk to Erica sometimes, your very nice assistant, since we seemed to hit it off when we visited your place. I know how busy you are and how insane your schedule is becoming, the closer you get to the meeting."

"True. There's a lot of work to do. Lark knows that, though."

"Yes, she does. And she's trying to not stress you out, but I know she's concerned."

"Has she told you that?"

"No," Fiona said slowly. "Not in so many words. And I don't want to go into detail… Damn, it's hard to explain without betraying a confidence. I just want you to try and see if you can be sensitive enough to read between the lines with Lark. It's not easy with her, because as fantastic as she is, she's good at shoving things under the carpet, emotionally. She's been hurt badly several times, but nobody knew until I weaseled it out of her. She's always heroic and thinks she has to carry the world on her shoulders. She takes the blame for everything."

"She's so much a caregiver," Sheridan agreed. "I don't think I've met anyone as selfless and altruistic. So what do I look for when I read between the lines? You can't let me go in blind, you know. I need something."

"Just listen, pay attention to detail, and have an open mind. And please know that there isn't a single calculating bone in Lark's body. She's always trying to do the right thing, and if she does anything that seems out of character, it's for the right reasons." Fiona's voice sank. "I can't say more than this, or I'd violate her confidence in me completely. Promise me that you'll hear her out if y'all ever have a run-in about anything? While this is pretty cheeky of me, I can't risk alienating you or angering Lark. I just feel this is important."

"And a tad confusing. Does this have to do with anything in particular? Something Lark's going to tell me?" Sheridan felt her heart sink.

"Yes. Perhaps. And please hear her out, okay?"

"Of course, I will." Sheridan couldn't imagine Lark saying anything that warranted a sisterly intervention like this. Unless…unless Lark harbored regrets when it came to their budding relationship. Sheridan drew an inaudible, deep breath. *Don't panic.* "Fine. I'll try to remember what you've said and do my best. Lark's been wonderful to me and deserves nothing less." Sheridan respected Fiona and was always in awe of how the badly injured woman could go on with her life with such optimism.

"Thank you, Sheridan. And there's one more thing. My parents are hosting an exhibition at the gallery the weekend after the stockholders' meeting. I know the business thingy isn't over by then, but you are most welcome to join us."

"Fantastic. What artists?"

"Just one. Me."

Sheridan was stunned. "You?"

"Yes. I paint, and this is my tenth exhibition. Usually they're pretty popular, so if you come the first day you might want to show up a little ahead of time."

"I collect local artists. How come I've never heard of you?" Sheridan was puzzled. She loved to browse local art galleries and find new treasures.

"You may have. I work under the name Mitchell Hirsch."

Lark Mitchell. Arthur Hirsch. Feeling utterly stupid for not connecting the dots, Sheridan groaned. "I don't believe this. I have two of your paintings. And one sculpture."

"That's wonderful," Fiona said, her voice warm. "I hope you enjoy them."

"I do. God, I can be dense sometimes. Mitchell Hirsch. I was under the impression that Mitchell Hirsch was a man—"

"That ought to do it. The mistake, I mean. Very understandable."

"I look forward to the exhibition. Thank you for inviting me."

"Thank you for taking what I said about Lark the way it was intended."

They hung up, and Sheridan sat with her hand clasped around the phone. Fiona's comments hadn't exactly told her what her misgivings were about. *Reading between the lines. Not my strong suit.* Not when it came to personal relationships. And her relationship with Lark had gone from professional to personal so fast she was overwhelmed.

"You ready, ma'am?" Erica poked her head through the doorway.

"Sure." Sheridan put her cell phone on the desk and wheeled toward the conference room where her department heads waited. Perhaps Lark would be awake when she got home so they could talk more. She missed her.

❖

Lark knew she was being childish by hiding. She heard Sheridan come in, but didn't leave her room to say hello. Blaming her absence on the fact that it was almost midnight, she turned in bed and tried to find a comfortable position. Part of her wanted to pad over to Sheridan's bedroom and make sure she was all right, but she knew she wouldn't.

Her conscience was plaguing her, and it also kept her from putting Sheridan on the spot about their training sessions. The fact that Sheridan had so easily fallen back into old patterns, and spent at least twelve hours at the office every day, was reason enough for Lark to put her foot down. However, she couldn't. She'd betrayed Sheridan already, even if she'd had the best of intentions, and she had no right to ask anything of her. No right to cash in on any promises that Sheridan had made.

Lark's stomach churned and she turned on the nightstand light. Her laptop sat ready to be switched on. Hesitating for only a few seconds, Lark pulled it onto her lap and pressed the power switch. It didn't take long to access her chat software. Lark had hardly spoken to Sheridan this way since she'd come back from the lake, but somehow she craved the connection right now.

> *Grey_bird:* You around, Sheri_star?
> *Sheri_star:* You bet! Just got home and bathed. Feel like a
>   new person.
> *Grey_bird:* You're tired?
> *Sheri_star:* Beyond tired. But important things happen in
>   a few days, so better stay on top.
> *Grey_bird:* So how are you doing?
> *Sheri_star:* I'm back from the lake, but I don't feel quite…
>   back. Yet.
> *Grey_bird:* Sorry to hear that. What can I do to help?

Sheri_star: Nothing, I guess. Well, it's always nice to chat with you, but I need to fix things on my own.

Grey_bird: How's the PT going?

Sheri_star: Oh, God. I won't get any brownie points for that. I've hardly had time since we settled back in here.

Grey_bird: Your physical therapist happy with that?

Sheri_star: Hardly.

Grey_bird: And how do you feel about it? You were so excited about the training only a week ago.

Sheri_star: That was then. The circumstances at my summerhouse were close to utopia. I just don't know how to get back into the swing of things. At least not until after the major event that's coming up.

Grey_bird: I'd think you need to prioritize.

Sheri_star: I suppose. That's just it, though. I can't put the stockholders last. They're just as instrumental to the business as the employees. They need to come first.

Grey_bird: And you? Surely you're just as important. To the business and the people around you.

Sheri_star: Hey, it's me you're talking to. You should know better than to use platitudes like that.

Lark stared at the screen, unprepared for the annoyed words. Despite her best intentions, she was aggravated, and she tugged the laptop closer.

Grey_bird: That was uncalled for. I'm trying to understand and be supportive.

Sheri_star: To me it feels like you're trying to push me into a mold where I don't fit. I'm not the average cozy type that needs reassurance and pats on the back constantly.

Grey_bird: I don't think that's what I was doing. I was trying to point out that taking care of yourself is important too. And a selfless act.

> *Sheri_star:* That doesn't make sense. Being selfless for me is to put the company first. To honor my inheritance.
>
> *Grey_bird:* That's bull. That's absolute bull. There's no one in your family, dead or living, that expects you to kill yourself in order to keep the business happy. I don't believe that for a minute.
>
> *Sheri_star:* You don't know anything about me, or my family, really. You don't know what it means to be the fourth generation in a highly prominent and successful family.
>
> *Grey_bird:* You know, you really can be quite full of yourself. What on earth are you talking about? I may come from slightly humble beginnings, but I'm well aware of your world, and how it works. And as for successful and prominent, I know what it is to live up to expectations.

Lark was furious now, and a cold lump of ice in her stomach continued to grow.

> *Sheri_star:* You do. Yes, of course. Well, I don't see how this is going to help anything. We'll just end up angrier if we keep chatting.
>
> *Grey_bird:* So you quit. Like you always do.
>
> *Sheri_star:* You don't know what I always do.
>
> *Grey_bird:* I know how you think! You were the one who called me a closeted flirt, remember?

There was a moment of no communication, when Lark's heart hammered, no, roared in her chest.

> *Sheri_star:* Actually I didn't say that to you.
>
> *Grey_bird:* Yes. You did.

More cyber silence, drawn out, which made Lark's fingertips grow icy cold.

Sheri_star: No. I joked with her about that. Lark.

Oh, my God. Lark sobbed, dryly and painfully.

Sheri_star: How could I be so fucking stupid? Bird. Grey_bird. Lark.

Clinging to the laptop, Lark shivered as chilling beads of sweat formed on her forehead. It was impossible to move her frozen fingers.

Sheri_star: I guess I don't have to wonder any more. Your silence speaks volumes.

Forcing her fingers to move, Lark stared back and forth between the screen and the keyboard, panicking, aching, and hardly breathing.

Grey_bird: I can explain.
Sheri_star: Sure you can.
Grey_bird: I can. It may not be good enough, but I can.
Sheri_star: Well, Bird, I don't want to hear it.
Grey_bird: Please. I know you're mad and you have every right to be. But please. Can I come over?
Sheri_star: I don't think that would be wise right now.
Grey_bird: Will you let me explain here then?
Sheri_star: I'm logging off now.
Grey_bird: No! Please!

Sheri_star has left the conversation.

CHAPTER TWENTY-TWO

Sheridan slammed down the lid of her laptop. Her hair was still wet after the shower, and she shivered in her robe as she pushed herself farther up on the bed. Lark's betrayal, her out-of-the-blue devious attempt to…do what? Fly under Sheridan's radar? Fish for useful information, to use how? Tears of fury clung to Sheridan's eyelashes, but she refused to let them fall. *Was this what Fiona referred to?* Sheridan doubted it. This was by far much more serious than a "run-in."

A knock on the door made her gasp aloud.

"Sheridan? Can I come in?" Lark asked, her voice low and short of breath.

"Go away." Sheridan's throat hurt.

"We have to talk."

"We've talked enough. More than enough."

"Please. Let me explain. Let me in."

"I said, go away."

To Sheridan's dismay, the door opened and the dim light from the corridor fell into her bedroom. "You just do what you want, no matter what, don't you?"

Lark rushed up to Sheridan's bed and fell to her knees next to it. "Please, just hear me out."

"Do I have a choice?" Sheridan felt bitterness curl the corners of her mouth. "It's not like I can dash out of here, is it?"

"I was desperate to reach you. You shut me out when I began to work here, and I wanted to get to know you. I wanted to be able to find my way to you, to help you any way I could. You know there's something between us, something more than just physical therapist and patient. I just wanted…to help, to see you through this time…like I did. Eventually." Lark sobbed in short bursts.

"And when did you plan to reveal your little plot? When, Lark? When I admitted in the chat to my new *buddy,* Bird, just how fantastic, sexy, wonderful, caring, and *loyal* my physical therapist is, and how I couldn't even imagine facing any more days of my life without her?" Sheridan wanted to scream the words, but they came out as menacing growls. One by one they tore through her vocal chords, sliced through the air, and hit Lark.

Gasping for air, Lark put her hands up, palms forward. "No! I never meant for it to come to this!" She leaned forward, her hands now on the bedspread. "I wanted to see if I could find out why you were stonewalling me like you did. There was no obvious reason for it, other than your own fear. I wanted to know how deep that ran, so I could help you erase it, help you become independent and trust that you had a future."

"Trust?" Sheridan hissed and scooted sideways. "You cannot possibly talk about trust when it comes to how you lied to me. When I came groveling back to you, that day in Boerne, and you took me into the midst of your family, your very wonderful family, I was humbled by how you rose to being the bigger person. If I had known then, what I know now—"

"—then you wouldn't be as strong as you are, as fit as you are."

"Or as screwed!" Sheridan leaned forward and captured Lark's chin between her thumb and index finger. "You thoroughly screwed me over, and nobody, *nobody*, does that to me and lives to tell about it. Ever." She lowered her voice to a cold purr that her employees had learned to fear. "You're cute and sexy, that's true. You're obviously good at your job. It doesn't make sense that you'd stoop to such an insane plan in order to coax information out of me…unless it wasn't about my health at all, but something entirely different."

Lark blinked and a frown marred her forehead. "What are you talking about?"

"If you really got under my skin, you'd be able to find out things that might prove valuable to—just about anybody."

"What?"

"Industrial espionage comes in many shapes and forms."

The expression on Lark's face, even before she spoke, dispelled any such notions for Sheridan. "Sheridan! I admit I was wrong. I was dishonest and I wish I could take it all back. I never meant to hurt you, or us, and I want all this to just go away, to recapture the feeling we had at the lake. But never, ever, have I acted in a criminal way. I'm no industrial spy. I wouldn't know what to do with that information, and we never talk business. Online or otherwise. You *know* that!" Lark was visibly shaking, trembling from head to toe.

"I know." Sheridan did. This was personal. Hurtful and deeply personal. "We have the stockholders' meeting coming up in a few days. I can't afford to lose any ground when it comes to my physical endurance. We have to work together, and train, these last few days. We don't have much time, and in retrospect, the less time we spend together...the better." Sheridan sighed and turned on her side. "Go to bed, Lark."

"Sheridan—"

"Just go."

Perhaps it was the finality in her voice that made Lark quit objecting. Sheridan heard her rise.

"All right. See you tomorrow morning," Lark said without expression, which didn't help alleviate the pain.

Sheridan heard the door click shut, and she groaned into the pillow. The next few days were going to be hard. Worse, they were going to be heartbreaking.

Lark's fingers trembled as she pressed the speed dial for her sister. "Fiona?"

"Lark? What's up?" Fiona answered sleepily.

"Sorry to wake you. I need to talk to someone, someone who knows. Damn, I fucked up."

"Oh, Lark. She found out. Or you told her?"

"She guessed. I slipped before I had a chance to find the courage to tell her. Oh, God, Fiona. She's furious. And devastated."

"That's a good sign."

Lark tugged the pillow closer. "What? What can possibly be good about it?"

"She's devastated because she really cares about you. If she didn't, she'd be furious, fire you on the spot—again—and be done with you. Did she fire you?"

"No. Not in so many words. She wants me to keep working with her until the shareholders' meeting. After that I'm history, probably. She hates me."

"And you love her." Fiona's tender words made Lark break down at last.

"Yes. Yes." Lark hugged the pillow close and pressed her cell phone tight against her ear. "I messed up so badly, Fee. I thought I had more time to help her understand. I thought if I could just explain at the right moment, when all the pieces of the puzzle fit…then she'd understand."

"I know, Lark. I know. It just doesn't work that way. Life's idiosyncrasies interfere, and rarely do so in our favor." Fiona spoke quietly, her clear, bright voice unusually low. "But all isn't lost, sis. She's hurt and offended right now, and she has every right to be. You have to acknowledge that and give her time. As hard as it seems, this wasn't an unexpected reaction, was it?"

Lark knew Fiona was right and had no problem imagining how she would have acted, if the situation had been reversed. "I know," she said huskily. "You're right. Of course you're right."

"Try to sleep. I know it sounds like a cliché, but things could look very different tomorrow."

Lark doubted it. Sheridan's low growl, so disgusted and yet so devoid of feelings, still rang in her ears. "I'll try."

"Give me a call tomorrow. Anytime, really."

"Okay."

"Lark, sweetie, don't give up on Sheridan yet. This is as bad as it gets. Trust me. She just might surprise you."

"She hates me."

"No, she doesn't. She may hate what you did. She may even hate feeling like a prize fool. But I find it very hard to think that she could hate you." Fiona sounded so sure. "We'll talk more tomorrow. Try to relax and go to sleep."

"You too."

"Sure. 'Night, 'night."

"'Night."

Lark curled into the bedcovers and buried herself in the small pit she'd created with the pillows. The room was completely dark, except for the dim green light from her cell phone. She had kicked her discarded laptop under her bed, wanting the damn thing out of her sight. Lark had no idea how she'd make it through tomorrow, but knew she would, no matter what it cost her. She wasn't going to leave in disgrace or resign for some after-the-fact contrived reason. *But facing her will kill me. Over and over.*

❖

"God almighty. What's going on, Sheridan?" Mrs. D stopped on the threshold to Sheridan's study. "You look like hell." The unusual outburst from Mrs. D made Sheridan glance up, knowing full well that her smile was nothing more than a pained grimace.

"That obvious, huh?"

"You could say that."

"Well, I don't want to talk about it. Is everything packed? I want to leave for the hotel directly after work tomorrow." The stockholders' banquet would take place at the Marriott River Center Hotel, and Sheridan knew from experience that staying at the hotel saved both time and energy. *Especially now.*

"Everything's ready. All you have to do is show up and do your thing."

"Did you reserve a room for Lark?" Just saying her name out loud made Sheridan's scalp prickle.

"Yes, I did. She'll have a room on the same floor as you, a few doors down. Good enough?" Mrs. D raised an inquisitive eyebrow as she walked up to Sheridan.

"Yes. I might need her…services."

"And something is definitely the matter, Sheridan. You look like a nervous racehorse as soon as you say her name. Did the two of you have another fight?"

"You could say that."

"Don't tell me you're thinking of firing her again?" Mrs. D looked alarmed. "She's good for you. In more ways than one."

"I used to think that too. Guess I'm not perfectly correct all the time. What a bummer." Sheridan didn't like the bitterness in her voice, but it seemed impossible to pretend that everything was all right.

"Goodness, what happened?"

"I don't want to talk about it."

"Whatever it was, it can't be worth throwing her out in the cold again, can it?"

"I won't have to. I'm sure she'll quit as soon as the stockholders' meeting is over."

"And where does that leave you—or Lark?"

Sheridan pinched the bridge of her nose. "God damn it. I have no idea. If I did—" She shrugged.

"You wouldn't sit here looking like a ghost." Mrs. D folded her arms. "Listen. Whatever has happened, and I'm not going to snoop, I still think Lark is the best thing that ever happened to you. If she made a mistake, or if you did, please, just think twice. That's all I ask." She stepped closer and ran a quick hand through Sheridan's hair. "I hate to see you so unhappy, honey."

The term of endearment, uttered with Mrs. D's usual matter-of-fact tone, nearly made Sheridan crumble. She caught her hand and held it briefly against her cheek. "I know. Thanks."

"And do you promise?"

Sheridan closed her eyes hard and forced her breath to become even. "Yes."

"Good." Mrs. D walked toward the door. "I think it's important."

The door closed behind her, and Sheridan pivoted on her chair, looking out into the garden. The sun poured down on the vast lawn, and something to the far left caught its rays. Moving closer to the patio doors, Sheridan saw reflections of light and squinted through the scorching sunlight. Lark was sitting with Frank near the patio railing, their two golden-brown heads close together. Sheridan pushed the patio door open and wheeled outside. The heat, so familiar and so scorching, washed over her, and she inhaled the familiar scent of home. She glanced at Lark and Frank again and frowned when she noticed how Lark was clinging to the dog. Sheridan rolled closer, her wheelchair soundless on the patio tiles.

"Frankie…oh, damn, damn, damn…"

Lark was crying, sobbing like a child into Frank's fur. The dog seemed to endure being on the receiving end of Lark's tears with a remarkable calm. Feeling like a Peeping Tom of the worst kind, Sheridan was about to wheel back to her study when she heard Lark speak again. Against her better judgment, she stopped with her hands still resting on the wheels.

"It's all messed up, Frank. I can't stand how it…is…and I can't make…it…right. She hates me. And I don't blame her…" Lark pressed against the dog, and Sheridan could barely hear her words. "I don't want to be here, but I can't let her down again. It hurts so bad to be around her. I just want to go home."

When Lark's tormented words seared her, Sheridan swallowed repeatedly. She managed to turn the wheelchair around and go back inside, unable to listen any more. She looked over her shoulder, but neither Lark nor Frank seemed to have heard her. Sheridan doubled over when the pain behind her eyelids sent flashes before her eyes. Four more days. They would leave for the hotel tomorrow morning and get ready for the opening banquet, and that meant keeping a cool appearance for the rest of the weekend. Surely she could pull that off. Sheridan sighed and straightened up. But from what she'd just witnessed—could Lark?

CHAPTER TWENTY-THREE

The faint whispers died out gradually as Sheridan began her solitary journey up the aisle between the round tables. Some of the luncheon guests at the luxurious hotel obviously didn't know whether to look away or stare openly at her.

Her gray eyes dared all the people present at the stockholders' banquet to pity her. She propelled her wheelchair through the vast ocean of people, her back ramrod straight and a half smile on her firm lips. She wore her hair in large locks swept back from her face, which looked deceptively devoid of makeup. Dressed in a Saville Row black suit over a silver gray shirt, she appeared immaculate.

Lark waited in the wings by the head table, cursing everyone who gawked at Sheridan. *Don't they realize how hard this is for her? Why the hell did she have to make her usual entrance?* But Lark knew why. True to tradition, Sheridan, like her father and grandfather before her, opened the yearly stockholders' meeting by hosting a banquet for all major participants. Tradition also meant "marching past the troops" as the Wards had always done. *I wonder how many even tried to dissuade her. I know I did, and she bit my head off.* Lark shuddered at the memory. Sheridan had merely stared disdainfully at her, a scornful eyebrow raised to make it clear to Lark that she was way off base.

The banquet was the opening point for a week of events, crowned by the Ward Enterprises Inc.'s stockholders' meeting. Sheridan's personal staff had prepared for this event for months, and in a way it was liberating to start the show. Lark sighed in silent relief as Sheridan approached the head table, managing the ramp without problems before she elegantly circled the long, elevated table and wheeled to her seat in the middle. The two men who flanked her rose quickly, looking quite forlorn since there was no chair to hold out for her. Sheridan parked the chair and engaged the brakes. "By all means, take a seat, gentlemen."

Sheridan turned around and nodded briefly to the man by the door who controlled the electronics. He turned down the dimmer, which threw most of the Grand Ballroom into semi-darkness, and directed a spotlight on Sheridan.

It didn't matter that Sheridan couldn't use her legs anymore; she was every bit the president of Ward Enterprises and commanded the audience with a mere glance as she began her welcome speech in a clear voice. Her face illuminated by the stark light, its shadows and planes emphasized, left no one uncertain who ruled the show.

Lark sighed inaudibly. It broke her heart to realize how much she was going to miss Sheridan.

❖

"Ladies and gentlemen, stockholders, senior employees, welcome to the yearly stockholders' conference here at the Marriot River Center Hotel. I am honored to be here before you, after a year of great financial success, as well as amazing discoveries and inventions created by Ward Industries' scientists. This year I have invited representatives for all groups of employees, no matter their duties, since I've learned we can't function without each other."

Sheridan paused for a few seconds to allow for the surprised glances around the room and the murmurs to die out.

"I also want to take this opportunity to thank everyone who sent cards and flowers, and who called to wish me a speedy recovery. As you can see, I'm here, thanks to modern medical science, as well as the people around me who supported me. The Ward dynasty lives on, and together we will greet the future with all the amazing things it entails.

"Let me first tell you about an exciting new development, a new medical research facility we are about to build in Louisiana…"

Sheridan kept talking, looking at her notes only a couple of times. She was inspired, driven by her rampaging emotions as well as a desire to prove herself, to show every potential doubter in the audience that she was back in charge.

Briefly, the image of Lark flickered by, and Sheridan nearly stumbled on her words, correcting herself at the last second. She refrained from gazing over at the far left where she knew Lark was observing her performance. Just knowing Lark was there, no matter their ruined relationship, was reassuring.

"I look forward to this upcoming year, with the discoveries and successes ahead waiting to be enjoyed," Sheridan concluded. "This year has been challenging on a personal level, but devoted employees have kept Ward Industries on its course during my brief absence. This means that the company is strong, and its culture healthy. And that, ladies and gentlemen, is all that really matters."

Thunderous applause hit Sheridan in wave after wave, energizing her. She knew her speech was much like a returning conqueror's, and obviously the audience thought so too. Her eyes burned with unshed tears as the people at the tables closest to the head table rose, followed by the ones behind them. The standing ovation lasted for at least a minute. Sheridan drew a deep breath, as if she were inhaling the feeling of victory. This was it. She'd been struggling so hard for this moment and now she was back. Swallowing her unshed tears, Sheridan forced a broad, triumphant grin onto her lips. She *was* back, but under the euphoria of success simmered a persistent feeling that the achievement was devoid of true happiness.

❖

Sheridan kept a half-smile on her lips throughout the banquet, knowing very well how her once-so-statuesque frame appeared to others now, after her illness. Fighting to remain upright, although she admitted the defiant posture killed her back, she moved the wheelchair skillfully between the tables toward the exit. Where the hell was Lark? She'd remained close throughout the event but was nowhere in sight now.

"Here I am." As if on cue, Lark showed up at Sheridan's side and placed a bottle of water in her hand. "And here you go. You didn't eat much, and you didn't drink anything."

Glaring at Lark, Sheridan grudgingly admitted she was right. "Thanks." She studied Lark over the bottle as she drank and noticed signs of fatigue. Her normally golden eyes were definitely dull brown, and her naturally pink, full mouth was pressed into a straight line. "You okay?"

"I'm fine. I can tell it's time to go." Lark didn't attempt to push the wheelchair, which was impossible anyway since it had no handles on the back. She merely stepped toward the exit, and Sheridan was about to follow her when something hit her in the head from behind, making her drop the bottle in her lap where the water ran freely across her pants. "Shit!" The word escaped Sheridan's lips before she managed to clench her teeth around it. Raising a hand, she felt the back of her head while she pivoted the wheelchair with the other.

Lark whirled around, taking in the situation in a second. "Sheridan!" She rushed forward, removing her employer's hand from her head. "Let me look. What happened?"

A woman standing close by stared at them in horror. She was holding a square purse, with hard metal edges. "I'm terribly sorry," she gushed. "I was adjusting my shawl, and… Oh, Ms. Ward. What can I do to help?"

Realizing it was an accident and not an attack, Sheridan began to calm down. She looked in dismay at her lap. *Damn, it looks as if I peed in my pants.* "Nothing, thank you. I'm quite all right." Her lips felt stiff as her annoyance still flared.

"You sure?" Lark's low voice, followed by soft fingers in Sheridan's hair, made her suddenly forget everything else.

"Yeah. Let's get out of here."

Lark nodded and withdrew her hand from Sheridan's hair, and the loss of the careful touch left Sheridan feeling robbed of something vital, even life-sustaining. Irritated at her dramatic thoughts, she nodded toward the woman with the purse before she wheeled out the ballroom doors. "You have the key?" she asked Lark.

"Sure."

In the elevator, Sheridan leaned back in the wheelchair and looked at Lark. She was dressed in a cream, tailored, sleeveless dress, with a simple string of pearls around her neck. Her hair shone like dark copper. *First I was a bitch for weeks, and now this last big fight…no wonder she's had enough.* Sheridan tried to disregard the stab of panic. *And who am I kidding? I was always the company bitch.* Still, watching Lark's tired face, her normally rosy cheeks so pale and the smooth forehead now wrinkled, bothered Sheridan. The loving, free, and devoted Lark she'd known at Lake Travis barely resembled this strained woman.

"Let me check the back of your head," Lark said when they had reached the suite. "That was one mean-looking purse. Sharp edges."

"All right." Sheridan refused to acknowledge how much she liked the touch of Lark's hands in her hair. For so many months, only health-care professionals had touched her. And then Lark. Another pro, sure, but…she was Lark.

Lark carefully parted Sheridan's hair in several places, examining her scalp. "There's a small bump. Looks like she didn't manage to break the skin, at least. Thank God." Lark sighed.

Turning the wheelchair, Sheridan caught one of Lark's hands, obviously startling her. "You still want to talk?" she asked, her voice stern.

To her alarm, tears welled up in Lark's eyes, clinging to dark brown eyelashes like perfect diamonds.

❖

Despite the fact that her vision was distorted by tears, Lark saw the look on Sheridan's face change into an expression close to fear. She involuntarily stepped back, her nerves too raw to endure a closer inspection.

"Answer me." Still demanding, Sheridan now sounded almost breathless.

"I can't…" Lark held up a hand. "I honestly can't. I tried the other night. I thought I could explain, but I…I don't know what I could say that would fix things." This wasn't what she'd planned. A formal letter of resignation lay in her briefcase. It was the only right thing to do.

"What do you mean?" Sheridan growled, her fists rolled up and rigid in her lap. "I thought you wanted to talk, to explain."

Lark refused to answer and stared at her hands. The black fabric clung to Sheridan's legs, reminding Lark why they'd hurried to the suite. "You need to change. What do you want to wear?" She turned to walk into Sheridan's bedroom.

Snaking out faster than any reptile, one of Sheridan's strong hands caught Lark's wrist. "Just a robe. And you're not off the hook. You owe me an explanation."

Lark stopped briefly. "Later. You're soaked."

In the bedroom, Sheridan slid over from the wheelchair onto the foot of the bed. Lark moved in front of her. Kneeling, she undid Sheridan's shiny black shoes and tugged them off carefully while

Sheridan undid her own trousers and Lark reached around her, ready to pull the trousers down as Sheridan lifted her weight by pressing her palms against the bed. After she pulled off the wet piece of clothing, Lark hung it neatly over the back of a chair. "You can manage now, right?"

"No. Stay." Sheridan was clearly still giving orders.

"All right. What else can I do?"

Sheridan sucked her lower lip in between her teeth. "Is there a limit to what you would do?"

"As long as it's in my job description, no." Lark's heart began to hammer in her chest.

"Smart answer. But then you're a smart woman, aren't you?"

"What do you mean?"

Sheridan smirked, sitting with her elegant, long legs bare; they didn't appear painful and immobile at all. "Your job description is pretty arbitrary, isn't it? You're supposed to meet any of my needs. You even lied and went behind my back to meet my needs, right?"

Lark's breath caught in her throat. "I can't do this anymore." The words came out staccato, Lark's emotions burning through her like wildfire. "I failed you. I failed as a professional. I sacrificed my principles in several ways because…because I thought I had to. And no matter what I say or do, I can't take it back. I can't undo it!" Lark flung her hands in the air. "I don't see the point in extending the pain any longer, for either of us. I quit."

The silence between them seemed to stop the world.

❖

Sheridan's heart bled. She knew the phrase was a cliché and such things didn't happen unless you suffered a coronary, but that's how she felt. Life seemed to leak from her heart because Lark was going to leave. The dream was over and the last drama now a moot point. "When?" Sheridan's voice hardly carried the short distance between them, which equaled an oceanic vastness.

"According to our renegotiated contract, I can leave with two days' notice. I would have liked to give you longer to find a replacement, but…I just can't stay on like this. But with the salaries you pay, you shouldn't have any problem finding someone."

Flinching, Sheridan heard the unspoken words. Lark didn't have to continue. *With my not-so-winning personality, it will be a nightmare.* "Why not leave right away? Why wait?"

Lark seemed to calm down. "You need help. I know you're capable of fending for yourself, but these upcoming days will be tough. I'm sorry…I shouldn't have let myself get drawn into this conversation now." She took one step closer. "Let me help you with the robe—"

"No. I'll manage. Leave me."

Hesitating, Lark regarded her and a range of emotions—regret, sadness, and possibly anger—flickered over her sensitive features. Sheridan wondered if she should at least be pleased that among all those feelings, none registered as pity.

As Lark left the room, Sheridan slumped to the side and hid her face against the coarse fabric of the bedspread. *More loss. Can I cope? Can I?* She stayed in that position for a few minutes, breathing deeply to regain control, before she sat up and unbuttoned her jacket and shirt. She pulled them off and tossed them carelessly on top of the damp pants. Not wearing a bra, she pulled the robe toward her and moved from side to side to wrap it around her body.

Sheridan pulled herself up against the pillows. As she took one and held it close to her stomach, she closed her eyes to try to ignore the physical pain, as well as the emotional torment. *Her hands. Why do Lark's hands contradict what she says? When she touches me, it's as if she can't stop herself, as if she wants to.* Sheridan tried to rouse the anger, but couldn't. Instead the hurt blazed through her again. From day one, Lark was always so professional and loyal. When everyone else among Sheridan's staff either didn't know what to say or do, or behaved as if Sheridan had not only lost the use of her legs, but also her brain, Lark's calm personality was like soft cotton against raw nerve endings.

Sheridan refused to let the pain take over. Instead she kept her eyes closed and the pillow pressed against her chest. Burying her face into its softness, she willed herself to relax. If she just could sleep some… Drowsily she floated in and out of a fretful dream state.

"I don't want to leave. I have no choice."
Careful hands pulled the pillow from her arms, wrapping her in

a soft embrace. "The truth is ... I never wanted to leave you in the first place." The hands made slow circles on her back. "You're all that matters to me. My heart's breaking, and I can't even tell you face to face."

Sheridan moved toward the warmth, the hands, but couldn't open her eyes. She tried to speak, but failed. No words, not a sound, came from her lips.

"You did your best to test me, to drive me away, and now I can't see any other solution than to grant your wishes." She felt a soft kiss on her forehead. "But, before I go, I want something."

Desperate to ask what, Sheridan moved restlessly in the tight embrace--still wordless, soundless.

"I want something to remember. I want a piece of your heart to take with me."

Sheridan tossed her head back and forth, frantically trying to communicate with the beloved voice. Finally she broke free, drew a deep breath, and called out a name.

"Lark!"

CHAPTER TWENTY-FOUR

Lark leaned against the backrest of the couch and examined the envelope that held the end to her life in Sheridan's presence, turning it over and over between her fingers. So much had happened between them, and her decision to quit, rather than have Sheridan fire her again, hadn't been easy. A small part of her kept trying to be optimistic, and its accompanying voice spoke of the closeness, the tenderness, and the fun they'd shared at the lake. The thought of never holding Sheridan close again, never feeling her pulse race with Lark's own, provoked pure, white-edged pain.

Groaning, Lark squeezed the envelope, inadvertently wrinkling it as she tried to pry her mind away from her agonizing thoughts. One weekend, two more days, and this experience would be over. She'd go home to Boerne and spend a few weeks there, perhaps help out with the gallery and work with Fiona some more. And then?

Lark shrugged inwardly. It didn't seem important what she did after that. Her work was important to her, but right now, she had no desire to find another job. She had enough put away not to have to work for years. Maybe it was time to go on a prolonged sabbatical. Travel, maybe. Lark sobbed, but turned the sound into a cough, determined not to fall apart. Not yet.

"*Lark!*" The outcry from Sheridan's bedroom was bloodcurdling.

Lark flew up from the couch and dropped the envelope on the floor as she ran toward the bedroom. Flinging the door open, she stopped on the threshold and stared at the woman on the bed.

Sheridan was crushing a pillow against her chest, her upper body shaking as she was obviously trapped in a nightmare. *About me?*

"Lark! No!" The strangled groan propelled Lark toward the bed.

Tears streamed down Sheridan's pale cheeks, the firm, curvy mouth trembling.

"Sheridan! It's just a dream. Wake up." Lark took her by the shoulders and shook her gently. "I'm here. I'm here now."

"No more…" Sheridan was still trapped in her private hell.

"I'm here. Sheridan, it's Lark. You're safe."

Nothing seemed to reach the shivering woman.

Lark embraced her firmly, unable to witness such torment. She held Sheridan tight, rocking her. "Shh. You're okay now." Then she heard a deep breath from Sheridan and suddenly a profound stillness. Lark stopped rocking, but didn't let go. She buried her face in Sheridan's damp locks, expecting a terrible eruption for having the audacity to offer consolation.

"Lark?" The husky whisper was such an anticlimax, Lark almost laughed.

"Yes."

To Lark's astonishment, Sheridan raised one arm and wrapped it around her waist. "I'm sorry." The scent of fresh soap and the faint musk-based perfume Sheridan used filled her senses. Lark tried to focus on what Sheridan was saying, but all she could think was how *good* and *right* it felt to hold her.

"I know." Lark kissed Sheridan's hair. "I'm sorry too."

"For what?" Sheridan pulled back enough to squint up at Lark.

"For destroying your day of triumph, the day you showed everyone that you're back in charge and back to stay. You worked so hard for this."

Sheridan pulled free and rolled away from Lark, whose empty arms ached. *Nothing's changed. She still loathes me.*

Patting the pillow next to her head, Sheridan gave a tired smile. "Won't you lie down with me, Lark?"

❖

Lark's eyes turned a brilliant gold "What?"

"Please, don't make me ask twice." Sheridan held her breath while she studied Lark's cautious expression. Lark, so strong, capable, and often surprising, looked at her with obvious apprehension.

"All right." Lark kicked off her pumps and lay down. "Here goes."

"So it does." With a contented sigh, Sheridan let her eyes roam freely. Lark's dress revealed more than she thought Lark realized right now. The top, where one part of the front overlapped the other and gave the illusion of a generous décolletage, fell apart, revealing a cream lace bra holding firm breasts.

Sheridan drank in the sight unabashedly. *So luscious. Like velvet and satin.* Farther down, the skirt of the dress had ridden up her slender thighs, showing off naked, long legs. No stockings. *Oh, my.*

"What's wrong?" Lark's eyes were a darker golden color now. "You don't have nightmares normally, do you?"

"Sometimes I do," Sheridan confessed. She had fantasized, spent many nights, awake or asleep, imagining and dreaming. *Of you. Just like this. And then losing everything. Just like this.*

"I'm sorry." Lark's troubled eyes roamed over Sheridan's body, and her soft, pink mouth smiled sadly.

"There's a remedy for all this," Sheridan said huskily. "There *is* something you can do to help me lose my nightmares and stop the pain. However, I'm afraid it's not mentioned in your job description."

"Then tell me anyway," Lark whispered. "Let's just say I'm off duty right now. I've gone home."

Home? Sheridan closed her eyes briefly. "Kiss me."

Lark flinched visibly. Her lips trembled, and she stared at Sheridan with something resembling panic.

Sheridan, in turn, was filled with dread. *Oh God, oh God, I was wrong. I take it back. Please, I take it back.* The horrified litany never made it past Sheridan's lips.

Suddenly, in a flurry of movement, Lark was on top of Sheridan, pressing her mouth on hers. Gasping, Sheridan parted her lips and let Lark's tongue inside to probe and taste. Finally able to engage her arms, Sheridan pulled Lark closer and kissed her deeper, ravaging the mouth so willingly attached to her own.

Finally breaking loose, Sheridan gasped for air, then pressed her greedy lips onto the skin she'd studied only moments before. She tugged at Lark's dress and pushed the top of it down, then gasped when she realized she'd inadvertently trapped Lark's arms in the process. Not above using this advantage, Sheridan slowed down and stared hungrily at the heaving chest before her. The lace bra strained over firm breasts.

"Let me?" Sheridan looked at Lark. A two-second pause almost stopped her heart from beating.

Lark raised her chin and arched against Sheridan. "Yes."

Sheridan latched onto the left nipple, gently biting and sucking it through the lace, and reveled in the whimpering sounds of pleasure that came from Lark. Impatiently, she pushed the bra up and revealed two hard nipples, as hot pink as ripe raspberries. Sheridan licked them, nibbled and chewed them. She couldn't get enough. When they were finally too raw for even a puff of air, she helped Lark completely out of the top of the dress and released her arms.

Lark unhooked her bra and tossed it on the floor. She gazed at Sheridan with a devious expression in her eyes, then suddenly reached up and slid the robe off her broad shoulders.

❖

Sheridan's dark brown nipples pebbled and awaited her touch. Lark didn't know where she found the courage, but she pushed the terry-cloth robe open all the way down. Sheridan wore lace boxers, and Lark stared at the triangular shadow beneath the flimsy fabric.

"You like what you see?" Sheridan asked hoarsely.

Her mouth watering, Lark could only nod. She'd seen Sheridan undressed many times before. *Never like this, never so vulnerable and strong at the same time.* "You're beautiful." Her own voice startled her into action. Leaning forward Lark took a taut nipple into her mouth and sucked it lingeringly, increasing the pressure on it until Sheridan cried out.

"Oh. Oh." Sheridan pushed herself off the bed and farther into Lark's mouth. "I've needed this…you…so much. For so long. Damn you." She was sobbing now.

Lark pinched the abandoned nipple as she moved on to the other, biting it, lavishing attention on the puckered skin with her tongue. Grunting, Sheridan obviously tried to remain in control of her raging desire, but failed.

"No!" Sheridan's hands shot out, and she grabbed Lark by the shoulders before she rolled them both over. Ending up half on top of Lark, Sheridan kissed her deeply, probing every part of her mouth.

As her heart thundered, Lark surrendered. She knew the built-up energy between them—the lust, the fight, the overwhelming emotions—was all going to come crashing down at this instant. It didn't matter anymore how the hurt and anger had plagued them. All that counted right now was the flurry of emotions that wouldn't be denied any longer. Lark knew Sheridan was going to take her.

❖

The soft fabric of Lark's skirt lay bunched up in a ring around her waist. Sheridan's eyes burned at the sight of the silk and lace underneath. *Don't shred them. Careful now.* She moved down the bed, grateful for all the training that allowed her to move as effortlessly as she did. Nuzzling Lark's panties, she reached up under the skirt and found the waistband, then tugged at it.

Lark raised her hips and allowed Sheridan to remove her underwear. Sheridan groaned quietly as she pushed the garment down silky smooth legs. Lark surprised her by willingly kicking them off when Sheridan couldn't reach any farther down, then spreading her legs slowly, in a gesture of trust and surrender.

Sheridan moaned aloud this time and knew she couldn't turn back. She had to have Lark, even if it was only this once. *Mine to have, this one time.* She had to take what was offered and use it well, or she'd go insane. As she maneuvered her body in between Lark's toned legs, she inhaled the special scent that was a bit flowery, but mostly all Lark. Soft, downy hair, trimmed but not shaved, didn't manage to hide the damp folds, swollen and slightly separated, underneath.

To Sheridan's amazement, Lark reached down and used both hands to part them farther. "Please. Touch me." There was anticipation in Lark's voice.

Please? Is she crazy? Doesn't she know how much I need her? Want her? Sheridan rested on her elbows and let her tongue skim along the wet sex. Avoiding the protruding bundle of nerves, she licked and tasted every part of Lark, making her whimper and shiver—long, reverberating shudders that shook the bed.

"No, no, no! Take me!" Lark cried out when Sheridan had enjoyed her taste for minutes that seemed like an eternity. "You owe me. You owe me for all the pain, of what I had to do…all this time when I fought my principles, my feelings for you…forbidden fruit…" Tears streamed down flushed cheeks. "You owe me, damn it!"

Startled, Sheridan tried to grasp what Lark was saying. *I owe you, do I?* She couldn't think clearly. As she flattened her tongue against the trembling clitoris and coaxed it farther out, Sheridan could think of only one thing. Lark was going to come, and come hard. And it was going to be because of her, Sheridan.

❖

Lark soared. She climbed toward the orgasm, sometimes almost having it within her reach, but it eluded her time after time. She groaned and spread herself farther, making more room for the woman between her legs.

"Sheridan," she groaned. "It hurts. I need to come."

"Yes. It's time."

Lark felt Sheridan move to the left, then several of her fingers pressed against her and moved inside, filled her up, while the skilled tongue massaged her clitoris.

"Sheridan!" The convulsions hit without any warning, and Lark clenched her teeth as her body arched off the bed. The prickling needles of pleasure erupted from her sex, spread through her system, throughout her legs and abdomen, in wave after wave. She was filled with sorrow, yet she was undulating willingly under Sheridan, whose fingers still took her. *This is it. This is what I'll have to remember, to take with me. This one moment.*

Her fingers still inside, Sheridan hauled herself up along Lark's body, her robe half on, half off. "You're amazing. You're wonderful." Her voice was a strange mix of fury and reverence, and Lark buried her face against the damp skin of Sheridan's neck.

"Is it over?" she managed.

"No. Touch me," Sheridan replied darkly.

As a dying woman gaining reprieve, Lark pushed her right hand between their bodies and moved her fingers in between Sheridan's legs, underneath the boxers. The molten heat and copious wetness made her gasp, and without thinking, she pushed on and went inside. Feeling immediate flutters of an impending orgasm, she used her thumb to circle Sheridan's large, swollen clitoris.

With a strangled sound, Sheridan pressed her cheek against Lark's shoulder as deep sobs shook her tall frame. Tears seeped from her eyes and ran down both their cheeks, mingling with sweat.

"You're close," Lark murmured. "You're…close."

"Yes!"

Lark felt the flutters inside Sheridan turn into waves, which in turn built up to oceanic convulsions that tugged at Lark's own body and sent her across a second precipice. As she heard the heartbreaking cries from Sheridan, Lark closed her eyes, knowing they moved toward the end. She carefully withdrew her hand and instead wrapped both arms around Sheridan. "I don't want to leave."

❖

Sheridan lay resting against Lark's shoulder. Her heart rate was slowing, as was her breathing. Her mind, however, was whirling as she examined Lark's words. *She doesn't want to leave. Or was that lust speaking?* The faint tremors inside Lark defied that last worry.

"Why?" Sheridan asked.

When Lark didn't reply, Sheridan realized she would have to take the next leap of faith. "I don't want you to leave me either. I want you to stay."

"Why?" Lark repeated Sheridan's question.

Fair enough. Digging deep into the recesses of what remained of her courage, Sheridan raised her head and, looking up into the marbled eyes, saw nothing but guarded kindness. "I can't imagine my life without you. No matter what we said or did the last few days. I just can't."

Lark's eyes turned a softer brown. "Anyone can help you with the PT."

"Yes, I know that."

"So why do you want *me* to stay?"

"I…" Sheridan closed her eyes briefly. "Because you reach me like nobody else can. I still have questions about why you chatted with me under false pretenses, but when I realized that my anger over that couldn't match my anguish over you leaving—"

"What do you mean?" Lark was apparently not beyond prodding for an honest answer.

Resentment flashed for a second and made Sheridan tighten her grip around Lark. "This, damn it! The way you touch me. How you don't let my fucking body turn you away…turn you *off*, for that matter." Her voice sank into a husky whisper. "With you, I feel like I can be well again, whole again, even if I'll never walk."

Lark smiled, a tremulous movement of lips. "You mean a lot to me."

Is she staying? Barely able to breathe she pushed on. "And?"

As Lark's warm hand cupped Sheridan's cheeks, it sent the message even before she spoke. "If you truly want me to stay, I'll have to mean more to you. More than your assistant." She raised her head and brushed her lips across Sheridan's. "All the time I've worked for you, I've felt as if I belong here. Even some of your other employees have commented on it. It tore me apart when you were the only one who couldn't see it. I struck up a chat conversation with you because I wanted to get to you, know you, and not entirely for selfless reasons. I was attracted to you from day one. It was so hard to see your pain. I wanted to do everything to help you."

"I see," Sheridan whispered. *Oh, God, I could have lost her.* "I do."

"Can you forgive me for lying to you? It wasn't easy for me, and I promise I won't do it again."

"I believe you." Sheridan held Lark close against her and let her hands roam the skin on her back.

"Thank God." Lark kissed her again. "My heart's been shattered since Thursday."

"I know. Mine too." Lark felt small kisses against her neck. "I don't want to lose you."

"You won't. Oh, God, darling." Lark twisted in Sheridan's arms and kissed her. "How could I ever leave you? I love you."

Stillness. It was so quiet that Lark was sure she ought to be able to hear Sheridan's heartbeats. She held her own breath not to miss a thing.

"I love you too." Sheridan spoke in a barely audible whisper as she pulled the discarded robe around them both. "And I've been in so much pain, and pain makes me mean."

"I'm sorry I went behind your back. It was wrong, no matter how good my motives were."

Lark's straightforward words, her willingness to take all the blame and not make excuses, were like soft wool around Sheridan's bruised heart. "I forgive you. And I'm sorry too. Forgive me for being such a callous bitch. I do need to be taken down a notch or two sometimes."

"Not true." Lark caressed Sheridan's back repeatedly in languid movements. "You just need someone to care for you and make you feel loved and accepted. Like the rest of us, really."

"And could you?"

"Be the one, you mean?"

"Yes."

"I want to be that person for you." Lark kissed Sheridan's neck. "I want to be the one to love you, care for you, and wake up next to you. And I'm greedy. I want you to be that one for me too."

"I'd like that." Sheridan captured Lark's wandering mouth with hers. Returning the kiss, Lark curled up against Sheridan, who felt safe and content as they snuggled under the robe.

Sheridan knew they still needed to talk about some things, but for now she was relieved and relaxed enough to sleep. She heard Lark yawn, a funny little squeaky sound that made her smile.

"Don't let go," Lark whispered and buried her face against Sheridan's neck.

"I won't. Ever."

Their breathing had gone from labored, after their lovemaking, to slow and regular, since they were on the verge of sleep. Sheridan knew her nightmares wouldn't reoccur. Not with Lark right there, holding her like she was the most precious woman in the world.

EPILOGUE

This is amazing, Fiona!" Sheridan looked up at the large painting in the center of the exhibition. "When did you do this?"

"I finished it two days ago. It's one of my best." Fiona spoke with a confidence that Lark hadn't heard before.

Lark gazed at the painting and wanted to express how it had torn at her heart as soon as she saw it, but she couldn't find the words. The painting radiated such love and tenderness that Lark had to swallow repeatedly to keep from bursting into tears. Fiona had painted a moment in Lark and Sheridan's life: Lark knelt next to Sheridan's wheelchair and tied her shoestrings. Her face was turned up, and a world of love and adoration shone from her face as she looked at Sheridan. Sheridan, in turn, was depicted with strong brushstrokes, her beautiful face in profile as she leaned forward, one hand around the back of Lark's neck.

They had sat like that so many times, for different reasons. Lark thought back on the week after the banquet, a hectic, crazy week during the days—and a gloriously passionate week during the evenings and nights. Sheridan had insisted that Lark move into her bedroom, openly, and Mrs. D's nearly tearful reaction to that change had at first startled Lark, until she realized Mrs. D's tears were those of joy.

"How are you doing, honey?" Arthur asked from behind them.

Lark turned and circled his waist with her arm, not taking her eyes off the painting as Arthur squeezed her shoulders.

"Fiona's broken new ground, hasn't she, Daddy?"

"I think we can safely say that she'll sell it all, and the critics will eat out of her hand after this."

"She deserves it." Lark glanced around her at the paintings, everything from indigenous plant life to people and landscapes. There were even a few sculptures, painstakingly made out of clay with Fiona's one good hand.

"And she's happy. For you. And for herself." Arthur motioned toward Fiona. "Erica's part of that reason."

"Who would've guessed?" Lark murmured. Tall and blond, Erica stood next to Fiona and greeted the art connoisseurs who formed a long line outside the door. Fiona kept glancing up at Erica, and Erica in turn constantly touched Fiona's hair and shoulders.

"Neither of us took into consideration her sexual orientation or her desire for romance," Arthur said with a sigh. "I suppose we were too busy making sure she was physically as healthy as possible."

"I fell into that trap too. I'd pour my heart out over loss and betrayal, and she never said anything. God, how blind can we be? And then she painted this extraordinary portrait of Sheridan and me."

"Don't beat yourself up. Your mother said these exact things to Fiona yesterday, and you know, she said that she'd given up on having anyone remotely interested in her, in her life, years ago."

Lark winced. "But still—"

"I know, honey."

"Lark, are you all right?" Sheridan wheeled up, a concerned frown on her forehead.

"Yes, I'm fine. Just taken aback by this painting."

"You like it, right?" Sheridan asked, searching her eyes.

"I love it. It almost makes me cry, though. So much love and understanding between us, and for us."

"Glad you see it that way. I just bought it."

Happy, but not surprised, Lark kissed Sheridan. "If I didn't love you already, Sheridan, saying that out of the blue would've sent me over the edge."

"Hey, don't want you falling off any edges, Bird." Sheridan raised an elegant eyebrow.

The use of the online nickname sent thrills through Lark, who wrinkled her nose back toward Sheridan. "Too late. Been there, done that."

"Done what?" Fiona asked, next to them.

Lark smiled at her. "Fallen in love."

"And it suits you. Never seen that glow before."

Lark stole a glance at Erica, who stood just behind Fiona. Elegant and composed, she looked as protective as any of Fiona's family members. "And am I wrong to assume that you're glowing too, sis?" Lark asked Fiona. "You have that certain…something."

"Oh, please." Fiona pursed her lips and took Erica's hand. "No such cheesy comments, please. I'm an artist, I'm paid to glow."

They all laughed, and Lark knew she'd never been this happy. *Nervous, true. But happy.*

"Sheridan, Sheridan, can Frank come out in the backyard with us?" Michael's young voice pierced the gallery crowd.

"Michael! No running in here." Doris hurried into the gallery after her enthusiastic grandson.

"Please, Sheridan?" Michael leaned over the armrest of Sheridan's wheelchair and hugged her clumsily. "I can train him how to play baseball with you."

"You can? That sounds fantastic." Sheridan ruffled Michael's dark hair. "Doris, it's all right. They can play with Frank. It's actually good for him to socialize as much as possible."

"Thank you!" Michael dashed out of the gallery before his grandmother had any opportunity to caution him again, slaloming between the customers and art critics.

"You're sweet to the kids, Sheridan. Thank you." Lark's sister turned to hurry after her son, muttering under her breath as she left, "Three children. I must've been out of my mind."

"Want to go watch them play?" Lark asked.

"Yes, let's make room for more of those eager people waiting outside." Sheridan turned to Fiona. "Thank you, for the lovely portrait. And for helping Lark not give up on me."

Fiona nodded slowly, her eyes darting back and forth between them. "You're most welcome, Sheridan. I should say the same thing. Thank you for Erica."

Lark looked back over her shoulder as she and Sheridan made their way to the private entrance to her parents' house. Her mother and Arthur stood with Fiona and Erica, and there was something so right, so happy, in how they interacted with each other. Lark hoped Fiona would find bliss like she had, to help erase some of the bad memories. Or not erase, perhaps, she corrected herself. Perhaps help to learn to live with the bad memories.

When they passed the empty kitchen Sheridan stopped in front of her. "You look thoughtful."

"I was just pondering something you said to me, something that means more to me than anything in the world." Lark knelt next to Sheridan and wrapped her arms around her.

"What? And when?"

"When we made love for the first time, you said something so unexpected, it's been on my mind a lot this week. It nearly makes me cry."

"Then please quote me, but I don't want to make you cry."

Lark buried her face into Sheridan's shoulder and inhaled her musky scent. "You said, 'The way you touch me. How you don't let my fucking body turn you away...or turn you *off*, for that matter. With you, I feel like I can be well again, whole again, even if I'll never walk.'"

"It's all true."

"I've never loved anyone like I love you." Lark kissed Sheridan softly. "Ever."

"I don't think I've loved anyone, period. Not since mother died. But you...I love and adore you." Sheridan coughed and held Lark close. "So what do you think? Should we go out there and show the kids how baseball's really played?"

Lark threw her head back and laughed. "Just what these kids need, a healthy dose of competitiveness!"

"Come on." Sheridan wheeled through the house and out the patio doors to the backyard. She stopped and pivoted as soon as she crossed the threshold, her eyes twinkling. "Let's go play, Bird."

About the Author

Gun Brooke, two-time winner of a Golden Crown Literary Award, lives in a small Viking era village in Sweden. Cheered on by family and friends, she writes full time, both romance and science fiction. Gun also creates digital art and is proud to provide her first cover for her sixth novel, *Warrior's Valor, Supreme Constellations Book Three*, coming from Bold Strokes Books in 2008.

Books Available From Bold Strokes Books

Wall of Silence, 2nd ed. by Gabrielle Goldsby. Life takes a dangerous turn when jaded police detective Foster Everett meets Riley Meideros, a woman who isn't afraid to discover the truth no matter the cost. (978-1-933110-90-5)

Mistress of the Runes by Andrews & Austin. Passion ignites between two women with ties to ancient secrets, contemporary mysteries, and a shared quest for the meaning of life. (978-1-933110-89-9)

Sheridan's Fate by Gun Brooke. A dynamic, erotic romance between physical therapist Lark Mitchell and businesswoman Sheridan Ward set in the scorching hot days and humid, steamy nights of San Antonio. (978-1-933110-88-2)

Vulture's Kiss by Justine Saracen. Archeologist Valerie Foret, heir to a terrifying task, returns in a powerful desert adventure set in Egypt and Jerusalem. (978-1-933110-87-5)

Rising Storm by JLee Meyer. The sequel to *First Instinct* takes our heroines on a dangerous journey instead of the honeymoon they'd planned. (978-1-933110-86-8)

Not Single Enough by Grace Lennox. A funny, sexy modern romance about two lonely women who bond over the unexpected and fall in love along the way. (978-1-933110-85-1)

Such a Pretty Face by Gabrielle Goldsby. A sexy, sometimes humorous, sometimes biting contemporary romance that gently exposes the damage to heart and soul when we fail to look beneath the surface for what truly matters. (978-1-933110-84-4)

Second Season by Ali Vali. A romance set in New Orleans amidst betrayal, Hurricane Katrina, and the new beginnings hardship and heartbreak sometimes make possible. (978-1-933110-83-7)

Hearts Aflame by Ronica Black. A poignant, erotic romance between a hard-driving businesswoman and a solitary vet. Packed with adventure and set in the harsh beauty of the Arizona countryside. (978-1-933110-82-0)

Red Light by JD Glass. Tori forges her path as an EMT in the New York City 911 system while discovering what matters most to herself and the woman she loves. (978-1-933110-81-3)

Honor Under Siege by Radclyffe. Secret Service agent Cameron Roberts struggles to protect her lover while searching for a traitor who just may be another woman with a claim on her heart. (978-1-933110-80-6)

Dark Valentine by Jennifer Fulton. Danger and desire fuel a high stakes cat-and-mouse game when an attorney and an endangered witness team up to thwart a killer. (978-1-933110-79-0)

Sequestered Hearts by Erin Dutton. A popular artist suddenly goes into seclusion; a reluctant reporter wants to know why; and a heart locked away yearns to be set free. (978-1-933110-78-3)

Erotic Interludes 5: Road Games eds. Radclyffe and Stacia Seaman. Adventure, "sport," and sex on the road—hot stories of travel adventures and games of seduction. (978-1-933110-77-6)

The Spanish Pearl by Catherine Friend. On a trip to Spain, Kate Vincent is accidentally transported back in time...an epic saga spiced with humor, lust, and danger. (978-1-933110-76-9)

Lady Knight by L-J Baker. Loyalty and honour clash with love and ambition in a medieval world of magic when female knight Riannon meets Lady Eleanor. (978-1-933110-75-2)

Dark Dreamer by Jennifer Fulton. Best-selling horror author, Rowe Devlin falls under the spell of psychic Phoebe Temple. A Dark Vista romance. (978-1-933110-74-5)

Come and Get Me by Julie Cannon. Elliott Foster isn't used to pursuing women, but alluring attorney Lauren Collier makes her change her mind. (978-1-933110-73-8)

Blind Curves by Diane and Jacob Anderson-Minshall. Private eye Yoshi Yakamota comes to the aid of her ex-lover Velvet Erickson in the first Blind Eye mystery. (978-1-933110-72-1)

Dynasty of Rogues by Jane Fletcher. It's hate at first sight for Ranger Riki Sadiq and her new patrol corporal, Tanya Coppelli—except for their undeniable attraction. (978-1-933110-71-4)

Running With the Wind by Nell Stark. Sailing instructor Corrie Marsten has signed off on love until she meets Quinn Davies—one woman she can't ignore. (978-1-933110-70-7)

More than Paradise by Jennifer Fulton. Two women battle danger, risk all, and find in one another an unexpected ally and an unforgettable love. (978-1-933110-69-1)

Flight Risk by Kim Baldwin. For Blayne Keller, being in the wrong place at the wrong time just might turn out to be the best thing that ever happened to her. (978-1-933110-68-4)

Rebel's Quest, Supreme Constellations Book Two by Gun Brooke. On a world torn by war, two women discover a love that defies all boundaries. (978-1-933110-67-7)

Punk and Zen by JD Glass. Angst, sex, love, rock. Trace, Candace, Francesca...Samantha. Losing control—and finding the truth within. BSB Victory Editions. (1-933110-66-X)

Stellium in Scorpio by Andrews & Austin. The passionate reuniting of two powerful women on the glitzy Las Vegas Strip where everything is an illusion and love is a gamble. (1-933110-65-1)

When Dreams Tremble by Radclyffe. Two women whose lives turned out far differently than they'd once imagined discover that sometimes the shape of the future can only be found in the past. (1-933110-64-3)

The Devil Unleashed by Ali Vali. As the heat of violence rises, so does the passion. A Casey Family crime saga. (1-933110-61-9)

Burning Dreams by Susan Smith. The chronicle of the challenges faced by a young drag king and an older woman who share a love "outside the bounds." (1-933110-62-7)

Fresh Tracks by Georgia Beers. Seven women, seven days. A lot can happen when old friends, lovers, and a new girl in town get together in the mountains. (1-933110-63-5)

The Empress and the Acolyte by Jane Fletcher. Jemeryl and Tevi fight to protect the very fabric of their world: time. Lyremouth Chronicles Book Three. (1-933110-60-0)

First Instinct by JLee Meyer. When high-stakes security fraud leads to murder, one woman flees for her life while another risks her heart to protect her. (1-933110-59-7)

Erotic Interludes 4: Extreme Passions ed. by Radclyffe and Stacia Seaman. Thirty of today's hottest erotica writers set the pages aflame with love, lust, and steamy liaisons. (1-933110-58-9)

Storms of Change by Radclyffe. In the continuing saga of the Provincetown Tales, duty and love are at odds as Reese and Tory face their greatest challenge. (1-933110-57-0)

Unexpected Ties by Gina L. Dartt. With death before dessert, Kate Shannon and Nikki Harris are swept up in another tale of danger and romance. (1-933110-56-2)

Sleep of Reason by Rose Beecham. While Detective Jude Devine searches for a lost boy, her rocky relationship with Dr. Mercy Westmoreland gets a lot harder. (1-933110-53-8)

Passion's Bright Fury by Radclyffe. Passion strikes without warning when a trauma surgeon and a filmmaker become reluctant allies. (1-933110-54-6)

Broken Wings by L-J Baker. When Rye Woods meets beautiful dryad Flora Withe, her libido, as hidden as her wings, reawakens along with her heart. (1-933110-55-4)

Combust the Sun by Andrews & Austin. A Richfield and Rivers mystery set in L.A. Murder among the stars. (1-933110-52-X)

Of Drag Kings and the Wheel of Fate by Susan Smith. A blind date in a drag club leads to an unlikely romance. (1-933110-51-1)

Tristaine Rises by Cate Culpepper. Brenna, Jesstin, and the Amazons of Tristaine face their greatest challenge for survival. (1-933110-50-3)

Too Close to Touch by Georgia Beers. Kylie O'Brien believes in true love and is willing to wait for it, even though Gretchen, her new boss, is off-limits. (1-933110-47-3)

The 100ᵗʰ Generation by Justine Saracen. Ancient curses, modern-day villains, and an intriguing woman lead archeologist Valerie Foret on the adventure of her life. (1-933110-48-1)

Battle for Tristaine by Cate Culpepper. While Brenna struggles to find her place in the clan, Tristaine is threatened with destruction. Second in the Tristaine series. (1-933110-49-X)

The Traitor and the Chalice by Jane Fletcher. Tevi and Jemeryl risk all in the race to uncover a traitor. The Lyremouth Chronicles Book Two. (1-933110-43-0)

Promising Hearts by Radclyffe. Dr. Vance Phelps arrives in New Hope, Montana, with no hope of happiness—until she meets Mae. (1-933110-44-9)

Carly's Sound by Ali Vali. Poppy Valente and Julia Johnson form a bond of friendship that becomes something far more. A poignant romance about love and renewal. (1-933110-45-7)

Unexpected Sparks by Gina L. Dartt. Kate Shannon's attraction to much younger Nikki Harris is complication enough without a fatal fire that Kate can't ignore. (1-933110-46-5)

Whitewater Rendezvous by Kim Baldwin. Two women on a wilderness kayak adventure discover that true love may be nothing at all like they imagined. (1-933110-38-4)

Erotic Interludes 3: Lessons in Love ed. by Radclyffe and Stacia Seaman. Sign on for a class in love…the best lesbian erotica writers take us to "school." (1-9331100-39-2)

Punk Like Me by JD Glass. Twenty-one-year-old Nina has a way with the girls, and she doesn't always play by the rules. (1-933110-40-6)

Coffee Sonata by Gun Brooke. Four women whose lives unexpectedly intersect in a small town by the sea share one thing in common—they all have secrets. (1-933110-41-4)

The Clinic: Tristaine Book One by Cate Culpepper. Brenna, a prison medic, finds herself drawn to Jesstin, a warrior reputed to be descended from ancient Amazons. (1-933110-42-2)

Forever Found by JLee Meyer. Can time, tragedy, and shattered trust destroy a love that seemed destined? Chance reunites childhood friends separated by tragedy. (1-933110-37-6)

Sword of the Guardian by Merry Shannon. Princess Shasta's bold new bodyguard has a secret that could change both of their lives. *He* is actually a *she*. (1-933110-36-8)

Wild Abandon by Ronica Black. Dr. Chandler Brogan and Officer Sarah Monroe are drawn together by their common obsessions—sex, speed, and danger. (1-933110-35-X)

Turn Back Time by Radclyffe. Pearce Rifkin and Wynter Thompson have nothing in common but a shared passion for surgery—and unexpected attraction. (1-933110-34-1)

Chance by Grace Lennox. A sexy, funny, touching story of two women who, in finding themselves, also find one another. (1-933110-31-7)

The Exile and the Sorcerer by Jane Fletcher. First in the Lyremouth Chronicles. Tevi and a shy young sorcerer face monsters, magic, and the challenge of loving. (1-933110-32-5)

A Matter of Trust by Radclyffe. When what should be just business turns into much more, two women struggle to trust the unexpected. (1-933110-33-3)

Sweet Creek by Lee Lynch. A celebration of the enduring nature of love, friendship, and community in the heart-warming lesbian community of Waterfall Falls. (1-933110-29-5)

The Devil Inside by Ali Vali. The head of a New Orleans crime organization falls for a woman who turns her world upside down. (1-933110-30-9)

Grave Silence by Rose Beecham. Detective Jude Devine's investigation of ritual murders is complicated by her torrid affair with pathologist Dr. Mercy Westmoreland. (1-933110-25-2)

Honor Reclaimed by Radclyffe. Secret Service Agent Cameron Roberts and Blair Powell close ranks to find the would-be assassins who nearly claimed Blair's life. (1-933110-18-X)

Honor Bound by Radclyffe. Secret Service Agent Cameron Roberts and Blair Powell face political intrigue, a clandestine threat to Blair's safety, and the seemingly irreconcilable differences that force them ever farther apart. (1-933110-20-1)

Innocent Hearts by Radclyffe. In a wild and unforgiving land, two women learn about love, passion, and the wonders of the heart. (1-933110-21-X)

The Temple at Landfall by Jane Fletcher. An imprinter, one of Celaeno's most revered servants of the Goddess, is also a prisoner to the faith—until a Ranger frees her by claiming her heart. The Celaeno series. (1-933110-27-9)

Protector of the Realm, Supreme Constellations Book One by Gun Brooke. A space adventure filled with suspense and a daring intergalactic romance. (1-933110-26-0)

Force of Nature by Kim Baldwin. From tornados to forest fires, the forces of nature conspire to bring Gable McCoy and Erin Richards close to danger, and closer to each other. (1-933110-23-6)

In Too Deep by Ronica Black. Undercover homicide cop Erin McKenzie tracks a femme fatale who just might be a real killer…with love and danger hot on her heels. (1-933110-17-1)

Erotic Interludes 2: Stolen Moments ed. by Radclyffe and Stacia Seaman. Love on the run, in the office, in the shadows…Fast, furious, and almost too hot to handle. (1-933110-16-3)

Course of Action by Gun Brooke. Actress Carolyn Black desperately wants the starring role in an upcoming film produced by Annelie Peterson. Just how far will she go for the dream part of a lifetime? (1-933110-22-8)

Rangers at Roadsend by Jane Fletcher. Sergeant Chip Coppelli has learned to spot trouble coming, and that is exactly what she sees in her new recruit, Katryn Nagata. The Celaeno series. (1-933110-28-7)

Justice Served by Radclyffe. Lieutenant Rebecca Frye and her lover, Dr. Catherine Rawlings, embark on a deadly game of hide-and-seek with an underworld kingpin who traffics in human souls. (1-933110-15-5)

Distant Shores, Silent Thunder by Radclyffe. Dr. Tory King—along with the women who love her—is forced to examine the boundaries of love, friendship, and the ties that transcend time. (1-933110-08-2)

Hunter's Pursuit by Kim Baldwin. A raging blizzard, a mountain hideaway, and a killer-for-hire set a scene for disaster—or desire—when Katarzyna Demetrious rescues a beautiful stranger. (1-933110-09-0)

The Walls of Westernfort by Jane Fletcher. All Temple Guard Natasha Ionadis wants is to serve the Goddess—until she falls in love with one of the rebels she is sworn to destroy. The Celaeno series. (1-933110-24-4)

Erotic Interludes: Change Of Pace by Radclyffe. Twenty-five hot-wired encounters guaranteed to spark more than just your imagination. Erotica as you've always dreamed of it. (1-933110-07-4)

Honor Guards by Radclyffe. In a wild flight for their lives, the president's daughter and those who are sworn to protect her wage a desperate struggle for survival. (1-933110-01-5)

Fated Love by Radclyffe. Amidst the chaos and drama of a busy emergency room, two women must contend not only with the fragile nature of life, but also with the irresistible forces of fate. (1-933110-05-8)

Justice in the Shadows by Radclyffe. In a shadow world of secrets and lies, Detective Sergeant Rebecca Frye and her lover, Dr. Catherine Rawlings, join forces in the elusive search for justice. (1-933110-03-1)

shadowland by Radclyffe. In a world on the far edge of desire, two women are drawn together by power, passion, and dark pleasures. An erotic romance. (1-933110-11-2)

Love's Masquerade by Radclyffe. Plunged into the indistinguishable realms of fiction, fantasy, and hidden desires, Auden Frost is forced to question all she believes about the nature of love. (1-933110-14-7)

Love & Honor by Radclyffe. The president's daughter and her lover are faced with difficult choices as they battle a tangled web of Washington intrigue for...love and honor. (1-933110-10-4)

Beyond the Breakwater by Radclyffe. One Provincetown summer, three women learn the true meaning of love, friendship, and family. (1-933110-06-6)

Tomorrow's Promise by Radclyffe. One timeless summer, two very different women discover the power of passion to heal and the promise of hope that only love can bestow. (1-933110-12-0)

Love's Tender Warriors by Radclyffe. Two women who have accepted loneliness as a way of life learn that love is worth fighting for and a battle they cannot afford to lose. (1-933110-02-3)

Love's Melody Lost by Radclyffe. A secretive artist with a haunted past and a young woman escaping a life that has proved to be a lie find their destinies entwined. (1-933110-00-7)

Safe Harbor by Radclyffe. A mysterious newcomer, a reclusive doctor, and a troubled gay teenager learn about love, friendship, and trust during one tumultuous summer in Provincetown. (1-933110-13-9)

Above All, Honor by Radclyffe. Secret Service Agent Cameron Roberts fights her desire for the one woman she can't have—Blair Powell, the daughter of the president of the United States. (1-933110-04-X)